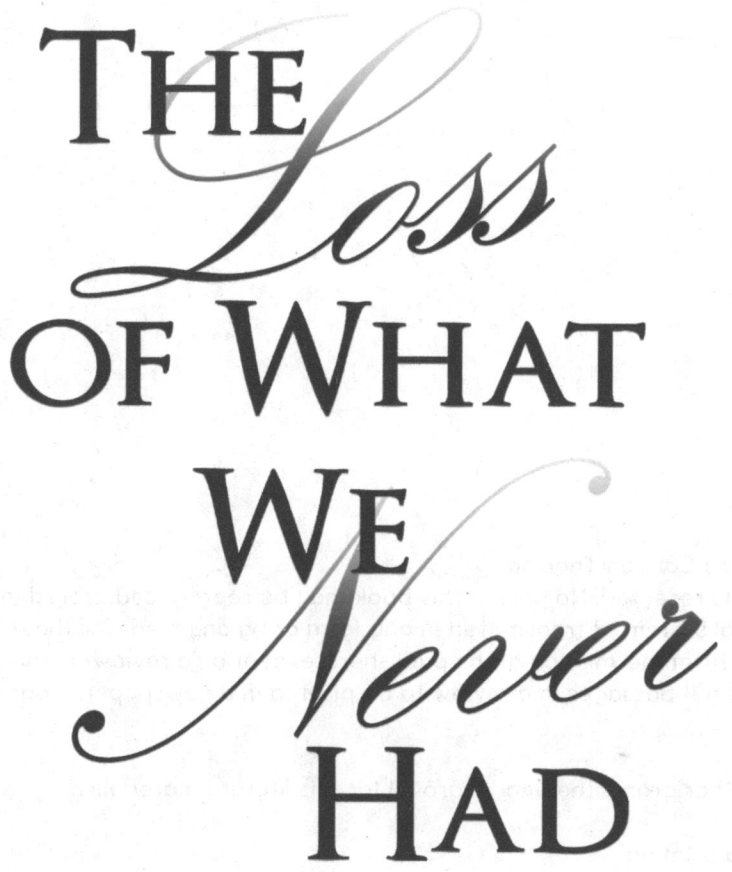

THE LOSS OF WHAT WE NEVER HAD

CAROLYN THORMAN

Black Rose Writing | Texas

ISBN: 978-1-68433-409-4
PUBLISHED BY BLACK ROSE WRITING
www.blackrosewriting.com

Printed in the United States of America
Suggested Retail Price (SRP) $18.95

The Loss of What We Never Had is printed in Calluna

*As a planet-friendly publisher, Black Rose Writing does its best to eliminate
unnecessary waste to reduce paper usage and energy costs, while never compromising
the reading experience. As a result, the final word count vs. page count may not meet
common expectations.

This work is for Richard

THE *Loss* OF WHAT WE *Never* HAD

I

The severed head of a Muslim woman lay in the weeds. No body, just the head, face-up, dark eyes accusing the sky. A hajib caught on a nearby cactus fluttered like a gold butterfly in the Mediterranean wind. Sand dried on the woman's forehead and on the blue triangles tattooed on her cheeks. I say woman, but she was more a girl, eighteen, maybe twenty. My Weimaraner, Mozart, sniffed the ground where a shoulder would have been, and I reined him in. As a doctor, I'd treated accident victims, terminal illnesses so I'd seen my share of bodily-carnage. But this... sleek, blue flies lazily circled the woman's lip. There would be eggs. My mouth burned with gastric acid. My stomach clenched into a fist. My vision blurred. When the only woman in my surgical rotation group, I'd perfected techniques to control nausea—don't gag, don't swallow, spit. The police; I needed them here, now. Except now of all days to have left my phone on the kitchen counter. When I met with the police, they would expect objectivity; a physician's clinical impressions of the scene.

I forced myself to look down at the victim's smooth olive skin, trying to pinpoint exactly where the sword or hatchet—or maybe a garrote—had struck. Third vertebrae? The site of the wound covered in sand as if the killer had deliberately buried the stem of the spine. From the tattoos, I assumed the woman was a Berber from the Rif Mountains in Morocco, about fourteen miles across the Straits of Gibraltar. Maybe she was an illegal immigrant crossing into Spain, maybe she had gotten herself mixed up with a human trafficker. In Texas, we call them coyotes.

The ground around the remains was rusty-red and wet. It occurred to me the killer might still be lurking in the tall tangled grass. I scanned the beach. No joggers. No morning hikers. Only the Mediterranean shimmering along the horizon like the silver blade of a knife.

Mozart lunged at a gecko. "Knock it off, dammit." A jerk of the leash and he reared, spun a half-circle, and dropped to all fours. Then realizing my frazzled nerves were overcoming my civility, I apologized. "This isn't the doggie's fault."

A gust smelling of fish lifted strands of the victim's black hairs from her temple. Why was the braid still intact? A handle while the killer worked? Another wave of nausea. I spat out a mouthful of bile and wiped my mouth on my sleeve, thinking how throwing up is such a useless defense against emotional trauma. The problem isn't in the stomach, it's in the brain.

I wrapped the leash around my wrist. "We're out of here."

Turning to leave, I saw the trampled footprints and broken branches. The girl was a fighter. It looked as if the two ruts marked the trajectory of the feet as her body was dragged off. Why did the killer leave the head? Could be the monster was an Islamaphobe making a sick political statement. Or this was an honor killing, punishment for some sort of unauthorized sexual event on her part—or alleged to have been on her part. The victim might have pissed off a husband or father who left her head as a message. Or a warning.

I assumed police procedures in Spain were similar to those back home in Texas. I paused for a last look to be sure I hadn't missed something that would be useful to the authorities. A final glance at the victim's eyes and all at once, I was overcome with the weird feeling I had seen this face before. Impossible. Chalk it up to temporary disorientation. I groped through my pockets for a cigarette, thought better of it and took out a blister pack of Valium I bought from the waiter in a tapas bar. The pill went down without water.

Once more, I started to leave, then hesitated. It seemed crass, downright immoral to abandon her here, so vulnerable, and exposed. Hesitating, knowing full well I shouldn't disturb a crime scene, on the spur of the moment, I decided respect for the deceased trumped police protocol. I walked over and untangled the hajib from the cactus shrub and draped it over her face, tucking it securely under her hair. Not to conceal the poor soul's identity, but to honor her death. I crossed myself with all the reverence I could muster, through the helplessness I felt.

Just as I returned to the path, Mozart leaped forward, his paws churning sand, seventy pounds of dog scrambling for traction. A few feet beyond the clearing, a man stood half-hidden in the weeds. He was tall, at least a head taller than the five-foot-high esparto stalks. His features blurred in the shadows of shifting leaves. All I could make out was dark hair and a red sweatshirt with its hood thrown back. For a minute he remained stock still, then took off through the crackling underbrush. For certain, he saw the head and had a good view of me watching him. Would he assume I was the killer? That's the case, he'd have to believe my hundred and fifteen pounds or so could manage a struggling victim while executing a clean cut. A normal guy would have joined me, yelled, or whipped out his mobile. But his creepy sneaking in the weeds. But the way he flailed at the stalks... my gut said this was the killer. And anxiety and paranoia would make him think I could finger him in a police line-up. Past behavior is the best predictor of future behavior. A guy who killed once—go figure.

Mozart was harassing another gecko, and as I pulled him off, a pamphlet on the ground caught my eye. An untrampled new tourist-promotion freebee from the Spanish Tourism Office. I unfolded the pictures arranged in a collage: Malaga's Picasso Museum, sailboats in Puerto Banus, the crenelated towers of the Estapona castle. Someone had circled a cathedral on the Seville Road with a red Magic Marker. Perhaps the killer himself. Something for the Guardia Civil. Did the local police speak English? Before I went to the station, I'd stop by Casey's, my British neighbor who spoke Spanish and might even go with me.

The shortcut to my apartment hugs the service road of the A7 that runs from Cadiz to Barcelona. Mozart's ears blew flat with each passing truck. Diesel fumes served as a proxy for air. Amazing, how despite a decapitated head bleeding out on a beach, the world appeared as I'd last seen it. The planet humming along as usual, indifferent to the outrage of an execution-style death. My high-rise was still standing. The stork's nest was still intact atop the tiled roof. The cafes, boutiques, and bars on the ground floor waiting for customers.

A marble pillar stood at the entrance to Puerto Esperanza, the name above a logo of a lion prancing through flames. A row of wrought iron benches faced the promenade. I collapsed more than sat, and leaned back, relieved the tourists and baby carriages had retreated to their air-conditioned vacation rentals. My skin tingled as if an insect crawled the back of my neck. I turned half expecting a man in a red hoodie loomed over my shoulder. Who was the victim, and where was the rest of her? My mind circled possibilities. It could be that he decapitator was a terrorist with the jihadist cell rumored to be based in Marbella. Or, another possibility, the killer was one of the deranged Christian fanatics calling themselves the

Knights of Constancia, the crackpot Catholic outfit hell-bent on kicking Muslims out of Spain.

A light breeze stirred the palms. A sparrow bounced through freshly mowed grass. Gradually the horror of the head and fear of the killer were losing their grip. My mind resumed its orderly pace and coalesced around one comforting thought—tomorrow I would be hightailing it home. My hearing before the Texas Board of Psychiatry to defend my license was three days away, and I needed to be there. My passport was in the carry-on, along with Mozart's photo ID ready to be clipped to his crate in the Malaga airport. Bills and apartment rent pro-rated and paid. And last night, I authorized my estate agent to market Dad's property.

When I came to the coast two weeks ago, I hired Zacharias DeLeon, a Spanish land developer to renovate and sell my deceased father's summer home. The trip to Spain to administer the sale was a favor to my mother as I wasn't a beneficiary of Dad's will. But that was another issue. Right now, the problem was to unload the property at a decent price. Fortunately, Zak was perfectly capable of managing the deal without me.

The iron slats of the bench were hot as a griddle, and I slid to the far end shaded by palms. Thoughts of Zak merged with images of the bloody sand, the churned earth, and the woman's face. Only all of a sudden in my memory the gold hajib was not on the ground but draped over the girl's hair. Because for sure the face on the beach was the same face belonging to the woman I'd seen last night when Zak and I were in the restaurant. Coincidence? You bet. But there it was. I closed my eyes to perfect the recollection.

• • • • •

Zak and I were finishing coffee when a Cadillac SUV bumped onto the sidewalk and stopped directly in front of the Gato Gordo's floor to ceiling window. A tall, dark-skinned Arab in a leather jacket over a tee-shirt climbed out of the driver's seat and sauntered inside as if he owned the place. A slender woman in a black kaftan followed a few deferential steps behind. She's was in a gold scarf, and like many women from the Rif Mountains, blue triangles were tattooed on her cheeks. The Arab parked her at a corner table and returned to ours. "Good evening," he said in careful English.

Zak threw down his napkin and barked, "How did you know I was here?"

"I find what I need."

"You don't need a thing," Zak said.

"Yes, I do. What you owe me and more."

Zak drew his wallet from his hip pocket and fished out a handful of euros. The Arab counted slowly, bill-by-bill, then looked up. "Not long enough."

Zak turned away and lifted his coffee cup.

The Arab's voice was calm, reasonable. "I need petrol to get the woman where she wanted to go."

I pretended not to listen, nor speculate on what Zak was talking about when he said, "Which isn't very far."

The Arab studied the euros in his hand. "But there is over-the-time."

"Shut up," Zak said.

Except for a missing incisor, the Arab's dazzling smile would have been perfect. "Please remember," he said, "you know what I know about our secret of where she's going to go to be with her baby."

Zak sighed, took out his wallet again and handed the Arab a few more bills. I faked interest in the bullfighting poster behind the bar. The Arab bowed with his hand over his heart and threaded his way through the cluster of tables, where the woman sat huddled in the corner. When she adjusted the hijab, I caught a glimpse of her long braid.

Zak's eyes followed the Arab's departure, then he leaned closer to me. "Sorry for the interruption. The guy put a new transmission in the company truck and says he paid out of pocket more than what I gave him."

Zak's lie was not one bit convincing. He patted my hand and launched into a lengthy diatribe against Arabs who cheat, and Moroccan Arabs whom he said are the worst of the lot.

I cut him short. "We'd best be going."

• • • • • •

I got up from the bench and gathered strength to move on. Panting, Mozart struggled to his feet. "You can finish your nap at home."

The noon sun blazed a path through the trees. The earth sweltered and gasped while it burned to a crisp. A white utility truck barreled down the A7. Heatwaves curled up from the asphalt like tiny cobras, and a shrub of yellow Heliopolis trembled in the dust. Incredible to think that only yesterday the Muslim woman had been relegated to a corner table where she sat as if resigned to the anger she might have overheard, and to the angry world into which she was born. How quietly she sat, calm, at peace as if already dead and above it all.

2

The afternoon heat overpowered the asthmatic air-conditioner in the lobby of my building, where the smell of roach spray competed with the smell of bleach. The queasiness in my gut stayed with me as I led Mozart past the elevator, which he hates, and up the narrow stairs.

My apartment was on the fourth floor, my neighbor, Casey, had a two-bedroom on the third. His door with the spray of silk flowers over the brass plaque read Harold L. Crandall, and under it, Casey O'Brannigan. Although his name suggested Ireland, he said he was from Cardiff. I gathered he was about thirty-five, around my age, and until a few months ago had been some sort of analyst with Her Majesty's Foreign and Commonwealth Office in London. He quit to become an ex-pat in Spain with his partner, Harold, a nice guy, twenty years older than Casey, an American who this time of day would be manning the bookshop he owned in the port.

I knocked. No answer. Casey was skittish about opening the door to strangers. "It's me, Paige," I called hoping my voice carried through the heavy oak. "Paige Glasgow, your American upstairs neighbor who—"

"No need to shout." Casey cracked the door, then swung it wide open. "Christ on a bike. Here, I'll take Mister Mo." He grabbed the collar. "What have you been into?" He held Mozart while he closed the door, then let him loose. "Look at your hair," he said. "And blimey if I don't see sweat. Didn't know you had it in you."

Casey glanced at my foot, and I leaned to brush off my sneaker. "Probably dried blood," I said. "No, it's only sand."

"Why'd you say blood?"

"It was all over the ground."

"Where?"

"I'll explain in a minute. Right now, can you go with me to the Guardia Civil to report a murder?"

"What the devil—? Whose?"

"If you're not busy because my Spanish is terrible. If you're tied up, it's okay to say no."

He glanced at the front of his shirt. "Let me get into something a bit smarter."

"We don't have time."

"Only be a minute."

The tails of his wrinkled button-down shirt hung outside his jeans, the trendy British schoolboy disguise that went along with his tousled brown hair and round blue eyes—doll's eyes I imagined would open and close automatically if I tipped his head. I say disguise because something about him didn't ring true, a lack of authenticity, an overeager desire to impress. His sound-bites of wisdom not as spontaneous as he'd like others to believe. And the way he checked his pulse every few hours. 'Doing it since a nipper,' he had explained.

Really? A habit a bit too sophisticated for a kid. Nevertheless, Casey was a good neighbor and a good sport.

"Meanwhile, go sit down," he said. "You look like the dog's dinner."

I chose the wing-backed chair, and Mozart leaped onto the sofa. Casey left the bedroom door slightly ajar. "I can hear you," he called. "And I'm listening. What happened? Where?"

I kept it bare bones: the head, the guy in the weeds—"

Casey interrupted, "Did you sick up?"

"Almost. Why I chose psychiatry rather than surgery, what my father wanted me to do."

"That's the spirit."

I went on to tell him about Zak and to describe the woman when she was alive in the Gato Gordo.

"You're sure the victim was the same person as the woman in the restaurant?"

Casey couldn't see me nod. "I'm absolutely certain," I called.

"You do understand, love, "Casey called, "that you, Zak, and the Arab were the last to see the poor lady in one piece."

"Maybe Mr. Hoodie, if he was the killer."

"A passerby. This was the Arab's work, no doubt about it." Casey at his most authoritarian. "The victim wasn't on that beach on her own." Casey's voice carried above the whine of bathroom plumbing. "Arab ladies can't go to the loo without a male escort, and it has to be a Muslim male. Thus, the Arab with her. And remember Zak gave the guy money. You've heard of contract killings?"

Casey emerged and smoothed the front of his silk shirt. "My outfit works for you?"

"Casey, for heaven's sake, my head's in a fog, I've just discovered a murder, and we have to go get the police, and it doesn't matter if you're wearing a tent, a bathing suit or nothing at all, we're out of here."

3

A ratty strip mall bordered the lot next to the Guardia Civil station, a low white building with a gold and blue crest on the door. Instead of parking at the station, Casey pulled into the mall. The smell of garlic burning in rancid oil drifted from the corner restaurant. Neon strips lit a grinning Buddha cross-legged at the entrance.

On the beach a few hours ago, the sand had blazed white and hot. Now the usual afternoon cloudcover veiled the face of the sun. A woman walking a Yorkie stopped to open an umbrella, and an elderly man quickened his pace. Casey set the emergency brake and turned to me. "The key to dealing with coppers is to keep it simple. Let's practice. Pretend I'm the interrogator. *Hola, Señora,* what brings you here?"

"When I was exercising my dog, I came across the decapitated head of a Berber woman."

Casey nodded approval. "How do you know she's a Berber?"

"The tattoos, I'll explain. Then I'll say how I covered her face and how when I was leaving to call you—you meaning the police—a man in the weeds saw me and took off, and after—"

"No, no, no. Bring up Mr. Hoodie and the cops will go ape-shit and we'll be in the station all night: photos, line-ups."

"But to find the murderer—"

"That's their problem, love."

Casey had a point. We went on with the rehearsal. "After I left the site where I found the head, I remembered I'd seen the exact same face the night before when she had been with an Arab man who knew the estate agent I hired to—"

"Stop, stop," Casey said. "Think it through." A drop of rain slid down the windshield. "I'm Mister Copper. Tell us, Señora Glasgow, exactly how much money your estate agent paid the Arab. You don't recall? Give me an estimate. Tell us again, how to spell this agent's name." Casey turned on the windshield wipers, and the frayed rubber slopped wearily back and forth.

"Turn those damn things off," I said. "Sorry, didn't mean to snap."

"Mention Zak and the cops will be all over him," Casey continued. "Might even lock him up while they hunt down the Arab, who if he did it, which he did, is halfway through Mauretania by now leaving your sexy Spaniard swinging in the breeze."

"I could be accused of withholding information," I said.

"Let me think what's best to do." Casey drummed his fingers on the wheel. "Better to protect yourself. If the police detain either Zak or the Arab, and it turns out they're innocent, if Spain is anything like the UK and the USA you could be hit with a civil suit, malicious prosecution."

"There's certainly no malice on my part."

He leaned to turn on the defroster, and shouted over the roar of the vent system. "Their solicitors will dredge up plenty."

I hit the toggle switch and waited for the whirl of air to wind down.

"For instance," Casey went on, "the prosecution can paint you as an Islamaphobe,"

"Bullshit. I—"

"Temper, temper." A quick smile, and he seemed to choose his words carefully. "You tend to get rather, well, cheeky."

"I do not."

"Oh, yes you do."

Outside, the asphalt was patent leather reflecting the red, blue, and green neon framing the Buddha. Being the child of a rage-alcoholic, I worked at maintaining exemplary self-control, Dad having demonstrated the high costs of anger with broken crystal, ruined dinners, and family vacations shot to hell. As a result, I'd trained myself to smile politely at colleagues when all along I wanted to break their necks. To appear nonchalant at criticism while my ego seethed.

"Admit you have a testy streak," Casey said.

"Maybe," I said to placate him. Manipulative, sure, which I believe is perfectly okay as long as you understand it isn't okay at all. "But just because you're right about my temper, doesn't give you the right to rub it in."

He ran his hand through his unruly hair. "Sometimes, you're a real nutter."

In the foyer of the station, we sat on steel chairs bolted into the floor. The air smelled of pine disinfectant. White woodwork shone with fresh enamel paint. I brushed Mozart-hairs from my summer sweater and wondered if the snagged threads were noticeable. Next to Casey in his navy linen jacket, I felt like a bag lady.

A commotion came from the loading dock entrance—two Guardia Civil cops dragged a young guy down the hall. A white skull cap covered his hair, and a scraggily beard brushed his collar. For sure, his checkered shirt, jeans, and plastic shoes came straight from the bazaar. He shouted in Arabic. The officers shouted in Spanish while dragging him along upright, a cop on each side, the prisoner's feet scraping the tile. The two other guards brought up the rear, one with the strap of his baton looped around his wrist. All at once the guy went limp.

I got to my feet and turned to Casey. "I'll explain I'm a doctor."

He grabbed the hem of my sweater. "Oh no you won't."

"He might have a head injury," I said.

"Yeah, right. A condition called passive resistance."

The prisoner regained strength, then collapsed again with a stream of, "*Allahs.*"

"Where're they taking him?" I asked.

"You don't want to know."

When they paused in front of us, the cop unclipped the baton from the arsenal at his waist and slammed it against the prisoner's shoulder. The crack of bone. The poor fellow screamed, choked and when I saw tears running down unchecked, I leaped to my feet again.

"Sit down." Casey snapped.

One glance at his face and I did. "They're kicking this fellow around because he's a foreigner, and he's poor and a—"

"Terrorist. Check the beard and cap."

"Because he's dark-skinned, probably an immigrant and who—"

"Just bombed an orphanage."

I managed to ratchet my anger down to a red film behind my eyes, telling myself, butt out, you're not in Texas. Then remembered shit like this happened there, too.

The cop glanced our way and grinned. When the crew rounded a corner, I heard the ping of an elevator.

Casey said, "I'm warning you, keep your mouth shut around here. The Guardia Civil has a nasty history. They were Franco's boys, his personal goon-squad. A fascist legacy and to this day a formidable force, even if they..."

The click of approaching heels cut him off.

The officer wore an oversized leather jacket of what could have been elephant hide. The insignia of the Guardia Civil—a cluster of brass sticks crossed by a sword—was pinned to his collar. We were ushered into a tiny cubicle where a purple vine drooped from a Talavera pot atop a file cabinet. According to the nameplate, the officer was Alfonso Gonzales Garcia. Short and burly, he had thinning brown hair and cheeks shot through with the lavender capillaries of a drinker. The middle finger of his left hand was missing, and I wondered if that's why the desk duty.

He stifled a yawn and drew a pencil from the Lavazza coffee can used as a holder.

"English?" I asked.

Garcia looked directly at Casey and replied, "Very, very small. Passports, please."

"My neighbor's here to interpret," I said, handing him my passport.

Garcia asked for both our names and addresses. At the word 'Texas' he lifted his hands from the keyboard and quietly laughed. "Turn me over your gun."

"I don't own one." Remembering Casey's warning, I added, "Sir."

Garcia scratched his head with the eraser end of the pencil, then dropped it back in the can.

A spider the size of an apple seed shot out from a manila folder. Garcia rolled a sheet of paper into a swatter. The spider scurried around the blotter and into the hole of the pencil sharpener mounted on the desk. Garcia dropped the swatter and gave the sharpener's handle a quick turn.

The interview resumed. After a drawn-out exchange, Casey said, "He wants to know what you're doing in Spain?"

Casey must have explained 'to fix up my father's house.'

Garcia wanted to know if I hired a contractor. Casey turned to me and said the government wanted to know, for it tracked self-employment and VAT taxes with a vengeance.

"Tell him Zacharias DeLeon, Great Estates."

We slogged forward. "Garcia wants to know why you were off the path."

"Tell him my dog went into the weeds."

"No ropes on her arms?" Garcia asked in his very small English.

"No rope."

Garcia frowned. "The law says all Spanish dogs—"

"Mozart's American."

Casey touched my arm and whispered, "Don't be a smart-ass."

The three of us plowed on, English to Spanish, Spanish to English. Then gradually I realized Garcia did seem to follow about twenty percent of what I said. But without thinking, I turned to Casey. "Don't forget to tell him about the guy in the weeds."

Garcia quickly lifted his head. "A witness-man?"

Casey's foot dug into my calf, and too late I knew I'd said too much.

Garcia zeroed in despite my insistence I knew nothing about the guy in the hoodie. More back and forth, until finally Garcia closed the laptop, swept up our passports, ducked under the trailing plant and disappeared.

"Twenty-three, twenty-four..." Casey was taking his pulse, and I interrupted with, "Where's Garcia off to?"

"Printer. I warned you not to bring up Mister Hoodie."

Embarrassment at my stupid mistake put me on the defensive. "My mind isn't working right. But what if Mister Hoodie is the killer?"

Casey shrugged.

Garcia returned with the smell of cigarette smoke on his jacket. He tapped a number in his cell phone.

"I bet he's calling their men in the field," Casey said. "Trigger the search for the remains."

Returning to the computer, Garcia silently re-read the screen. His cell buzzed. "*Sí?*" He continued speaking as he returned Casey's passport to him. He closed the call and refreshed the computer screen

"Sir?" I asked. "Where is my passport?"

Casey repeated the question in Spanish.

Another exchange and I heard exasperation in Casey's voice, a patronizing tone in Garcia's. The dialogue reached an impasse. Garcia held up his hands as if he had nothing to hide, nothing to give. "*Abogado,*" he said finally.

I tightened my grip on the arms of the chair. "Why on earth do I need a lawyer?"

Casey kept his eyes on Garcia, but spoke to me, "If you want your passport."

"You're kidding." Stunned, my thoughts came in fragments: my plane ticket, my license, my practice, my income, my life.

"He says they need you in-country to identify the guy in the weeds. You can't leave until the case is adjudicated."

"That's crazy. In Texas, I think there has to be a hearing before they can detain a witness. No one can just take away—"

"They can do anything they want."

"I'll call the embassy."

"Steady." He put his hand on my arm. "No point in getting your knickers in a twist, love. The embassy's a waste of time because not even the almighty US of A will mess in the internal affairs of another sovereign nation."

All at once, the tiny spider shot out from the pencil sharpener. Garcia pounced, quickly grinding the bug into the green blotter, hard, harder. He lifted his hand and examined his thumb.

Ignoring the carnage, Casey went on. "You've no recourse with these people."

"What if they never find who did it? I can't live in Spain forever."

"Agreed." He appeared thoughtful. "I suppose after a decent length of time, maybe hire a Spanish solicitor. The coast is crawling with English-speaking firms catering to ex-pats."

The angrier I feel, the softer I speak, a trick I use with patients to maintain control. At least the illusion of it. I rose and loomed over Garcia, with both of my fists on his desk. "You have no authority to confiscate the property of an American citizen."

"Actually, they do," Casey muttered.

"Shut up," I snapped. Then to Garcia. "My passport. Here, now. *Aqui ahora.*" I fought the onslaught of a meltdown, but nevertheless my self-control went down in flames. "Or I'll take your fucking building apart stone by stone and your shit-for-a-brain along with it."

Garcia brushed at the front of his jacket as if my words were crumbs. He said something to Casey, then with a tired sigh, rose and lumbered out of the cubicle.

"He's getting it," I said with a flush of triumph.

"No, he just went back to the printer."

Once more, my skin felt on fire. "I'll be on that plane tomorrow, passport or no."

"Don't be daft. Even if you do manage to sneak out of Spain, USA border control might not let you re-enter—at least easily—without Spain's exit stamp."

I am ten years old, trembling and terrified as Tommy, the fat fifth-grade bully corners me on the playground shouting, "Trapped like a rat. Trapped like a rat."

Garcia returned with a sheaf of papers, scribbled his signature on the bottom of a document, spun it around and pointed to a line above my printed name.

"I'm out of here." I turned away and leaned to pick up my bag.

Casey took the form and began to read, tracking each word with his finger. "Actually, it's quite well written. A simple and accurate summary."

"I won't sign anything."

"Oh, yes you will." Casey handed me the pen. "You're in enough bloody trouble."

•　　•　　•　　•　　•

A half-hour later, I sat on Casey's sofa with Mozart's head on my lap. My nerves, my skin, every inch of me felt super-sensitive and raw, as if I had showered with steel wool. Each time I tried to focus on the here and now, my mind's eye saw the woman's long black braid in the rust-colored sand.

"We're in time the catch the soccer game, Spain's playing Germany," Casey called. He emerged from the kitchen and stood in the doorway with a dishtowel tucked into the belt of his jeans. "You still look like the dog's dinner. But after a drink and food—"

"Please, no, I can't think of food."

"Then, drink." He went to the Ikea unit that ran the length of the wall. A few muttered "Damns," and the clink of bottles as he rummaged in the bottom cabinet. "Aha, here we go, your brand of Malaga, Leon Dulce Vineyards. Or might whiskey be called for?"

"Malaga's fine." I had mentioned loving the pungent wine that tasted the way bottled flowers would taste. Casey dropped the screw-top cap into an Inca pottery bowl, an artifact from digs when he studied—or read, as he put it—anthropology at Oxford. Harold's fourteen novels rested on the top shelf out of reach, out of date, out of mind. Casey held the wine bottle to the light. "The old boy's been nipping."

The tension in my stomach held its grip despite the comfort of Casey's apartment. The cozy hodge-podge of flea market furniture, Whistler's mom rocking over the mantle, the tattered Herez carpet under the coffee table, the Portuguese earthenware stacked on the sideboard. The décor somewhere between student housing and starter homes brought memories of the loft in Houston, where Grant and I lived during our residencies— happier there than in the McMansion that came later.

"I can't seem to get the sight of her blood out of my mind."

Casey drew his Jameson from the cabinet. "I mean, love, it's not as if you haven't seen plenty of gooey deaths."

"It's not the gore. it's the cruelty that gets through to me. The sadism. I see it everywhere—victims the police bring to the emergency room, graphic wounds on the covers of junk paperbacks and on junk TV. Not to mention what I saw as a child." My stomach tightened. Casey turned from the sideboard and silently stared at me. "My father," I added as if apologizing. I could told Casey about the nights I lay listening to Dad scream at my mother in his shrill falsetto voice, and my mother's whimpering in reply. "Cruelty is a disease of the soul," I said. "With no cure." I made sure Casey was preoccupied with measuring whiskey into a tumbler, before I eased another Valium from my pocket.

Casey spun around. "Aha. Caught you red-handed. What have you got there?" A short laugh. "And to think you won't write me a simple script for hydrocodone for my bad back."

"I've told you a hundred times, I'm not licensed in Spain. And right now, I'm not licensed at home, either, until the hearing in Texas. And even after that..." I blocked the thought. "I just have a few Valium from—never mind where."

"Come on. Out with it."

I sighed, knowing Casey would hound me until I told him. "The waiter in the restaurant."

"Which one?"

"The Slow Boat to China."

"I mean, which waiter?"

"Tall, thin, dreadlocks, one gold earring."

"Red hair?"

I nodded.

"That would be Diego." Casey moved to the chair opposite the sofa. Mozart jumped down from beside me and ambled over to rest his muzzle on Casey's knee. The Malaga felt thick as honey going down. "The girl on the beach was so young. Who could murder a kid for a breach of morals? Honor? Oh, please."

Casey cleared his throat, signaling I was in for in for an educational moment. "All societies," he began, "have the right to enforce their social controls."

Typical Casey, driving me nuts with his indiscriminate approval of every dysfunctional social system in the universe, except our own, which he regularly trashed.

"Honor killings however, are a no-no," I said.

"Only that's not what this was. Because honor killings are meant to send a message. All you women better play by the rules." Casey at his pompous best, raising his index finger. "Take stoning for adultery. The entire village is expected to grab a rock and pitch in. Whereas your victim's murder was in secret, which tells me this was about something else." He swirled the whiskey in his glass and waited for it to settle. "I'd bet my Gucci boots she was done in by the Catholic crazies. The so-called Knights of Constancia. You probably have no idea how many of these Franco left-over fascists are hidden in plain sight? One might be your plumber, your cleaner or priest."

Casey probably exaggerating again; he tended to be histrionic. Although there was no ice in his glass, he stirred his drink with his finger, then wiped it on his thigh. "What gets me, you would think with social media, the world should become a unified whole. Instead, it's breaking into a thousand mini-nations—Catalonia, the Basques, the South Sudanese. Every dialect wants its own flag. Every religion wants a seat in the UN. Now here come these daft Knights holding rallies, stirring up the unwashed unemployed, yelling '*España por España,*'kick out Protestants, Jews, Muslims, Unitarians—every non-Catholic so we can have Queen Isabella all over again, the Iberian Hitler, the angel of genocide. Only sorry, gents, this isn't the Fifteenth Century." Casey eased Mozart's head from his knee, stood and crossed the room to reach for my empty glass. "You look a tad better, either my ranting or the drink. Want more?"

"Please."

"More of my ranting?"

"It's therapeutic," I said, wondering if for him, or for me.

He filled the glass to the brim. "Furthermore, the Knights are gaining numbers. They've infiltered parliament, local governments, I even heard your elegant Spanish estate agent, Zak DeLeon, is one of their officers."

"I don't believe it."

"Among other roles in the organization, he's a fundraiser. The church is selling parish dinners at two-hundred euros a plate, collecting for the statue of the Virgin they're putting up in full view of the Muslim villages along the Moroccan coast." Casey shook his head slowly. Can you imagine? Talk about in your face. And the Virgin is not even wearing a veil." Casey gave a snort of a laugh and finished his drink. "Want to know the cat's ass? The Pope's coming to the dedication. Whole thing's political. King Filipe donated the land, although that little fact is strictly hush-hush."

I studied Casey's face, the deceptively innocent blue eyes. "How do you know all this?"

He gazed off in the distance, then faced me as if having settled on a credible reply. "My former colleagues in the Queen's Madrid Office. We talk. I keep in touch. Weddings, awards ceremonies, holiday parties. That sort of thing, you know."

No, I didn't. Since when did the British Foreign Office staff share inside information with a former mid-level bureaucrat, an ex-agent, expat. This was more than collegial. Was Casey back on the agency's payroll? If so, then say it.

While refilling his glass, he spoke over his shoulder. "Be prepared. You, me, the Knights will kick us out of Spain, too."

"Speak for yourself. I'm Catholic."

"American Catholics don't count." Carrying his drink in one hand, Casey headed to the small TV mounted on the wall. "Let's help Barcelona beat the shit out of Berlin."

Mozart's was dozing at the end of the sofa. "Time to go home," I told him as the band played the last note of the Spanish national anthem. "Kibbles," I shouted over the roar of the crowd.

4

Zak DeLeon jumped from the dock down onto the deck of the Strega, his Valencia 36, the high-freeboard sloop he commissioned from Davila Maritime, four generations of Cadiz shipbuilders. He paused at the ping of his phone. A text from Paige, 'Change of plans,' she wrote. 'Stuck in Spain, possibly for the rest of my life. We need to get together.'

He'd get back to her later. Standing before the open hatch, he shook his head in annoyance, the third time this week Candy forgot to close the door. He snapped on the cabin light.

"Turn that off." Candy lay on the bunk, her arm shielding her eyes from the overhead. She was in her 'Nebraska is Corny oversized tee-shirt. "Shit, Zako, you woke me up. Where've you been?"

Zak crossed the narrow passageway to the galley that was nothing more than a microwave atop a mini-fridge you had to stoop to open. He stared at the half-eaten wheel of brie, a Styrofoam box, and bottle of Bushmills. He lifted the whiskey and unscrewed the cap.

"I saved leftover takeout." Candy swung her feet to the floor. "You want I should heat it up?" She tugged at the hem of her skimpy denim shorts. A tall blonde, she had the sharp bones of a model. Going to fat, but she still carried hints of her glory days as a runner-up for Miss Omaha.

A year ago, they met on the beach in Marbella. Candy, a dropout from a Spanish language study group: Zak, on a roll. A real estate boom and northern Europeans snapped up every condo and villa on his inventory. Brits with tiny dogs, Swedes with bottled water, and Japanese with videos to capture it all. Americans came for flamenco workshops, wine-tastings and self-improvement programs like the language-immersion group that brought Candy.

At first, charmed by her naiveté, Zak gradually realized her shallowness was not necessarily stupidity, but an inability to sequence facts into cause and effect. Useless and empty, her brain was a camera without film.

"There's cheese, too. Where've you been?" she repeated.

"Kurt and I were ironing out a work-scope." Zak splashed whiskey into a glass and took it to the chart table where he sat on the leatherette bench. "For a contract with a woman from Texas who's renovating her dad's finca."

"You knew her from school in the States?"

"Actually, years ago my father worked for her father when the old guy entertained his American doctor friends in what he called his villa." Zak shrugged. "It's not a villa. It's just a house. I hadn't met the daughter until last week."

Candy groped for her sneakers under the bed. "What's Miss Texas look like?"

Zak lowered his glass.

"So's I know what I'm up against."

"Candy, this is business, like, making a living."

"I bet she's thin."

He pictured Paige's slim legs exiting gracefully from the passenger seat of his

Porsche. "I didn't notice."

Candy leaned over him. "Because you like them skinny." As if in danger of being overheard, she whispered, "You two getting it on?"

The breeze from shore carried the accordion strains of *Red Sails in the Sunset* The Italian guy serenading the tables on the promenade.

"Candy...." Zak pinched the bridge of his nose with his thumb and forefinger. "This is my first big contract in months. My stock's down the toilet, no bids on the high-rise I've put up for sale, my back's kicking up again. And you're giving me a hard time?"

He couldn't tell Candy he could have murdered his employee, Bassem, the little shit of an Egyptian, coming into the restaurant demanding money while the mother of the baby, the Knight's hostage, was right behind him. Earlier in the day, Zak had been out of the office when Kurt, his manager, had allowed Bessem to take the company van to drive the mother to see her kid. A decision so stupid, it boggled Zak's mind. Kurt had probably fallen for Bassem's pitch about a kid needing its mother. Sentimental drivel.

" Why's your face all scrunchy?" Candy asked.

"Kurt overstepped his authority." Zak held the bottle of Bushmills to the light and emptied the last of it into his glass. "Approved something behind my back."

Candy gave a melodramatic yawn and reached for her pack of Davidoff's. "Back to Miss Texas." She slowly unwound the cellophane strip, stopped and looked up. "So, what is it with you two? I mean, regarding you and me?" She slid the pack of cigarettes aside. "I got rights."

"No, you don't."

The accordionist swung into *Lady of Spain* and Candy crossed her arms over her chest.

Christ, here come the sulks.

To his relief, she unfolded her arms. "She got big hair? Spray stuff?"

"I think she wears it in a knot in back." No need to mention the sexy loose strands Paige tried to keep pinned. "Her name's Doctor Glasgow, and she's actually on the mousy side."

"A doctor doctor?"

"What's wrong with that?"

"So, where's Mr. Glasgow?"

"I didn't ask."

"If she's fixing the place up, I bet there's a boyfriend. See, she sets up housekeeping way outside the States so no one back home will find out."

"I told you she's renovating her dad's finca for sale."

"You believe that?"

"Why not?"

"Sucker."

He studied Candy through wisps of her cigarette smoke, wondering why he was so pissed when he had already decided to dump her. Easier said than done; easiest if he, himself, simply walked out. That's exactly what he'd do. Walk out. Then he remembered he owned the boat.

He finished his drink and headed down the narrow passageway toward the hanging locker. Candy opened the DVD and sat cross-legged on the bunk, staring at a rerun of 'The Death of Life,' a novella with English subtitles. The Strega rocked gently in the wake of a passing cruiser. When the hull steadied, Zak rummaged for a tee-shirt.

An hour later, Candy unfolded the bunk-extender and made up the mattress with sheets and a quilt. "You coming to bed? Yes? Or no?"

God, she grated on his nerves. "Don't shout."

Lying beside her, Zak wondered how to gather the strength to weather her tantrums, come the breakup. She could be nasty. It might be tricky to kick her out without screams for money, possibly from a lawyer. He rolled away and listened to the whispery rustle of her nightgown as she gathered it above her waist, a signal he was expected to obey. She flung her leg over his, her fingers scampering up and down his spine.

"Quit that."

The hand went away. "What's the matter? Miss Texas squeeze it out of you?"

"Give it a rest, Candy."

Her breath in his ear. "Tell me, you been a dipshit all your life? Or did an attack just come on."

She climbed over him to get out of bed. In the galley, she slammed a cabinet door, and he concentrated on the accordion melody drifting through the porthole. The scent of Paige's Chanel filled the air, and Zak wondered if it were possible to hallucinate a smell.

Candy coughed. Zak sighed, punched the pillow into shape, and lay back. That Candy was an idiot. Wasn't her fault. He started to rehearse his breakup speech, his explanation, and apology before remembering he had nothing to apologize for.

. . . . .

Four in the morning and unable to sleep, Zak sat in the galley staring at the computer. He glanced at Candy stretched flat out and snoring, turned back to the screen and brought up his e-mail. Ads: Corte Ingles, Lidle's sale on *hamburgesa*. Nothing yet from Family Heritage, the genealogy service he hired to document what he already knew. What was taking so long? All they had to do was chart the branches of the tree connecting the Valdez's to the DeLeons. Written proof and Zak could inherit the realm.

The Valdez family's claim-to-fame-was the Duke who fought with the Spanish Armada that went down when the British took Gibraltar. As if anyone gave a rat's ass about the obese stone fit only for off-shore investors and Barbary Apes—assuming there was a difference. For his loyalty, the Duke was awarded vineyards, a river, and an entire village. If Zak was lucky, he'd wind up owning the shawl of brilliant white houses draped over the hillside. A town with a church with a Mudejar tower, a Citroen dealership, four tapas bars and narrow streets winding up from the valley to the castle atop the hill.

The castle generated income from visitors paying to see the torture chamber that existed only in the imagination of the Spanish Tourism Office.

Imaginary, that is, until the Office hired a contractor to install cells, loop chains from iron rings in the wall, and build a gallows purportedly of oak but with the sheen of freshly hewn plastic.

Sometimes on his way to Jerez, Zak would turn off the 381 and inch his Porsche through the alleys snaking up to the ramparts. Run his hand over the walls and breathe the chalky smell of damp stones. Gaze over his plains where the family-owned every bodega, dressage horse, and pedigreed bull from the mouth of the Guadalquivir to the Costa del Sol. His, all of it. His. No matter that he wasn't the landowner of record. The deed was in his DNA.

And although knowing the interior of the Valdez castle like the back of his hand, Zak would take the tour. He mingled with the busloads of sightseer women in sleek polyester, and the sightseer men in vests fitted with the important straps and pockets seen on war correspondents.

Guides would point out the pint-sized chair built for a sixteenth-century physique where the nobleman sat while he ordered the slaughter of peasants. A crock of shit. One more deception promoting the god-awful packaged tourism that cheapened history and trivialized art.

Candy stirred. "You're up. Sick or something?"

"Go back to sleep," he said.

Candy yanked the quilt over her head. If it were possible to flounce laying down, she flounced onto her side.

Zak closed the genealogy site and opened an email from Kurt, his name above his title, Fiscal Officer, Great Estates. Kurt also served as a volunteer, the fiscal director of the Knights. Zak brought up the template designed for authorization for acquisitions. It showed two crates of AK-47s from Huan Lee imports, and a shipment of Kevlar body-armor from a supplier in Munich whose name was new to Zak. Nevertheless, he entered his electronic signature.

He exited the site and opened the resumes for the Knights' new recruits. All heavy hitters: a vice-president of Valencia's Ford Motors, the owner of Los Cosas boutique, a lawyer from Opus Dei, and Doctor Ramon Garvez, Chief of Surgery at Marbella General.

The welcome packet they would send included the Archbishop's blessing under a photo of his Excellency taken at the summer palace where years ago—right after the Madrid bombing—Zak and Archbishop Raphael De Alba had created the Knights of Constancia.

Hours after the Islamic terrorists struck the Atocha station, Zak stood behind the police barrier as rescue teams picked through the wreckage. Watched them drag bodies and body parts from the crumbled cement, tangled wire, and rebar sticking straight up like index fingers accusing God. Smoke curled to the yellow sky. The rubble exhaled its foul breath of cordite, diesel, and burnt rubber. Sickened, Zak turned away, then forced himself to turn back as medics salvaged limbs and guts. Slowly Zak began to realize how carefully the rescuers gathered and examined each fragment of flesh. Then it dawned on him, the medics were attempting to reassemble remains into a semblance of a whole. Or, if that wasn't possible, the rescuers were placing each limb and each organ on its own separate gurney. One stretcher. One life. With a sudden burst of pride Zak saw this as a symbol, a revelation, one small gesture that defined his people, his nation's desperate attempt to maintain its integrity despite the attacks of invaders. And they're back, he thought. Back to reclaim what they call their Andalusian heritage. Fuck 'em.

The next day Zak gained an audience with Archbishop de Alba, who upon hearing Zak out, explained, 'Time's come to revive the famous, infamous Inquisition. Not necessarily the torture and gore, unless—never mind. But to foster a new militant movement, a push-back initiative. Unfortunately," Father went on. "The popular focus is on the previous Inquisition's downside."

Well, yes, Zak thought. Downside, certainly. But was Father onto something big? A new Freemasons or Opus Dei? Or was he just a nut?

"They forget Isabella's accomplishments: victory and unity." Father continued. "So, it's up to us to assure that Spain's purity is sustainable." Father was sitting at his desk and rolling a Mont Blanc pen in his fingers. "We are all of one blood." He drew himself up full height. "We are Spaniards. God's aristocrats."

God's aristocrats. Zak hid a smile. But just because Father was arrogant, didn't mean he was crazy, A new movement meant money. Church, community and even Vatican grants and donations.

The following nights Zak and Father drafted the by-laws and budget for a watchdog group they jokingly called the resistance and officially dubbed the Knights of Constancia. Fidelity, the Archbishop said, loyalty to the majesty of Spain. The mission statement read, 'to deter the destructive effects of diversity,' "Because," Father said, "only fools believe minorities fight for equality. They fight for supremacy."

A week of revisions while Father paced the creaking oak floors, and Zak designed templates on his laptop. Once Zak threatened to quit when Father insisted all Board members be donors. Once Father refused to sign off on a transparency statement. Their differences resolved; they drafted legislation to be introduced in Parliament. None with a snowball in hell's chance of passage. A property surtax levied on non-Catholics, language they lifted from the Emirates. A bill barring building permits for synagogues or mosques. Father argued for military expenditures for a cadre of special forces to be deployed against refugees. Overkill, Zak insisted.

The documents were indexed, tabbed, and packaged with a cover letter to Madrid and copies to Rome. "You've met our diocesan lawyer?" Father asked. "Roberto Defalla? No? Never mind. He'll file for incorporation for the Knights of Constancia."

• • • • • •

Candy sneezed.

Zak closed the list of new recruits and said aloud, "God's aristocrats. I love it."

Candy raised her head. "Who's the it?"

He opened a new document and pretended not to hear.

She rolled to one side, pummeled the pillow into shape and repositioned it behind her head. "Or is the 'it' Miss Texas's money?"

"Candy, just for once can you think before opening your mouth."

"American doctors are hip-deep in it," she said.

"Go to sleep."

The Strega rocked in the gentle rhythm of the waves, an occasional bump of the fenders against the pilings. Zak's eyes focused on the screen, but his thoughts were on Paige's silky loose hairs blowing against her pale cheeks, her slim hands and endless legs. How she leaned towards him across the table, leaned into him as they walked the esplanade on the way to his car. He glanced at Candy and imagined Paige stretched out atop the sheets and wondered what that would be like.

5

The day after the debacle at the police station, on my hands and knees, I wrung out the scrub-rag and draped it on the rim of the bucket. I sat back on my heels to catch my breath as Bach's fugue on the radio was wound down. Counterpoint—me, Zak... I brought the thought up short. Who was I kidding? What relationship? There wasn't one unless you counted the conversations about the cost of cement. We had no connection other than renovating the summer house. In fact, he might even be ripping me off on the cost of materials. Don't be stupid. Tell the Guardia Civil about Zak and the Arab in the restaurant. So, what if they use Zak to find the Arab and indict them both? Case closed, I'll get my passport and go home.

The ledge of the ceramic baseboards held a rim of sandy grit. I dipped the brush into my power mix of Don Limpio and ammonia. I'd relegated Mozart to the deck until the floor dried. A knock on the door, and he let out a hound-dog yip. Wiping my hands on my jeans, I got to my feet. The pounding escalated. The doorknob rattled. I thought of the Gestapo and the infamous knock on the door in the middle of the night. But this was Spain, not Germany. And Franco was dead. The sudden wave of my fear was the fear of the irrational, the anxiety of being in a place where I didn't know the language and didn't know the rules. Not the everyday rules of traffic and no smoking signs, but the unwritten rules of how the society really worked.

"Hold it, I'm coming." I turned off Bach and crossed the living room before the pounder splintered the wood. Mozart's barks became howls. He stood on his back legs with his front paws propped on the screen "Careful, watch those claws," I shouted to him. At the front door, I slid back the security chain.

Two Guardia Civil officers stood in the hall, one tall, one short. "*Señora,*" said the tallest. He wore his black beret at a slant, exposing a stubble of blond hair. A finial of a nose presided over a round chin, his front teeth prominent as a beaver's. Polish? No, more likely, Galician from up north around Coruna. Light from behind his head shone through his pale blue eyes, as if unfiltered by gray matter.

His short, wiry partner had the bushy black eyebrows of the Basques. Both wore khaki tunics and boots. I looked for guns but saw only batons, miniature baseball bats strapped to their belts.

"*Hola, Señora,*"the Basque said.

"Sorry, no *Español*. English? I forgot the correct Spanish 'you' so tried both. "*Usted? Tu?*"

He tipped his hand back and forth and smiled, large teeth with brown necks as if the enamel were rusting from the bottom up. "Don't worry." He tapped the brass badge on the front of his jacket. Leather? In this heat? Under the badge, a name-tag read Raul Perez Guadiano.

His partner, the Galician, Juan Varega Martinez, craned his neck to keep an eye on Mozart. "Bites?" Juan said.

"You mean my dog?" About to assure him that Mozart's sole enemy combatants were fleas, I said as I often said to workmen I was leery of. "He can be vicious. It's the breed, Weimaraner's are German. Although I took him to dog school."

"*Bueno,*"Raul said as if relieved.

"He bit the trainer." I lied.

A whiff of Don Limpio drifted from my damp t-shirt. "Excuse the way I look; I wasn't expecting anyone." Raul nodded impatiently at the door I held half-closed. "Let's see both your ID's."

Each photo showed the Guardia Civil logo and a reasonable likeness to the bearer, but the cards were so blurred by the yellowed plastic covers, I demanded the men remove them. The expiration dates, issuing dates, and emergency telephone numbers on the flip sides appeared bona fide. But the pictures were no clearer than when encased in plastic, fuzzy as if the camera or the subject had been jerked back and forth.

I returned the ID's and motioned to the sofa. The men preceded me into the living room. Neither sat.

"Your owner passport, please," Raul demanded.

"I don't have it. Your people took it yesterday at the station."

"You who whom?" he asked.

"They said it would be held until a legal issue gets resolved."

27

The officers exchanged looks.

Strange. Wouldn't the passport confiscation be in the computerized record? And wouldn't these guys have seen the entry? I tried to recall if Casey mentioned that the passport confiscation was in the printout of the interview with the intake officer. Come to think of it, where was my copy? Then I remembered I left it in in the door-pocket of Casey's Audi.

"Because you," Raul said in an accusatory tone, "must have gave a report to a different department."

"Different from what?" I asked.

"We're from the Department of Verification," Raul said.

"Okay, so you're a verifier," I said, my suspicion about the guys escalating. "But why are you here in person? I was told officers rarely go off-site, why my friend and I had to file the report at the station and waste a whole day."

Raul's eyebrows moved slightly, as if too heavy to rise. "Friend?" He took a notepad and pen from his hip pocket. "Name of friend?"

This was getting silly. "What do you want?"

"Your report copy for verification."

"I think we're finished here "I looked to the door. "Feel free to leave."

While Raul formulated a response, Juan wandered the living room, lifted a pillow from the sofa, put it down, and flipped the pages of a Norton anthology with such indifference, I wondered if he could read. From behind the screen, Mozart yapped twice, then sat quivering with excitement.

"We'll leave when we get it," Raul said.

"I told you I don't have it."

"She lies," Raul called to Juan as if I weren't there.

"Who you are you two, anyway?" I asked. "You don't know what goes on at your own headquarters."

A scraping sound as Mozart ran his paw down the screen. I spun around and yelled, "Stop it."

Juan's jacket sleeves hung to his knuckles. The gaps between Raul's legs and his boots was at least half an inch wide—as if the men were in rented costumes. This was a scam of some sort. Raul had a mean streak and something about Juan—he was either bipolar or smoking funny stuff. Crack? On the other hand, it was possible the men were authentic—shabby uniforms reflecting Spain's chronic fiscal crisis. Whoever they were, what was the worst they could do to me? Other than rape, murder, kidnapping, theft... Instead of blood, my heart pumped fear through my system. An acidic unfamiliar body fluid moistened my palms and filled my mouth.

Juan had invented a game—darting toward the balcony, then jumping back as Mozart flung himself against the screen, He laughed a methamphetamine laugh, prolonged and shrill.

Raul snapped at Juan in Spanish.

If I tried for the door, they could block me before I got out. My phone was in the other room. Screams might or might not get through the thick plaster walls. For the first time in my life, I wanted a gun.

With his hands on his hips, Raul looked around the room, taking in the IKEA sofa, marble floor lamp, and the Picasso print over the couch. His eyes lingered on the rag draped over the bucket. His hand moved to the baton at his belt. "Who else is in this place?"

"I do my own cleaning."

"We find out."

I moved in front of him. "You need a warrant." Bluffing, as if I knew Spanish law.

"Not necessary." He opened the lower door to the credenza. "When the one who is supposed to cooperate isn't, we have the right to look for why." He pulled a stack of paperbacks to the floor, stepped over them, and crossed into the bedroom.

My mobile was on the nightstand. I started around him, but before I could get to the phone, Raul pocketed it and shook his finger at me as he would admonish a child.

"Give that back. I'm calling my lawyer." Another bluff. I didn't have a lawyer.

Mozart whimpered.

"You be quiet,"

Raul pawed through the desk drawers, then tackled the papers on top. He studied a Cortes Ingles receipt for a pair of jeans. "Go ahead," I said. "Feel free to look. Don't mind me." With my arms crossed and tapping my foot, I leaned against the doorway to the bedroom, pretending indifference. Watched the light from the window change from cream to gray, the clearly defined square shadow on the wall fading as the sky grew dark rain clouds.

Raul tossed aside calendars, credit card statements, a ten-page brokerage summary, and a paper on medication compliance I was editing. Meanwhile, Juan rummaged in the dresser and giggling like a teenager, held up his hand and twirled a bra from his index finger. Neiman Marcus's industrial style, no-frills, white.

Two strides and I grabbed my underwear. "Fucking pig." I tossed it back in the drawer and slammed it shut. "Grow up. Three minutes to get out of here before I —"

A silver streak and Mozart barreled through the doorway, skidded around the corner of the bed with his nails fighting for traction.

"*Cuidado,*" Juan screamed.

I turned to the living room and the jagged hole in the screen. "Mozart, over here, boy. Be good." He knocked over the pole lamp as he shot past.

Juan pushed me aside on his way to the front door. Mozart blocked his path, leaped and with his paws on Juan's chest began licking his chin. I reached, grabbed for him, and found myself holding a collar, but no dog.

Juan unclipped the baton from his belt.

"Don't you dare," I shouted.

He wound the strap around his wrist and raised the club higher. A downward swish cut the air. He missed.

"Son-of-a-bitch," I yelled.

Mozart danced under Juan's arm. Once more, the guy lifted the baton positioning for a backhand attack. If I could throw him off balance—I lunged. Juan retreated; arm still raised. My kick hit his shin. Undeterred, he aimed the baton at Mozart and held it in mid-air just as Mozart galloped off. The baton swung down—the crack of bone—mine.

I clawed at the dresser on my way to the floor and found nothing to grab. Gasping, I watched the room spin as I lay on the carpet that smelled of dried wine and the dust collecting since the Visigoths. Listening for voices, I heard only the click of Mozart's feet in the kitchen and the hum of the refrigerator. Then came the slam of the door, sounding as if from a great distance. The men were gone. I rolled on my side, straightened my legs gratified to find them in working order. I flexed my arms. All intact, more or less. Gathering strength, I attempted a deep breath and stifled a scream. The air was a paring knife coring my lungs.

Mozart lapped water in the kitchen, his metal bowl clanging against the cabinet. I loosened my t-shirt from my jeans and ran my hands over my torso. The worst scenario, punctured lungs. I risked another breath. Shallow, but air was getting through.

Fetal position worked best. Lay quietly. Stabilize. Call Casey downstairs. Only Raul had my phone. A doctor. An X-ray? I tried to recall exactly where I'd had seen the billboard along the A7 towards Marbella. The sign pictured a smiling physician, a British flag, and in English, Manchester Emergency Medicine.

I talked myself through the plan. Take it step by step. Car keys from the jacket pocket. Where's the remote for the garage? On the kitchen table where I'd left it. Don't forget the wallet to pay the clinic. How much in there? A few hundred euros and three credit cards.

I struggled to a full-blown stand. So far, so good. Careful, take it slow in case of a jagged bone. Vicodin. Thank heavens I'd saved a few from a root canal. To be on the safe side, I took two Advil and a valium.

I shut Mozart in the bedroom with his water. Crossing the hall, riding the elevator was a piece of cake providing I didn't breathe. The garage door was open to one of the ferocious downpours that swamped the coast for about ten minutes before roaring off to Portugal. I made it into the front seat of my rented Renault and managed to exit the garage without side-swiping a neighbor's BMW.

No windshield wiper on the planet could outpace the downpour overflowing the gutters. I wound through the narrow street and turned onto the ramp to the interstate, which was now a waterfall of foaming mud. Inside the car, condensation coated the windows, lifting my arm to the defrost toggle switch brought back the paring knife.

I remembered the physician's billboard as being right before the entrance to the tunnel at Puerto Banus. The rain was letting up. One mile past the Caeseras Road, another mile past Estapona, and mixable dictu, the sign with the Union Jack. The man in the white coat smiled directly at me over the caption, "We Speak Your Language."

"Praise God," I said aloud.

· · · · ·

Later that afternoon, I lay on the sofa strategically positioned so I could watch the boats rock in the marina, the sea, and the dark line of the North African coast. I adjusted the ice pack on my back and eased my leg out from under the seventy pounds of dog draped over my feet. Yo-Yo Ma came from the stereo, but instead of a distraction, Bach's exuberance only sharpened my anxiety. Three broken ribs, two men, why me?

"Self-pity is irrelevant, and irrelevance wastes time." My father's voice was as brutal as the surgeon he was. With a cigar in one hand and a Jack Daniels in the other, he would preach, "The old Occam's razor. Strip the problem to the bone. No digressions, no speculating and if you're too lame-brained to control maverick thoughts, cut them from the herd."

I tried to cut the two maverick thugs from the herd. They wandered back. Were they Guardia Civils—if that was the correct plural—or imposters? No burglary, the invaders were after my police report. Someone in the station must have spotted me, and told whoever was interested, why I was there. Who might care? Only three people—or maybe two. Zak, the Arab, and the tall, dark watcher-in-the weeds, who might be the Arab himself. Between the restaurant and the murder, the guy would have had time to change from his leather jacket into the red sweatshirt. But an Arab—possibly an undocumented immigrant—would hardly have confidants inside the Spanish police force.

That left Zak, who paid the Arab, but what for? Zak might worry I'd tell the police about him being in the restaurant and passing money to an Arab as the woman looked on. All a big maybe. All I knew was, from now on each knock on the door and unidentified number on the phone would bring a cold sweat.

The prescription meds from the Manchester clinic turned the room to a soft haze and muzzled the jaws biting my chest. My thoughts drifted from the woman's head on the sand, to my broken bones, to the rathole of a clinic and the gentle touch of the British doctor.

• • • • •

The sign outside for the Manchester Clinic was inviting and bright. Inside, the place was a dump. Shabby, but clean—the smell of bleach stung my eyes to the point of tears. The institutional green walls and white tile with blackened grout gave the waiting area the feel of a day room of a state mental hospital. Goodness knows I had seen enough of them. The clinic's privacy curtains sagged from rusty hooks. A sullen clerk slapped across the room in loose sandals and handed me a medical history form on a clipboard. The signage, the paperwork—everything in English including her question, "National insurance, no?"

"No."

"No insurance?" She shouted as if my ears, not my bones, were the presenting problem. "*Vale, vale.*"

Anywhere, anytime, somewhere a Spaniard is yelling "*Vale, vale.*" What does it mean?

She lay the completed form it on the counter. "Before the treatment, one hundred seventy-five euros." She gave me a receipt and ushered me into an exam cubicle where Doctor Tony Berringer was pulling on latex gloves; he gave me a weary smile, his gaze reflecting either boredom or exhaustion. Gray streaks in his blond hair accentuated his tan, weathered skin. With a cool touch, he palpitated my back and politely and clinically correct, worked his way around my breasts. Exam finished; we sat in the consultation cubicle. Posters warning of AIDS and Hepatitis brightened the flimsy partitions. Barringer explained why he couldn't show me the X-rays. "Against government policy."

"But I'm private pay, not on Spain's nickel."

"And you're not in America."

"If you read the intake form, you'll know I'm a doctor."

"With ribs seven through nine snapped like pretzels," he says.

I draw back. This man did not suffer fools gladly.

"And some murky cartilage around number nine," he added. "I can't determine more without a scan. Meanwhile, my dear, nothing to be done but rest, a deep breath every hour or so to keep the lungs tip-top, ice, pain medication as needed. How'd it happen?"

The truth would result in his calling the police to report an assault. My apartment combed for fingerprints. Questions. From my brush with the Guardia Civil, I knew the outcome would bring nothing but more grief in my getting out of the country. "My dog jumped on me, and I fell against the dresser."

A prolonged stare, his thoughts written on his face, victim protecting the boyfriend who beat her up. "Dogs will do that."

I held out my hand to Mozart's height. "He's a big boy."

"I'm sure he is."

A smile might have indicated I knew he knew I was lying. Folding the prescription, I turned at the entrance of the cubicle. Then suddenly turned back, for some reason, not wanting to leave. I felt safe, here, with this tired, but careful physician. Funny how the aura of a person transcends his physical self. Despite Barringer's cool professionalism, or perhaps because of it, I wanted to rest my head against his cheat, wallow in self-pity and cry. Odd, because I never cry.

He looked up from what he was writing. "Anything else?"

Yes, but what? I recalled a line from a poem and heard myself say, "A cup of tea, made for me without asking,"

I hurried outside, the embarrassment of what I said hot on my heels.

Mozart shifted his weight on my legs, bringing me back to the sofa and the blue water and blue sky behind the glass door. The roar of a diesel engine trumped the memory of the clinic, and I propped myself up on my elbows. A fishing boat rounded the jetty and plowed courageously through rough seas. A magnificent arc of spray soared over the rocks, and gulls keened above the foaming wake. "Marvelous," I said to Mozart. The word pushed through my ragged breath.

Bach's fugue was played out, the apartment quiet but for an occasional gurgle from the drain in the floor near the toilet. A hint of sewer gas in the air saying it was time to pour water, better yet, bleach, down the drain to kill the smell: one more aggravation coming from the plumbing, pipes probably dating from Ferdinand and Isabel.

I half-dozed and awoke with thoughts jumping out of sequence. Maybe the woman-the girl I called the beheadee was the Arab's wife. Or a lady of the evening. A stupid outdated phrase, but useful, I liked it. Was the murder about some sick sex thing? Was Zak into leather garters, whips, chains? One more reason to keep the police out of it.

An important question haunted me while I hovered near the gates of codeine heaven—why on earth did I care enough about Zak DeLeon to cover his ass?

6

Three days after the visit from the thugs, my broken bones still aflame, I pulled out of the garage into the morning sun on my way to the family's summer house. Today Zak and I were to go over the work-scope for the renovations. This as a favor for my mother, who was too frail and disorganized to negotiate a real estate sale on her own. I had no stake in the property. According to Dad's Spanish will, Mom inherited the summer house. Dad's Texas will give Mom a life estate in the Houston house and bank accounts. Upon her death, instead of me as the beneficiary, the remainder would go to the Houston Museum. 'Your father said you make enough money, Mom said.

But this wasn't about money. It was about love and a father wanting to care for his kid after he was gone. One who wanted to remain in his child's life even after his own death. Thinking of my father brought back the painful hollowness in my gut, the hunger beyond the need for food. And I wondered, as I always did, how it was possible to feel the loss of something I never had.

I turned onto the interstate and lifted my arm to open the sunroof. Big mistake. The knife paring my lungs, struck. I pulled onto the shoulder and rested my forehead on the steering wheel until the Vicodin kicked in.

The pain in remission, I eased the car onto to the highway. Taking as deep a breath as my chest allowed, I settled back to enjoy the whitecaps flashing offshore and the lantana spinning purple in the exhaust of passing cars. Miraculously, the temperamental Renault's transmission was on good behavior, the gas tank full, and for the first time the car's sound system radio picked up radio Gibraltar. The broadcast was a repeat of last night's TV news showing a mosque in Cadiz in flames, firemen, police cars and two body-bags on the sidewalk. The Knights of Constancia claimed credit. The announcer quoted the group's chief of public relations, "There will be another Inquisition, but this time we will get it right."

Wonderful, I thought. Bring back Franco's paradise of firing squads and mass graves. Give the world one more nation of medieval barbarism and silence. Casey was right, the Knights did go for high visibility; the spectacular Cadiz mosque bombing, the inflammatory speeches to inflame the Islamophobes. The announcer went on, "A spokesman for the Sons of the Emir report no progress on negotiations with the Knight's for the release of the baby held hostage. Iman Tariq, the infant's father, warned of repercussions."

Tinny background music took over the news, and I lowered the volume. In front of me, a line of red tail lights crept past the entrance to the McAuto. I inched around them and took a right onto the 381 toward Seville. The four-lane highway wound over the gentle hills of the wildlife refuge. Eucalyptus trees flanked the road. Bulls earmarked for the ring grazed among sheep and dainty white goats. A few miles farther, a low wall sheltered an adobe cottage where chickens goose-stepped around a dusty courtyard. The Spanish countryside was pretty enough, but not quite right. The landscape lacked the freshness, the innocence and pristine glory of America. I pictured Big Bend at the curve of the Rio Grande, the Louisiana marshland graced with long-legged cranes. Spain's tired earth seemed spent, as if too many feet had roamed the forests, too many hooves trampled the fence lines and too many plows scarred the fields. History had exhausted the leaves, the dirt, even the stones. America's nature was spontaneous—Spain's was resigned.

A few miles north, I took the potholed track that passed the abandoned cathedral. Just as I remembered, there sat the ruins. I parked, turned off the ignition, opened the window, and listened to the tick of the cooling engine, and the peep of a ground bird. The air carried a whiff of rosemary and brought back the summer day when Dad and I explored the ruins a decade ago. "I'm sure you can't grasp the impact of the Visigoths," he said with a sigh as if worn down by my stupidity.

During the Spanish Civil War either the Republicans or Falangist's bombed the bell tower into a field of cubist blocks. Dad and I picked our way around the rotten planks at the entrance to the narthex, passed through the doorway that had no door, then crossed to the ankle-deep marble rubble of the chapel's floor.

"A shame one of the Goth's architectural beauties was reduced to this," Dad said. The fragments of an icon lay atop a severed pillar. The Virgin's face elongated, Byzantine style, but strangely enough she held a Celtic Cross. A twisted iron candelabra lay half-buried in the earth amidst shards of ruby-red votive cups, candles once lit by prayers going up in smoke.

The distant whistle of the silly tourist choo-choo train that ran from Algeciras to Rhonda brought me back to the here and now. Looking both ways before backing out, I noticed tire tracks in the mud. The deep corrugated grooves led to the only wing of the cathedral still in one piece. The vehicle must have been hauling quite a weight. A delivery? Or a busload of tourists? No hotels nor gift shops within miles.

I have profound respect for the sixth sense, the truth that comes not from the brain, but from the gut. Dreams, love at first sight... knowledge beyond statistics and peer-reviewed publications. Data is not truth. I looked down at the flattened weeds and the skin on the back of my neck tightened. A trail left by someone who never should have been there. I swung onto the main road and picked up speed.

Our family house baked in the noon heat. I pulled up in the drive and cut the engine, the silence broken only by the dialogue of two crows. A bee buzzed the wisteria. I was early. Since I'd given Zak my keys to let in workmen, I couldn't get into the house. I decided to wait in the car. With the air conditioning full blast, I leaned back to ease my shattered bones. From the window, I could see beyond the house, over the valley and all the way to Gibraltar rising from the sea like a great humped-back whale.

So many vacations spent here, my mother sleeping off her depression meds and Dad working the golf course, leaving me free to explore, read and think about the kings and queens and Bishops and knights who once led processions through these woods. Since I'd last been here—about a year ago—the grounds appeared the same. Only a few signs of neglect: the yellow fungus on the hibiscus, the raspberry shrubs went rogue and the dead branches on the boxwood I hid behind the day I caught my father with Jorge Castillo.

•   •   •   •   •

I was twelve years old picking raspberries and trying not to eat more than I dropped in the pail when I saw Dad and Jorge Castillo naked on the grass. Castillo was a Dallas doctor of pharmacy, Dad's friend, who scheduled his golfing vacations to coincide with ours. Why was he flat on his back? And what was Dad's head doing between Castillo's legs? A sickening wave of vertigo swept over me, when I forced myself to accept what I suspected they're up to. I'd best get out of here, I thought. I turned toward the house before realizing I couldn't cross the lawn without being seen. The men would have to leave, eventually. I crouched behind the boxwood hedge to wait. Although I tried not to look, I did.

Dad's shoulders moved, quivered, and suddenly stopped. A tee-shirt beside him served as a napkin he used to wipe his mouth. Castillo's chest heaved—slow, then slower. Dad swung a playful punch at Castillo's stomach. Both men laughed.

"*Gracias.* You do good work." Castillo's speech the overly precise voice of a drinker trying to avoid slurred words. He ran his fingers through Dad's thinning hair. They lay whispering with their arms around each other. Dad shifted slightly, drew back his hand and slapped Castillo across the cheek. A yelp. Dad raised his arm and the smack of the following blow cuts the dense humid air. A low moan is followed by a muffled gasp—or maybe a sob. Dad rolled on his side and gently ran his palm over Castillo's chest. He must believe the pain was worth the tender strokes.

Sunbeams played among the branches of the magnolia. A wasp teased the lantana. A stork floated in lazy circles over the garage. Castillo raised his head. I realized if I'm able to see his eyes, he surely must see mine. He gave no indication. I crouched lower and watched through the mass of tiny leaves. When Dad kissed Castillo's forehead, I felt an unexpected surge of—what? Anger, fear? So hard to say. Something almost like jealousy—something like the envy mixed with shame I'd felt when my enemy, Barbara Wallace won the spelling bee. Dad is always so aloof, cold, downright mean. Yet here was proof he could love. So why not love me?

The minute the men doze off, I make a bee-line for the kitchen.

That night around midnight I was reading in bed. This was during my H. Ryder Haggard phase and lost in *King Solomon's Mines,* I failed to see Dad in the doorway. Sensing his presence, I looked up. From the way he listed against the frame, I could tell he was drunk.

"Jorge Castillo said he saw you, see us," he said.

Trembling, I froze, wondering what to do. One false move would have brought Dad's rage. A lamp tossed against the wall, a broken chair... I lowered my book as carefully as I would if a cobra were in the room.

He stared without blinking. "I hate you," he said and turned into the hallway.

Feeling abandoned and ashamed, I drew the covers over my shoulders and buried my head in the pillow, so no one could ever find me.

•　　•　　•　　•　　•

Zak was due twenty minutes ago. I turned up the fan on the air conditioner and picked up my memory where it left off. Dad never had to speak those words again. His patronizing smirk and total disdain of everything I was, and everything I did said it all. When he was dying in the ICU, feeble as he was, he pushed away my hand and told the nurse, "Get her out of here."

They say therapists choose the profession to resolve their own pain. Maybe it's true. The textbook explanations of Dad's symptoms hit the mark: attachment disorder, emotional hypersensitivity, disturbed identity, threats of suicide, and one botched attempt. It took my entire psychiatric residency before I faced the fact, I had a father with an Axis Two personality disorder. Was Dad gay? I must have come from somewhere.

The crunch of wheels on gravel jolted me from the past. Zak's Porsche rounded the curve of the drive. Following him was a black SUV the size of a Greyhound bus, its fenders streaked with mud. Both vehicles pulled up at the far edge of the paved courtyard. Respecting my vulnerable bones, I carefully slid from the front seat. Zak came toward me, apologizing for being late. He wore a crisp navy linen blazer. I brushed at the oversized jersey, the only top I could get into without a return of the knife in my chest.

A slam of the SUV's door and an elf of a man in a tight-fitting tee-shirt and Pepe jeans came around the tailgate.

"Kurt Shumaker," Zak said with his hand on the elf's shoulder. "Fiscal guru and the brains of Great Estates. He'll help with the estimate."

I held out my hand: Kurt's grip a miniature vise.

Zak selected a key from a ring, and as he fought the stubborn lock to the front door, Kurt walked backward while shading his eyes with his hand. "Ve must get genuine tile roofing. No fake plastic." Kurt's accent familiar. No wonder, for every winter half of Germany flocked to the Costa del Sol.

The lock clicked, and Zak and I stepped into the foyer. Aside from the musty smell of closed rooms, the place was intact. "No signs of vandalism," I said. "Castle security did a good job," I turned to Zak. "Come on, I'll show you around."

"I've seen it."

"Not my guided tour," I said over my shoulder. "Only three bedrooms. Single-story because Mom had a thing about fires and getting out in time."

I led him into the living room where Mom had converted what had been a charming Spanish *finca* into a tacky Texas Hill Country ranch. Talk about kitsch. Matching end tables with maps of Texas carved in the oak, a huge leather sofa that could seat a buffalo, and a bronze cowboy roping a calf—a Remington knock-off hauled from Dallas in her hand luggage. The wagon-wheel ceiling fan came in the mail from San Antonio, along with the machine-made Navajo rug. It was years before I realized not everyone's house reeked of vanilla pot-pouri.

"Furniture's from Perez Interiors near the bullring in Seville." I felt the heat in my face as I realized I must sound as if I were trying hard—too hard—to impress Zak. As if his opinion mattered. "Anyway," I added, toning it down. "A buyer might like the view from the terrace."

"Nice." Zak's reply too polite.

"Gif me a hand with ze ladder," Kurt called.

Zak touched my arm. "Be back."

I returned to the car, opened the trunk, and guarding against sudden movement, lifted the bag from the Super Sol. It held tostadas and Manchego. Did Zak like cheese? I came to my senses. Who gave a shit what he liked?

I lugged the groceries to the kitchen. Zak lay on his back, half inside the cabinet under the sink. A pipe wrench lay on the floor beside him.

"I have cheese," I said to a pair of boots.

No reply.

"Can you hear me?"

"Not now. Hey, turn the faucet, see what comes out."

As I reached for the tap, pain shot from my chest to my back. A strangled intake of breath and I grabbed the countertop.

Zak withdrew his head. "You okay?"

For some reason, I didn't want him to know about the attack, the report the creeps were after, the girl's head on the beach. I went with, "Mozart tripped me up, and I hit the corner of the dresser."

Slowly I steadied myself on the rim of the sink. A turn of the handle brought rusty water from the spigot.

"Allow it to run into pure," Kurt said from the doorway.

Half an hour later, Zak read from the notes on his iPad. "We're in for a new roof, tiles in the master bath, flagstone, and paint. Sticking with white?

"Semi-gloss."

He returned to his iPad. "Kurt's checking the foundation. Let me add up the materials he listed. We talked about a painting over the fireplace."

"I agree. Maybe something from a local artist."

"That's your own problem and expense."

I watched Zak tap the screen. He could be Irish, I thought, that dark hair and gray eyes. He had taken off his blazer and draped it over the sofa, the lining exposed, the way Dad folded his Brooks Brother jackets, careful with his belongings, his work, his patients—careful with everything except the people he was supposed to care about.

"How do you spell renovate?" Zak asked.

I leaned over his shoulder. "Only one *n*."

His shirt smelled of Foca laundry soap and a hint of citrus. I resisted the crazy urge to bury my head in the hollow of his neck, reminding myself this was no time to be romanticizing about a charismatic Spaniard.

"And all new appliances," he said. "Stove, washer..."

An hour later, I walked Zak to the driveway. Standing beside his car, he held up his blazer to fish through the pockets. "Keys in here somewhere." He found the Porsche fob and opened the door. "Call if you can't make it tomorrow," he said, folding his long legs under the dashboard. "Otherwise, we're on."

"Seven o'clock," I agreed.

He backed out, shifted into drive, and after side-swiping the row of hedges he shot off with a twig of boxwood caught on the grill.

7

Driving away, I took a last look at the house and tried to dismiss the sadness as I pictured my mother's clouded eyes and white hair. I should be in Texas, home. Surely, she was wondering why I was gone so long. I'd called Pete who was covering for me asking if he could handle my appointments awhile longer, explained that my passport was hung up. For the first time, I felt the ruthless force of homesickness. Ruthless, because romanticizing another place undermines the merits of the place you're in. I missed my sturdy Spanish-style house near the Gulf of Mexico, its white kitchen, and tiled patio. Would my house-sitter remember to set the timer on the outdoor lights? The almost tangible longing for the familiar came in thoughts of Sunday afternoons when I would make soup for the week. Pea soup with a ham hock: minestrone. Winter nights keeping up with the journals, sitting in front of the fireplace with Mozart asleep beside me. A past I never appreciated until I was far from it in the present.

The sun was beginning its decent into the late afternoon; one minute the fields in shadow, the next, glowing in mauve light. A hawk trembled in mid-air, its underwings flashing red against the sky. An afternoon when you could imagine the lion at peace with the lamb, swords forged into plows.

The ruined nave of the bombed-out church rose above the pines. What about a quick look inside, see how much I remembered from when Dad and I went exploring? Only take a minute. What would it hurt? I swung onto the access road.

The ruts from the tire tracks I'd seen that morning had dried to caramel; the esparto grass still slick after the heavy vehicle had flattened it to muddy straw. Halfway to the church, my tires sank into the mud. The wheels spun. In low gear, I backed up and gunned it. Startled, the car leaped to solid turf.

The tire tracks stopped at the chapel. I got out of the car, trespassing, but who cared? The center of the walk-way bore the single groove of a hand-cart, the kind used to move furniture.

The late sun graced the granite blocks; a gold cross topped the Visigoth cupola. With relief, I saw the magnificent stained-glass windows were unbroken, only the colors muted by eighty years of the dust from a forgotten war. A low hum from behind the building, and I paused—a generator? Marble angels, black with mold, knelt at the entrance. I approached the massive portals, and before I could try the door, it opened, and I was face to face with a Spanish grandmother.

She was one of the Mediterranean ladies who roosted on every door stoop from Lisbon to Athens; black headscarf, long black dress, black sweater and soft black shoes over thick brown stockings. Grandmothers who policed the comings and goings of everyone in the neighborhood, who scrutinized every package delivered, and judged every behavioral flaw that passed under their glittering eyes.

"Hola," I said, then, "tourist," trusting the international word to transcend language. It must have, for the woman gave a slight yellow-toothed smile. Her wrinkled skin was weathered, but her cheekbones were high and firm, not pretty, but once handsome was how I would remember her.

"I came to see the beautiful chapel." I touched my eye. The woman looked me up and down and apparently deciding I was harmless, motioned me inside.

Low wattage bulbs hung from wires crisscrossing overhead; the walls absorbing the light as quickly as the porous stones absorbed the humidity. In the center of the vast room, a child slept face-down on a mat inside a play-pen. Judging from the baseball bats on his pajamas, he was a boy who appeared to be about seven or eight months old. The play-pen was hand-carved with curved spindles topped by a mahogany railing. It rested on a pad of carpet, buffering it from the concrete floor. A brass fixture held the gate shut. An amulet hung from the handle of the knob; a wide-opened eye centered in blue glass keeping watch over the infant.

I don't like children. That is, as a demographic. I care very much about their well-being, but can't stand the fussing, screaming, and mismanagement of their body fluids. During my pediatric rotation, I chose to work exclusively with moms: well-baby education, post-partum depression, and medication safety.

I walked around the room with the grandmother behind me, admiring the arched ceiling and marble statue of the Virgin in a dark corner. The place was spotless with a faint smell of disinfectant. No one cleans like a Spaniard. At first, I assumed the woman was a caregiver for the ruins while she also watched her grandchild. But the assumption didn't jibe with what I saw. A heavy-duty cord ram from a hole in the wall to somewhere behind the appliances, a stainless-steel washer and dryer, a Bosch double-door refrigerator, a state-of-the-art stove vented with a downdraft, and a Penguini portable air-conditioner. All were lined up as if in a showroom. A hospital bed with lowered rails took up the opposite wall. A white Portuguese Matelassé sham matched the Matelassé spread. I suspected the woman slept here with the sides raised when she allowed the kid in bed with her; the rails, not a bad idea. A kitchen table, a crib, a changing stand, holding what could be a lifetime supply of Pampers. In a far corner, a recliner faced a flat-screened TV.

A perfect hideaway. Whoever set the place up had money. So why not keep the kid at home? Or in a posh daycare facility. I thought of the middle eastern amulet and the boy's thick curly hair. At first, I resisted the obvious—too melodramatic, too preposterous, too unlikely. But there it was, right in front of me—the kidnapped kid, the imam's son, the hostage. And what better place to stash him away than a ruined church in the middle of nowhere? The ideal site chosen by the revisionist group of crazy Christians. And what better minder than a Spanish grandmother?

Call the Guardia Civil. As I fumbled in my bag for my phone, it occurred to me the call would bring big trouble for the old woman. Based on nothing more than a hunch, I sensed she wasn't privy to what was going on—otherwise, she wouldn't have let me in.

She went to the table and pulled out a chair. An olive oil can filled with petunias sat in the center. She motioned for me to sit across from her. I hesitated, then realized she must be lonely here; no neighbors, only the kid day-in, day-out. I sat on the edge of the chair. "I can't stay...."

The woman pointed to the child. "*Enfirma.*"

As in infirmary? Sick? "The kid's sick?"

The woman seemed to understand that I got it. She crossed the room to the kitchen area. "*Medicina,*" she said, lifting a gallon-sized glass container of brown liquid. She shook the jar, poured a small amount into an enamel pot, and turned on the stove. The smell of cloves and something astringent filled the air. A minute later, she poured the stuff into a cup.

Kneeling beside the play-pen, she unlatched the gate. The baby stirred. Too lethargic, the cheeks flaked with a thin white crust. Dried tears? Mucus? His head lolled back, then drooped on his chest. The huge, dark eyes struggled to open. The woman groped under his flannel wrap, checking the diaper. Apparently, all clear.

Dehydration? The woman settled him on her lap, dipped a spoon in the cup, and held the spoon to his lips. He made a face, turned away, and batted at her hand. Two more tries and she scored. The next go around, he took a full mouthful and spit it on her dress, a direct hit. No rag in sight, 1 rose and found a roll of paper towels near the sink.

"*Gracias.,* "The woman dried the baby's chin, then her dress. "*Enfirma,,* she said morosely, as if resigned to being spit upon.

I spoke each word carefully as if slowness itself would translate. "Vomiting? Diarrhea? Hot? Pain?" 1 didn't even attempt meningitis or diphtheria...

"*No Ingles,* "she said, working the spoon. 1 got up and looked into the gallon jug. A few cloves, a sliver of garlic and a peppercorn floated in the whiskey—or brandy. The woman dandled the baby on her knee, "Ah, Hamid, Hamid," in a sing-song. She snaked the spoon toward him at an angle.

Radio Gibraltar had not named the imam's son. But Hamid fit. When 1 felt the child's forehead, 1 found his temperature elevated; a thermometer would help. 1 tried the word on the woman. No-go. 1 reached in my purse for a pen and drew a thermometer on a paper towel; lines, numbers in centigrade. The woman smiled as if humoring me. Maybe hand motions. 1 slid the pen under my tongue, then held the pen to the light and read aloud, "BIC", feeling like a nut.

The child dug at his eyes with his knuckles, then rubbed his ear. 1 reached and gently stretched the lobe as if the tympanic membrane would come out to meet me. I'd have given my right arm for an otoscope.

The cup empty, the woman returned the child to the play-pen. He tossed irritably, whimpered, coughed and fell into either a nap or a stupor. In my bag, 1 had Vicodin, Valium, aspirin and a few lint-covered vitamin C tablets. Aspirin might lower the fever. But with no medical history, 1 wouldn't risk it.

The room dissolved into a cave. My heart pounded uselessly as if trying to pound frustration into an otoscope, thermometer, stethoscope. Who cared if I knew the hip bone connected to the thigh bone? I had only what was in my brain, and right now, my brain was no help. Ask me to explain the relationship between acetylcholine and serotonin, ask me the dynamics of hemoglobin, and I could rattle off the answer. But without tools, I was worse off than a chimpanzee that at least had a stone to break an egg. I looked over at the gallon of *medicina,* the grandmother's technology light years ahead of mine.

Hamid rolled onto his stomach and kneeling on all fours, crawled to one side of the play-pen, grasped the spindles and struggled, unsuccessfully, to pull himself up. Without thinking, I loosened the kid's grip on the bars and swept him into my arms, his body against me warm, compact, and heavier than I expected. He whimpered and buried his head in my sweater. Something wet, his nose running against my neck. He needed so much, and I had nothing to give. I swayed, patted his back, and said with a catch in my voice, "I know a squirrel who would like to meet you."

The door flew open with enough force to drive the lion's-head ornamental knob into the wall. A rifle hung at the intruder's side. He was short, burly and unshaven, wearing the thick black pants, woolen cap and blue shirt of a farmer. Grandma quickly drew Hamid from my arms and lowered him onto the mat. The child screamed shrill piercing howls of indignation. The farmer took one look at me and leaned to slide the rifle from his shoulder. My breath stopped. Then he strode past the table to prop the weapon against the wall and let out a stream of angry Spanish. The woman crossed her arms and stared him down. He turned to me and pointed to the door. "*Fuera de aqui.*"

I got the message. "I'm going, I'm going," I said, dredging up my few Spanish words. "*Ayuda.* Please get help *por la niño,* I mean *el ninño,* who's *enfirma.*"

The man wiped his hand across his mouth and pulled out a chair.

I motioned to Hamid. "Doctor? Baby?"

The man studied me, pointed to the infant, and shook his head, no. "*Ahora.*"

He pointed to me, then to the door.

Rude, abrasive, he pushed the envelope of my patience. "I don't care if you don't care, but I do. Dumping a baby in this God-forsaken cave without sunshine or medical care."

The man's face remained impassive; I lowered my voice to get his attention, not knowing how much he grasped if anything. "I'll get el doctor who can start an IV, get an ambulance out here and—"

He half-rose and slid back his chair.

I nodded to the woman. "I'll be back," and walked out the door without closing it behind me.

Pulling away from the chapel, I gripped the wheel as if it were the guy's neck. Molecules of anger crashed against the walls of my skull. Ignoring a baby who was spiking a temperature. Allowing him to suffer, hot, aching— how nasty could the guy get? Spaniards. Look at the Conquistadors, I thought. Bad as Nazis, looting, killing. Cortez lives.

But blaming an entire nation wasn't fair. I took a deep breath and calmed down. The creep in the cave was just another one of the world's bullies. Yesterday the Americans bombed Mosul. Christian Knights blew up a mosque. Jihadists tossed a bomb into the ferry from Tangier. Compared to the rage that seemed to be sweeping the human race, neglecting a baby was small potatoes.

I turned onto the track leading to the entrance, driving slowly to avoid the ditch of pooled water and mud. Bumping over stony ruts, I heard an engine and looked up just as a black SUV shot from behind the church. How many black BMW SUVs would be in this corner of Spain? More than one would be a stretch. The driver had to be Kurt. For sure he saw my car parked at the church's entrance. Assuming the kid was the Knights' hostage meant Kurt was mixed up in the kidnapping. My stomach sank. Where there was Kurt, there was Zak.

As if my anger at the farmer were a weathervane hit by a cross-wind, it spun to become fear for myself. Was my fear real? Or overblown? In any event, Kurt and some of his very bad friends knew that I knew where the hostage was.

8

That night, all night, I wrestled with the bedclothes and the chocking fear Kurt or his fellow Knights would mow me down in a drive-by-shooting, or they would fire-bomb the Renault with me in it. Going back to the church was asking for trouble. But I had to. Having discovered the baby, and promised the grandmother, I felt a moral responsibility to get Hamid a doctor. Maybe into a hospital.

After combing the Net for a likely-sounding local pediatrician and finding not one who I sensed would come to the church with me, on a hunch I called Tony Berringer, the Brit from the walk-in clinic. He had mentioned he didn't speak Spanish. But that would make no difference to a baby in diapers. I called him with a lame-brained story about an elderly lady caring for a child of absentee parents, and the kid spiking a fever, and me a psychiatrist with no license to practice in Spain—blah, blah blah. He interrupted, asking, "When?" His agreement to come with me hinged on my agreement to wait until the weekend when his clinic was closed. When I got off the phone, I wondered why he said yes at all. Loneliness, I decided. I hadn't seen a wedding ring, not that I specifically looked for one, but I guessed the isolation of an ex-pat might be getting through to him. Everyday communication dumbed down to adding an "a" to English nouns and hand motions serving as verbs.

The apartment was too hot. I struggled to roll down the cheap microfiber blanket I'd picked up in Carrefour's. Thoughts of my bedroom in Houston once more triggered the longing to be home. Although my affairs were reasonably under control. Thanks to my lawyer, the hearing for my license reinstatement had been post-phoned. Mom was floating my expenses here, plus, of course, Zak's charges for services and materials for the summer house renovation.

Zak, I thought of heading to the kitchen for a glass of ginger ale. I returned to bed, adjusted the pillows, and lay on my right side, then tried the left.

From the three weeks, I'd known Zak I'd concluded he was charming, seductive, and grandiose. Based on experience, I knew if I confronted him, asked about the Arab, that instead of an explanation I'd probably trigger an attack of narcissistic rage. If he were in my office—not that he ever would be—I'd run down the indicators for a diagnosis.

But he wasn't my patient. He was a business friend. One with more impact than just being my property manager would suggest. Maybe it was his energy, dry humor, and intensity. What fun it would be to meet him in Madrid. See his reaction to the El Greco's, then sit outdoors in Retiro Park. Did Spanish hotels have those high four-poster beds? I stopped the nonsense mid-thought.

Once more, I was fantasizing a full-blown relationship before one got off the ground. A bad habit. Something wrong with my learning curve. Painfully, but to remind myself of what I almost forgot I learned, I relived events with Boot Riley.

A year after Grant's death I'd made the mistake of having sex with an oil-field roughneck who worked the off-shore rigs out of Galveston. Employment was sporadic. During slack seasons, Boot picked up handyman jobs. When he finished whatever he had fixed in my house, we would sit in the kitchen, where I'd listen to his complaints about Doris, his overweight and overwrought wife, while he rolled a joint from the shreds in his Tupperware box. "Just as well you don't use," he said. "Expensive habit."

Which I probably subsidized. He might have been overcharging: I could never bring myself to tally his receipts scrawled on the backs of envelopes. When he began dropping by just to talk, I should have paid attention to the flashing red lights

Hellos and goodbye hugs led to trysts on the sofa, where I told him 'no' again and again, not because I didn't want to, but because I was listening for the word 'love,' explaining, whenever my mouth was free, that otherwise, we might as well be crickets rubbing our back legs together.

He must have been startled that hot afternoon when my *no* was not forthcoming. Only my saying, 'I don't care,' while my greedy hands tore at his shirt.

Afterward, he leaned over the edge of the bed to grope for his shoes. My silk robe was on the back of the closet door. I looked good in blue: slip it on, we could hang out in the kitchen, then go back to the bedroom. I smiled up at him. "I'll fix coffee."

Without meeting my eyes, he fastened his belt. "Got to pick up Doris at the mall."

The following night we argued over his bills. Later I realized I started the fight. Some relationships can only end in anger. This was one of them.

Thoughts of Boot merged with those of Zak until I finally dozed off. After four hours of sleep, it was eight AM. Too late to go back to sleep, I was stuck with my mouth feeling like an owl's nest, and I could only get out of bed by offering myself a bribe. How about Marbella? I'd been wanting to explore the upscale shops. Then to appear civilized among the privileged Marbellians, I put on a dress. After a quick spin around a grassy strip with Mozart, we went to Casey's, Mozart's sitter.

He opened the door. "Breakfast time, love, want some?" He wore a nightshirt, of all things.

"Where on earth do you buy them?" I asked.

"My housemate whips them up on his sewing machine. Good old Harold's already gone to his bookstore to flog his outdated stock no one buys." Casey rubbed his head, the shaggy curls falling back in place.

"Coffee, if you have it. Can you keep Mo while I go shopping in Marbella?"

"No problem. See today's Sur In English?" The gossipy tabloid that was distributed free.

"No, why?" I followed him through the living room to the kitchen where he spread the newspaper on the table and skip-read aloud, tracing the print with his finger. "Police find remains of a decapitated young woman." Casey looked up at me. "The picture doesn't show much, you can understand why, too gruesome, but there's a description of facial tattoos, comments from the Sergeant."

The article went on with the statistics of violence on the Coast.

"Says here," Casey read, "the Guardia Civil investigating North African migrant communities. Evidence—they don't say what—suggests hate crime."

He slid the paper over to me and went to the sink to add water to the espresso machine. The picture showed a Guardia Civil officer standing amidst weeds.

I moved the paper aside. "Casey?"

He turned off the spigot.

"I think I found the hostage, The imam's baby."

"Sorry?"

"I said, I found the hostage."

"Christ on a bike. What I thought I heard." Leaning against the counter, he reached for his wrist and began counting his pulse rate.

"They're keeping him in a bombed-out church near Dad's place."

He broke off the count and asked, "You certain it's the right kid?"

I described the grandmother and the sick baby winding up with, "If you could come along to translate—"

"Of course. Happy to."

"We may need an ambulance. I suspect meningitis—"

"Count on me. Love to go with you. Absolutely love to," he added.

"Why so enthused? A day on the road can't be that interesting."

He lowered his eyes, raised them. "Curiosity, and all that." In a brighter tone, he said, "Harold can take care of big-boy. Right Mister Mo?"

Mozart raised his head from the sofa, then went back to sleep.

I left Casey turning pages of the newspaper, the tails of his nightshirt tucked between his knees.

•　　•　　•　　•　　•

I love stores, good ones, where there's no noise but the soothing scrape of hangers riding metal bars. And perfumed air pumped through the vents. I milled around through Ferragamo's, Gucci's, Burberry's, and Furla until I came to Sayyed Kavandi's Iranian Imports, where I lost it.

The warning to myself not to buy, was lost in the smell of dusty wool and cardamom tea. Tall and slim, Sayyed was graceful as a panther as he glided across the showroom. "Tea? Coke?" Sayyed asked and clapped his hands. A teenaged boy emerged from a back room carrying a brass tray with glasses of tea and a small plate of cookies. I sat on a regency chair and balanced the cup on my lap as the boy flipped rugs one-by-one to show me. Bijars, the scarlet work-horses, Kazaks and their alarming geometrics, and zany Ardebils sporting cartoon camels. "Stop. Go back. The Tabriz."

According to Kavandi's account of its provenance, the three-by-five was a clone of one in the palace of the now de-throned Shah Pahlavi. Lavender vines embraced a medallion of yellow lilies. The underside was signed by the weaver. But a dealer in Houston told me his first job in the Teheran bazaar was weaving signatures onto unsigned carpets. Oh, well.

"Euros?" I asked.

Sayeed started at three thousand.

I hung in at one-five until we settled on an even two-thousand.

The flipper-kid carried the folded rug to the car. Home, I unfolded it in front of the credenza and opened the balcony door to the western sun beaming down at the pale velvety Tabriz. From one angle, its background appeared to be cream: from another angle, ivory. Two thousand euros? Not bad.

Are you kidding? Of course, it was bad. What was I thinking? Without income, by this time next month, I'd be into my savings. I should have known better than to set one foot into Sayyed's. On the other hand, the sanctions against Iranian exports dried up the European market, making the rug a good investment. Rationalizing? You bet. I stroked the wool that was soft as mink. The Tabriz was far more than a rug. It was a work of art. A gift to the world from Persia, where poets are honored and where carpets fly.

Mozart came up behind me. I turned to him. "Not one paw on that rug." He advanced anyway, only to spin and yip at the knock on the door.

I rose, unfastened the latch, and faced Zak in the hallway. "Why so surprised?" he asked. "We were on for seven, weren't we? Or did I make a mistake?"

A leather briefcase hung from his shoulder. He wore the linen blazer he had on yesterday only tonight it was over a navy tee-shirt. He was one of the few men who could pull off a day's growth of beard without looking as if he slept under a bridge.

"I picked up wine," he said, opening the plastic bag. "Where should I put it?"

I led him into the kitchen, where he took two bottles and a box from the bag. He set the Malaga on the counter. "I remembered you like this goo. The rioja's for me. And this..." He held the box aloft. "Is for our furry friend." The Bocadillo box pictured a grinning Chihuahua. Mozart nuzzled Zak's leg. "Can he have one?" Zak asked.

"Make him sit."

"*Sentarse.*"

"He doesn't speak Spanish."

"Watch this. *Sentarse.*"

Mozart sat quivering, grabbed the biscuit, and trotted into the living room.

Zak turned to me. "Where's your wine glasses?"

If Zak wants to take charge, let him. "In the cabinet above the stove."

The drink he passed me was filled to the top. So many questions were poised on the tip of my brain all of them concerning the Knights, most importantly, was Zak a member? Was he involved in the kidnapping? The words "mother," and "taking her to her baby" spoken by the Arab in the restaurant came to mind. Zak understood the references. I would not confront him directly, rather, I would ease into it.

Watching him pour his own drink, I asked, "How well do you know Kurt?"

"Let's see—" He raised his eyes to the ceiling. "About five years. Why?"

"He strikes me as being kind of rigid. Opinionated. The way I would picture a man of convictions. Any chance he's one of the Knights?"

If Zak were annoyed, he didn't show it. "Who cares?"

I motioned for him to follow me to the living room, where I sat at the desk, and he took the sofa. I was working up the courage to ask if he, himself, was a Knight. And what did he have to do—if anything—with the woman's head on the beach? At that, he might get up and leave. I was prepared.

"It's that Kurt will be alone at Dad's house," I said.

"All my men are bonded," Zak snapped. He opened his briefcase. "Don't worry. Meanwhile, the bathroom tile's been delivered, and we're waiting on the lumber. Shingles come Monday." Zak held up original receipts stapled together.

Shades of Boot O'Rourke and his padded bills and Boot making a fool of me. And giddy me, playing into his hands.

"The bottom line—in dollars—is a thousand, three hundred, and forty-two cents," Zak said.

'Check's ok? I've signature authority on my mother's account."

Mozart rested his head on Zak's knee. "Still a hungry boy?" Zak asked.

"He's begging."

Zak nodded at the checkbook. "While you write that out..." He stood and headed into the kitchen with Mozart padding behind. "*Sentarse*" was followed by the clink of Bocadillos hitting Mozart's steel bowl.

With Zak out of the room, I reached in the desk drawer and took out the vial of Vicodin. Not a good idea on top of the Valium and wine, but the pain in my chest was writhing and whining. The tablet went down with the dregs in the glass.

When Zak returned, I tore out the check and asked, "Do you listen to Radio Gibraltar?"

"I run my ad over it, sure."

"They say anyone, the guy next door, the meter reader, anyone could be one of the Knights because the whole country's reverted to the old game of Christians and Moors still at each other's throats. Bystanders like me could be caught in the crossfire."

"This has something to do with Kurt?" Zak asked.

"I mean, these days you can't be too careful."

"What's gotten into you? You usually make sense." Zak studied the rim of his glass, then looked into my eyes as if totally baffled. "What are you really afraid of?"

"The entire world's terrified of drive-by-shootings, being beheaded—"

"Good Lord, your imagination's on overdrive."

I set the wine on the table and motioned to the glass. "Maybe too much of this." My laugh came out all wrong.

He got up to take the check and stared down at me. Then circled my chair and placed his hands on my shoulders, his thumbs gently massaging the tendons of my neck.

"You're probably uptight about the cost of the renovations. Plus, too many decisions."

The tendons melted under his hands. I stiffened my muscles so he wouldn't know how good it felt.

" You've nothing to worry about." He ran his palms down my arms, up to my shoulders again.

Maybe he was only weakening my defenses so I would trust him. For that's what seduction does, doesn't it? Weakens resolve, distorts judgment. The techniques of Boot Riley's seduction to loosen me up and wear me down. I braced myself, determined to ignore his hands wherever they went. But the body has a mind of its own.

I closed my eyes wondering if my suspicions about Zak were delusions brought on by the aftershock of the woman's head on the beach. Paranoia working its way to the surface of the brain the way a splinter works its way to the surface of the skin.

The heel of Zak's palm dug pleasantly along my spine, then inched lower. "Careful, it's still tender from the accident, remember?"

His thumbs returned to the neck, "What can I do to get you to unwind?"

I should have said, get your hands off me. But I didn't want to.

His fingers caressed my throat, temple, hair. "Nasty old pins." He pulled one out, and I tucked the loose strands behind my ear. He began taking out the others, one by one, leaning to drop them on the table.

My hair fell loose.

This has to stop. Go in the kitchen, get away from him. I glanced at the pins on the table. "You forgot the barrette."

He leaned and drew his cheek across mine, a hint of lemon from his rough beard.

The balcony door was closed, but the sound of the sea lingered in the captured air. Now his hand was gentle under my elbow, as it would be if I let him levitate my body from the chair, not that I had to. I followed him to the sofa on my own free will.

We lay facing each other side-by-side on the imitation leather cushions, his breath warm on my forehead. Two pairs of jeans lay crumpled on the floor. How had that happened? I felt his weight on me and mumbled, "This isn't a good idea." I ran my hands over the tight muscles of his back, every inch of him hard, the fever in his thighs firing mine. He slid my leg aside with his knee, and I must have gasped, for he asked, "Am I hurting you?"

"Probably."

A gagging cough came from across the room. I turned my head and screamed, "Oh, my God. Mozart, get off."

The dog stood on the Tabriz with his legs splayed, back arched, and his head lowered as green liquid spewed from his mouth.

"Drag him on the tile," I shouted and ran to grab him.

Zak leaped from the couch.

"He's slipped his collar," I said, reaching to pick it up. It lay in a pool of slime, and I changed my mind.

The dog gagged. "Zak, grab his fur,"

Mozart heaved, and thick yellow mucus splashed onto the medallion. A sour smell of grass and bacon, the essence of Bodacodillo, rose from the floor. With me pushing the dog from behind, and Zak pulling him by the scruff of the neck, we managed to slide him onto the tile and across the room.

"Quick, the balcony." Zak shoved the dog outside and closed the door. "Cold water, the sooner, the better," Zak caught his breath. "And every rag you've got."

I raced to the bathroom for a towel. Where did I leave the bucket? I tore into the kitchen.

"Too much to wipe up," Zak said. "Best thing's the bathtub."

"No way."

"Arab housewives wash them in the ocean. Colors don't run in saltwater."

The box of salt was in the cupboard, and I handed it to Zak, who was bent over the tub and swirling the carpet under the cold-water tap. Mozart's collar rode the waves, the rabies tag clanking against the porcelain.

"I think we caught it in time," Zak said.

"Two thousand euros."

"Oh, yeah? When'd you buy it?"

"Today."

He lifted his head. "Holy shit."

"The stain's coming out."

"Think Mozart needs a vet?" Zak wrung out a wad of fringe. "Maybe he's sick."

"He always does that when he overeats, it's a Weimaraner thing. But never before inside. Do you think the pink flowers on the hem will fade?"

"Can't tell while it's wet. Let it soak a minute, and I'll hang it on the balcony."

"Can't. It's against the management's policy."

"Fuck the management."

"Maybe so long as it can't be seen from the sidewalk."

Zak straightened, and instantly, my face went hot. I looked away, realizing how naked we were. Carefully keeping my eyes on his face, I reached for the rack at my elbow and pulled two towels from the rod.

"Adam and Eve." If he meant it as a joke, it didn't come off that way. "The first sin." He knotted the corners of the towel at his waist. "But not the last."

9

Leaving his Audi in the car park, Casey made his way through the crowd of tourists swarming Gibraltar's duty-free shops. He walked while studying the map that the sea wind was struggling to rip from his hand. He looked up. The building he wanted must be that high-rise across the street with the plate glass entrance. He waited for the light to change, the map flapping like a captured bird,

The lobby was cool, silent and dark, a vault of hidden currency and commerce. The white letters on the black directory board read AGS, Assertive Global Solutions, and in italics, International Conflict Resolution, Samuel Weber, President.

Alone in the lift ascending to the ninth floor, Casey propped his briefcase against his ankle, straightened and placed two fingers of his right hand on the pulse of his left. The doors slid open, and he stood between them while he finished the count. Eighty beats a minute. Perfect. Relieved, he picked up his briefcase and proceeded down the hall.

Weber's receptionist wore a summer jersey of ruffles and sequins. "You have an appointment?"

"Yes, this morning."

"Like, today?"

No surprise that she spoke American English. Weber, her boss, was retired US Navy, having gone out as Rear Admiral, Casey recalled, and immediately landing a plum of a consultancy with the Saudi's which led to a teaching stint at Annapolis. It must have gone sour because next thing you knew, he was launching AGS, in an entire suite of posh offices a strip-mall away from the Pentagon. The Gibraltar office was merely an off-shore haven needed to placate the tax-takers. No inconvenience. It was also a handy pit stop on flights to the Middle East.

The receptionist glanced from her computer to the digital wall clock. "Nice and early?"

"Eleven, was my understanding." Casey drew back the frayed sleeve of his blazer to check his watch. "Heavens, it's only nine-fifty."

"Mr. Weber won't be in for an hour?" A sentence spoken as a question.

Americans do that, for fear, a statement might be misunderstood as a commitment.

"I can get you something to drink while you wait?" She nodded at the community of orange plastic chairs.

Casey turned away in embarrassment. "I'll be back."

He chose a wobbly outdoor table at the bistro around the corner and laid his briefcase on the seat next to his. Not much in there except a few maps and a resume: keep up appearances. An attempt to inflate what he regretted he was, a day-laborer hanging around the door of the international security industry waiting for work.

No menu nor price list. The waiter loomed over his shoulder, and Casey ordered an espresso. A sudden break in his vow of austerity prompted him to add, "A croissant if you have one."

He sat back to consider how to handle Sam Weber, who would try to wheedle out the information Casey was selling before they agreed on terms. Not on your life. Pure gold it was Paige finding the hostage. Vowing she would never again set foot in a Guardia Civil station, she asked Casey to telephone the hotline to tell the authorities about the kid. He promised to make the call later from his mobile, a promise he had no intention of keeping. 'Be sure to say the child's sick,' she told Casey. 'Don't give any names.' Smart lady, for who could guarantee a Knight in the police force wasn't listening in. Or checking the log of calls. Not that a spy in the force mattered. The call would never happen. Only a madman—and he was not a madman—would throw the hostage's whereabouts to the bobbies when it was worth a fortune to the Muslims. Sell the information and be set for life. Well, a few years, anyway. But how to find a Muslim contact—a spokesman with whom he could negotiate the sale? How to access the commander, the czar, or sultan or whatever the top cat of the Army of the Second Emir called himself. One could hardly stroll into Friday mosque and say, 'I'm here to make your day.'

The answer was Global Solutions. Sam Weber had a telescope on the non-transparent world. The challenge would be convincing him to buy-in.

He would question the source. No one who knew Paige would doubt her conclusion that the child was indeed the imam's son. But Sam didn't know Paige from the Queen of Sheba. Would the situation sound credible? Have to pad it a bit, throw in fancy details: the informer was in top government, or an old Middle-East embassy hand—that sort of thing. If Weber bit, the rest was a cake-walk. Settle the price, and Bob's your uncle.

The waiter lowered the tray, unloaded its contents, and left the bill. Casey computed the tip, dropped two euros, reconsidered, and took one back. Consulting was feast or famine: up to your neck in contracts; then nada. And right now, he had to sock away enough to buffer the dry spells without relying on Harold. Although Harold was a prince of a house-mate, he might, or might not be around when Casey's HIV morphed into AIDS.

He turned his hand palm up. Too soon to check the pulse again. His self-imposed limit was three times a day. He reached for his wrist anyway. What could possibly be wrong with a harmless obsession that proved Casey O'Brannigan was alive? For now.

Ten fifty on his watch brought a replay of the morning's trip up the lift, and ruffles at the gate. This time she ushered him into the inner sanctum. The office could have been a celebrity theme pub with Sam Weber the star. A photo of him accepting a plaque from Donald Trump when Trump was merely a billionaire entrepreneur. A snapshot of Weber saluting Felipe before his coronation as King, of Weber's jolly wife astride a thoroughbred. The furniture was particle-board teakwood that would drive a Dane to drink. Mold darkened the wall-to-wall carpet.

Sam sprang from behind his desk. "As I live and breathe, what the hell you been up to?" The giant of a man put his arm around Casey's shoulders and led him to the sofa. "Take a load off the feet." Sam's sandy gray hair was as thick and unruly, his Italian suit rumpled as if he had just emerged from a jetway. Which was usually the case. Had Sam ever been seen without a wainscot? This one wore egg-yolk near the middle button.

"Been how many years?" Sam asked, their knees almost touching as they sat side-by-side.

"Actually, six months. The seminar I gave at the American base you kindly sent my way."

"Super outcome evaluations. Bet you're here on a fishing expedition for a repeat performance, right?"

Casey took a deep breath, "I've found imam Tariq's son."

Sam's face expressionless, then the smile made brilliant in a dentist's chair-side bleach

Machine, Casey guessed.

"Fantastic," Sam said.

He's clueless, Casey thought and went on to explain. "The hostage, the baby the Knights of Constancia kidnapped. You've heard of the organization?"

Sam shrugged.

"Good. Anyway, they're holding an imam's kid to make sure the unveiling of their religious statue comes off without the Emir's Army blowing them to hell. You've heard of that group?"

"A problem," Sam agreed, nodding.

"If the Emir's Army blokes restrain themselves, the baby gets returned. You know our local jihadists are backed by Saudi money. They want the kid home, and I know where he is. I'd negotiate the sale myself, but I don't have connections."

Sam peeled the scab of yolk from his vest with his thumbnail, then looked around for a place to put it. "Where do I come in?" He leaned and flicked the crust on the coffee table.

"I need a broker to contact the Emir's Army and negotiate the sale of the kid's whereabouts."

Sam got up, moved around his desk, and sat behind it. "Coffee?"

Good play, Sam, Casey thought. Controlling the conversation, time-out to gather the wits. "Thanks, but not for me."

"I forgot—you people drink tea."

"Nothing, thanks."

"Hey, don't be ashamed. My own wife drinks tea. Sarah," he called to the receptionist. She appeared, tugging her skirt over the leg-band of her knickers. Casey looked away.

"A pot of Bigelow's and the usual for me. And keep the damn door shut."

Were Americans born rude? Casey wondered. Or was it their awful food?

Sam turned back to him, "You sure this hostage is the real McCoy?"

"I saw him," Casey lied. "My informer took me to the site." Anticipating Sam's next question, Casey headed him off. "Sorry, can't name names. My informant's a London contact with embassy savvy. Leave it at that."

Sam pressed for details Casey created as he went along, God forbid he would be put to the test to remember what he said.

Sam did a half-turn in his swivel chair, swung back. "I might buy-in, but I will not sell the Islams information, and they go straight for the asset, and the acquisition goes south, they'll chop off my head. A nasty tendency. If I buy the information, the location of the asset—"

"Not asset, the kid."

"The kid. And sell the actual physical asset owned by myself back to the Islams. See what I'm saying? And you understand, of course, hostage reconciliation comes with considerable overhead."

"You mean recapture, not reconciliation."

"Reconciliation's what we call it."

The door opened, and Sarah entered with a tray bearing a Styrofoam cup of coffee, a carafe of water rapidly losing steam, one Lipton bag, and a handful of those little envelopes full of the horrible chalk Americans call cream. "Anything else?"

Sam waved her away.

Casey fixed himself a tepid cup as Sam settled back to spin out a scenario. "Here's what we're looking at. Hypothetical, you understand. First, we have to be in possession of the asset."

"Kid."

"To negotiate a clean exchange." Sam launched into a long-winded explanation of the pitfalls. A tedious description of vetting intermediaries, and of finding a neutral ground to park the asset.

"Whatever," Casey said.

Sam complained about risk assessment, the cost of cameras, vehicles, and armed facilitators.

"You mean mercenaries?"

"Facilitators, they're called."

Sam's stream of words became blather. The tributes to the expertise of AGS and praise of Sam's vast experience in hostage negotiation, half of the examples made up, Casey suspected, which made him wonder if Sam were lying more than he, himself, lied. His fingers hovered over his wrist; he drew them back. He listened until irritation got the better of him, and he broke in with, "And my take-home?"

Sam shook his head as if Casey should know better than to ask.

Thirty minutes later at the same outdoor table in the bistro, Casey tried to rid his head of Sam's idiotic jargon. They were to meet again the next day. Zoom in with the telephoto—as Sam put it.

A new waiter, and another coffee, this time an Americano. Casey shook down a packet of sugar and tore it open with his teeth. Overhead the noon sun bore directly onto the choppy Straits of Gibraltar, scorching the intrepid sunbathers on the ratty beach. Church bells chimed from a neighborhood higher up the Rock. A wooden-planked ferry glided toward the pier. Ragged

Moroccans came down the gangplank and into the unwelcoming arms of British customs.

Casey finished the dregs of the cup and was gathering energy to find his way back to the car park, when the caffeine fired every neurotransmitter in his brain: the Knights of Constancia were getting seriously screwed. And he was the greedy bastard throwing them to the dogs. Or rather, to the Army of the Second Emir who would bomb, shoot, rape and chop up every bloomin' Christian on the face of the earth. Never mind that the Knights were absolutely daft. They were Christian daft, civilized daft, whereas the Muslims were—well—Muslims. Worse, he was betraying Paige, bless her heart, violating the trust of this perfectly lovely lady. Casey glanced around at the other tables: shoppers with Marks and Spencer bags, a couple sharing a single compote of ice-cream. He felt their disapproving eyes staring not at a fellow human being, but at the despicable two-headed worm he was.

Jump ship. Call it off. Forget Sam, his facilitators, the lot of them.

And goodbye to the jewel dropped in his lap? He pocketed the extra packets of sugar and rose to leave. He looked down at his hand, closed his eyes, opened them to a vision of the hand of his future. The inevitable day when the bones were fragile as a trout's, the flesh thin as onion skin. He placed his fingers on his pulse, held them firm, counting, not letting go until satisfied the beat went on.

10

The purple sea sparkled lavender as if amethysts rode the waves. In the brisk wind, the huge contemporary windmills waved their arms hysterically above the whitewashed walls of an Andalusian village. Along the highway, electrical poles bore plywood platforms atop their cross-beams where storks could build their nests. Shaggy messy nests with strings and straws spilling over the rims, like sombreros upside down. I glanced over at Casey at the wheel and said, "When you get a chance, look it up. These big-guy-birds winter in Africa and blow in for the summer."

"Who does?" Tony asked from the back seat.

Casey downshifted and said, "You're blind? Storks, right in front of you."

Tony lowered his head to look out the side window. "The locals must build these special supports. I'm touched they're so kind to wildlife."

"Touched." Casey mocked under his breath.

I heard Tony's exasperated sigh from behind me and wondered how many of Casey's smart-ass remarks I could put up with. It might be a long afternoon. The other evening when I reminded Casey about visiting the baby in the church, I'd mentioned the doctor who X-rayed my ribs would be coming with us. Casey threw a fit, paced his apartment, stopping only to take his pulse, that bizarre habit. What got into him? He knew I had no prescription or admitting authority. I reminded him without a practitioner we might as well not go at all. At that, Casey backed off.

A low-flying stork dipped toward the windshield, then veered upward in a wonderful sweep of black and white. "They bring babies," Tony said.

"You believe that shit and call yourself a doctor?" Casey said.

I tapped his knee. "Don't be literal."

Casey was in his usual schoolboy outfit of a button-down shirt with its tail over the belt of his jeans. He ran his fingers through his unmanageable hair to flip it out of his eyes, a gesture I always found endearing. Until today.

"How much farther? Tony asked.

The closer we got to the church, the tighter the muscles in my stomach. The last words I said to the woman were, "I'll be back with el doctor." Doctor I had repeated. She seemed to get it, and I banked on her wanting help with the kid. But if she told the Knights, they might have moved him to another hideout. Or the farmer could be waiting with his rifle ready to blow out my brains.

Casey made a sharp left onto the church's access road and straddled the ruts, the Audi plunging through clouds of gray dust. Tony leaned forward with his hand on the back of my seat to steady himself as the car lurched over potholes. I half-turned to face him. "That's it up ahead. Bombed to bits in the Civil War. The chapel's all that's left, where they've hidden the baby. Left him in the middle of nowhere."

Tony's voice hardened. "Happened every day in Mauretania. Thugs holding out for a few dirham's ransom. The only way we Docs without Borders could function was to ignore the politics and treat whatever came through the door." Tony looked ahead through the windshield. "Lovely building. Gothic I'm struck by the solitude. Reminds me of Tintern Abbey."

"Exactly what my father used to say," I replied. "Visigoth, he told me. The opinion of an armchair archeologist. Casey, you can pull up there near the entrance."

We got out, and as I stood with my hand on the door handle, I said, "Listen. Hear a generator?"

Tony reached for his bag. "I'm right behind you."

The door was unlocked, and I ushered Tony and Casey into the medieval cavern of a room. When I took off my sunglasses, I made out the woman and the farmer playing dominos in the kitchen, a six-pack of Reina Cervesa under the table.

The woman rushed toward me, the ragged hem of her black skirt brushing the floor. "*Senora.*" With her hands on my shoulders, she kissed me quickly on the right cheek, then the left. The farmer did not look at us, acted as if we were not there. The woman must have taken care of him in her own way. He lifted a bottle of beer and topped his mug, plastic with a pink teddy bear decal. He was in what looked to be the same black baggy work-pants and black cap he'd worn the last time I saw him. No rifle in sight.

Tony leaned over the crib. "Come here."

I went up beside him. "His name's Hamid," I said. The child yawned, squirmed, and fell back into a stupor. I touched a tiny finger. "Why's the skin peeling?"

The grandmother tugged Tony's sleeve and held up the jug of her medicinal whiskey as if for approval. Tony sniffed the contents and shook his head. She looked at his black bag, placed her hand on her heart and stepped aside, either grateful for the intervention, or resigned to it.

Tony began undressing the baby. "Bloody hell. Poor little nipper can hardly breathe in all the shit. Spaniards aren't the worst. You should see Native American babies strapped to a board—never mind." His skilled hands drew the child's arm through a sleeve. He tipped the kid forward and gently rolled the shirt up and off, then hesitated at the leggings. I leaned over the rail and unfastened a complicated row of snaps.

"I don't like this lethargy." Tony checked the diaper. "Dehydrated, all right." He turned to Casey. "Over here, please, my Spanish won't cut it. Ask the grandmother if there's been vomiting, if he's been eating solids, taking liquids? Is she—?"

Casey held up his palm. "One question at a time." He spoke to the woman and launched a three-way discussion among himself, the woman and Tony in rapid-fire Spanish interspersed with English.

"Looks bad," Tony muttered as he read the temporal artery thermometer. He palpitated the lymph nodes and winced.

At the sight of the otoscope, Hamid shrieked, gathered a second wind and howled. Tony waited until the baby wound down then patiently examined each ear and the mouth keeping up a running narrative directed at me as if training an intern. "Dry lips, oral rash. Any experience with Kawasaki? Not the motorcycle, the disease."

"I know, I know." Tony's condescending attitude pissing me off. "It affects the coronary arteries, lymph nodes."

Tony nodded.

"Permanent heart impairment if untreated," I added drawing on the full extent of an in-service at Baylor. "Aspirin, which is funny," I added, "because it's usually contraindicated in children."

"We saw a lot of this in Mali," Tony said.

That's all he could say? No acknowledgement I kept up with the journals. I hid my disappointment behind a polite nod.

He went on. "The ambulance crew can start a pediatric IV."

The door opened with a gust of cool morning air and six masked men glided over the threshold and gathered near the entrance. The grandmother screamed and clutched the front of her dress. The farmer leaped to his feet, knocking over the chair behind him. I stepped back until I hit the wall.

"*Que quieres?*" The farmer shouted.

Fear slid from my mind to my knees that were about to give out. The Emir's Army here for their imam's kid. I reached for the rail of the grandmother's hospital bed. The soldiers wore black hoods and black gloves. All were in camouflage, but each tunic differed from the others. One guy in desert fatigues, another in jungle green. The tallest in the group—he seemed to be the leader—stepped forward and barked in Spanish.

From the kitchen, Casey replied, then translated, "He says for none of us to move. Not to panic. They've come for the baby."

"*Gracias,*" the leader said. No Castilian "th" lisp at the "c" in the way he pronounced the word.

"He's telling all of you to stay where you are," Strange, Casey barked the order as if he too was a thug with a gun. Wasn't he one of us?

Something to figure out later. I steadied myself against the bed's side-rails. A flash of the woman's head on the beach, of the BBC's discussion of a newly adopted method of beheading going viral in Morocco, a wire sawed across the victim's throat. "Get these men out of here," I begged Casey.

"Don't lose it, Paige," he replied.

The walls spun. Something was wrong with my eyes.

Casey rested his elbow on top of the miniature refrigerator watching the bad guys as he would watch visiting relatives.

Tony crossed his arms over his chest. "Do not touch this infant." Spoken with a quiet dignity that would put decent men to shame.

The leader snapped his fingers and led his men to the crib.

Tony called out firmly, "Casey, I want you to demand—hear me? Demand the baby be taken to a hospital. Emphasize die. Hospital. Now."

While Casey translated, the leader studied Hamid and scratched the back of his head through the mask.

With exaggerated movements, Tony felt the infant's forehead and lymph nodes, then stepped away motioning for the leader to do the same. But the man shook his head and turned to the guy behind him.

The soldier rested his rifle against the crib, reached down and slid his hands under Hamid. I dashed over and blocked his arm. "Animal," I screamed. "Animal, animal."

The soldier let go of Hamid and reached for the gun.

Tony whipped around and stood between me and the assailant.

The grandmother screamed.

The soldier tucked the butt of the rifle into the curve of his shoulder.

The grandmother shot over and with one hefty shove, pushed the soldier forward almost into my arms. The rifle clattered to the floor. Two other guys ran to help their comrade. Hamid's howls outdid the grandmother's, while Casey continued to yell, "Stop. Everyone. Stop."

The leader came forward, lifted the weapon from the floor and muttered, "A god damned clusterfuck."

Panting, I looked up trying to think if I heard right. "You're American?"

"*Que?*" he quickly replied.

A whispered exchange between the leader and the guy in the desert fatigues and he once again reached for Hamid. The baby's legs flailed against the crib. His screams echoed from the stone walls.

"He's only in a diaper," I said, my voice strangled.

Casey called out in Spanish, and the guy paused. "I said you wanted to dress the kid," Casey said. "He's telling you, hurry it up."

I struggled with the one-piece pajamas, while Tony rummaged in his bag and came up with a vial of what might be aspirin. Showing it to a soldier, Tony ran his finger under the writing on the label. "*En Español*" he pointed out.

The soldier shrugged.

I went to the changing table and handed over a carton of Pampers. When the soldier reached for it, I was hit with the blast of alcohol on his breath.

I glanced at the soldier beside him and did a double-take at the ring on his finger bearing the Naval Academy logo.

Relief loosened every muscle in my body. Relief? My next thought was, why? Simply because these were Americans? My people? What were they doing here?

The Annapolis man lifted Hamid from the crib. I tucked the blanket around the frail thighs. "Keep a good grip," I said loudly enough to mask the catch in my throat. The man lifted Hamid and held him awkwardly against his chest, looking around for the door. The grandmother sobbed softly as Hamid was carried past. I followed the guy outside where a white Ford Explorer was parked in the mud. A driver and a passenger sat in front. A soldier gripped my elbow to escort me back into the room. On my way inside, I heard, "Papillion." I turned and saw the desert guy pass Hamid to the passenger in the front seat. "Papillion," drifted across the driveway. Then, "The A 46." Followed by, "All the way to Antequera?" in English.

Inside, the room was cool, damp, and strangely desolate. Tony as fussing around the empty crib. I went over and joined him. "You hear the guy speak American? Were they real Muslims?"

Tony shook out the sheet. "Probably converts. Volunteer terrorists. A boy on the Net lured by the glitz of barrel bombs." He folded the sheet neatly and smiled at the grandmother. "The jihadists recruit on social media."

"Why didn't they kill us?"

Tony held a tiny blanket in mid-air. "I'd say any number of reasons. They didn't want to draw attention to the kidnapping, they hadn't planned on us being here."

A quiet whimper and I turned to the grandmother sitting sat at the table rocking back and forth. I walked over and touched her shoulder and asked Casey. "Can you lie? Please? Tell her the baby will be all right." A lie because assuming he'd be returned to his father, he would never be all right. The old woman looked up with red-rimmed eyes.

In the far corner, the farmer, on his knees, groped for dominos under the cabinet. Tony resumed putting the contents of his bag in order. He seemed resigned, as if having witnessed this scene too many times, in too many places that were as evil and strange as this one.

II

The Pajero Bistro

A rickety wooden walkway led from the street to the Pajaro, a combination tapas bar and beach-front restaurant. Paintings for sale by local artists covered three walls, the fourth opened to the sea. When it rained—as it was when Zak entered and shook out his umbrella—the Pajaro's owner, Heinrich Otter, rolled a ragged curtain of clear vinyl down over the opening. Theoretically, customers would stay dry while still enjoying the view. And indeed, they would have a view, Zak thought, if it weren't for the black mold breeding on the plastic.

Zak drew out a chair and waited for Kurt, who was at the bar buying cigarettes. The sale seemed more complicated than it should. Kurt and Heinrich in a huddle with their heads together until Heinrich held up his index finger and disappeared behind the curtain that hid the kitchen. Kurt turned and gave Zak a thumbs up.

Kurt had introduced Zak to the Pajaro, where the unwritten rule was to order only German brew and German tapas if there were such a thing. The steins and tacky Hummel figurines reminded Zak of a beer haus in Munich. But this was Torremolinos, and like everything else, in the decrepit resort, the Pajaro was in serious decline. Its hey-day in the seventies came after Franco died and the entire nation reeled in an orgy of topless bikinis, North African dope and home-grown porn. Torromalinos was hot: movie stars, royalty, and beach bums swarmed the vacation apartments and packaged-tour hotels. The splendor of Spain, Zak thought, its glory and gravitas buried with Franco. When the country's exhilaration of liberation settled down, and the economy shot up, Torremolinos was trumped by Marbella, Puerto Banus, and Estapona, the prestigious addresses moving west.

What was taking Kurt so long? The cigarette transaction a work-in-progress. And who's he trying to impress, Zak wondered, with that dark suit and shiny maroon tie. Dapper was the word. The watch on a chain across his vest would be an anachronism on anyone else. But Zak had to admit it suited Kurt to a T, as did the Ferragamo loafers. All in all, he looked more like the owner of Great Estates, than like an employee. Kurt's official title, Fiscal Manager and Director of Operations understated his true calling—a fixer. The salary from Great Estates would never cover his BMW 750, and three-bedroom condo in Puerto Banus.

"A man has to do a little of this, a bit of that." Kurt's banal wisdom.

Yet Zak knew there was far more in that small Gothic brain than just Germanic pragmatism. He told Zak he joined the Knights for the same reason Americans joined the Abraham Lincoln Brigade during the Spanish Civil War, to fight for the cause. He wasn't paid to serve as treasurer of the local Knights, no reward except, as he put it, fixing the broken world.

Or undermining it. Zak never knew what the guy was up to with his ties to banks tolerant of anonymous depositors, and ties to provincial administrators who waived fines. He even had a roster of customs officers willing to sign off on bogus bills of lading. Kurt said his most lucrative contacts were with suppliers with whom he bought and sold arms, gently used guns and grenades peddled to regimes in sorry need of change.

With three cartons of Marlboros under his arm, Kurt approached the table and chose the chair with the fewest missing slats. "Heinrich's tobacco's duty-free. Can you imagine such a thing?"

"Speak English, please," Zak said. "Your German-Spanish-French mix grates on my nerves. On the phone, you said the baby was kidnapped from the church. He's gone. What the hell happened?"

"So. As I started to explain before you insisted on one-for-one—" Kurt paused to break open a carton. "The Texas woman who owns the summer house found our hostage."

"How do you know?"

"When she left her father's house—remember? The day we were all there, I followed her to the church. Then later, for another reason, I talk to Veber. You've heard of Global Assets, the American company in Gibraltar?"

"Weber, The *W* in English, is pronounced like the one in water."

"So., He told me the woman told her British neighbor who calls himself an international relations expert, in other words, unemployed and useless."

Kurt unwound the cellophane strip from a cigarette pack. "She told this O'Brannigan—I don't know his full name—where the kid is, and he goes to Veber to sell the baby's location." Kurt thumbed his monogrammed Dunhill, trying for a light.

"Weber wanted to buy a baby?"

Instead of laughing, Kurt motioned to Heinrich coming toward them with a tray. "Ah, here it is. I ordered our usual."

In a white apron stained with orange grease, Heinrich lowered cheese, a small loaf of black bread and mugs with mud-colored beer showing through the frost. He held a plate in mid-air. "Who's for curried sausage?"

"Don't look at me." Zak pointed to the pickled herring. "That's mine." He lifted the mug and took a sip as if testing the vintage.

Kurt tapped ashes into an ashtray. "You ask why Veber? O' Brannigan knows the Muslim's will pay top price to get him back, but that means finding a mosque rat who speaks a human language, meaning a contact who can negotiate the price and the sale. He, himself, can't do this because normal people don't know where the rats hang out. Why he goes to Veber."

Zak studied Kurt's face looking for a clue as to why Weber would confide in a German accountant who worked for an estate agent.

"Why is he telling you this?"

"Too much caraway seeds in the pork. Otherwise, perfection."

"Kurt, I asked you a question."

"Let me finish it in order." Kurt lifted his fork. "O'Brannigan goes with the Texas woman and some doctor when they went to check the kid physically. It was sick or maybe just pretending."

"Smart kid."

"While the Texan and the doctor were there, Veber's militia-men went in and hauled off the little boy. Went like clock time."

"Clockwork."

Kurt speared a slice of sausage and held it out to Zak, red sauce dripping on the tablecloth. "Try it."

To humor him, Zak eased the portion to the edge of his plate.

Kurt set down his beer and winced. "Mud."

Zak eased the spine from a segment of herring, knowing full well that Kurt knew the kind of business Weber ran, but wanting Kurt to know he knew.

"Don't trust Weber. Americans have what are called beltway bandits. Let me explain." Zak trying to keep it light. "The beltway is the ring road around the city—like the ring road in Berlin." Giving Kurt the picture. "Consulting firms along the interstate are owned by military guys who worked for US contracts shops in Defense, then retired while their connections are still hot."

"Happens here, too."

Zak went on. "They stay on top of RFPs—that's requests for proposals— and know when to bid, to compete for the big ones."

Kurt seemed to be tracking the scenario.

"They go for costs plus exorbitant fixed fees," Zak went on. "Or negotiate overhead with former colleagues. Selling to any buyer, they play it close to the chest because who wants to be fingered selling AK 47s to both Assad and ISIS at the same time." With his knife, Zak scraped the shiny gray skin off the fish. "No morals get in the way. Weber's the worst."

"You know him, too?"

Zak slid another herring from the tray. "I hired him for a workshop on spy-craft for our new recruits to the Knights. But what were you doing with him in the first place? Why would he tell you anything about anything? Why—? Wait." Zak sat back, stunned by his insight. Or rather pleased by his knack for putting the facts together. "Weapons?" Zak said, awed by Kurt's audacity. "You sold to Weber's guys? Maybe the very ones used to take the kid from the Knights? From us? The organization you belong to? The cause you work for? The Christian Europe you swore you'll die for?"

"No, no, of course not." Spoken with such conviction, Zak knew he was lying

"It's the other way around. Veber called me. "Kurt tapped his chest. "Not wanting to buy. Wanting to sell. Dump his overvalued chicken-shit used materiel. Always, always I verify the provenance before I pay. I'm careful with serial numbers, models, and recent, shall we say, purposes, uses."

"You're saying you bought the weapons used by Weber's mercenaries. What a clever lie. But not good enough. Whichever way it came down, you're still screwing your own people."

Silence, before Zak asked, "Why are we having this conversation?"

Kurt closed his eyes as if looking for the best way to get off the hook. "Because I have to tell you, my boss, everything, always, what's going on."

Covering his ass, Zak thought. He knows, I know Weber. In case I happen to run into him and he slips. "Meaning you're afraid," Zak said. "If I found out through someone else, I'd make you a new body orifice—"

"Oh, my, how dramatic."

Zak continued through gritted teeth. "Our own asset. The kid we—" Zak searched for the word and came up with, "Borrowed. The only leverage we had."

Zak stared at Kurt as he would stare at a cockroach in the bathroom sink. The German lowered his head and tore off the heel of the loaf.

Zak finished the last of his beer to damp down his rage. An unexpected feeling of something similar to loss, but more like disappointment came over him. Kurt, his trusted right-hand man, now needing to be kicked out of the Knights and fired from Great Estates. And Zak would do it in a heartbeat. Except Kurt had his hand in every padded line-item buried in the books, records, accounts, labor. But the golden days of Kurt the confidant were over.

From now on I'll use him only for what I absolutely need, Zak thought. Which is how he's using me.

Carry-on, Zak thought. He slid the mug aside as if making room on the table for damage control. "Let's turn the situation around. How much will the jihadists pay Weber to tell them where the kid is?"

Kurt looked up.

"Would Weber sell the kid back to us, the Knights, instead of the Muslims?"

"If we offer more euros." Kurt dipped his napkin in his water glass and dabbed at a spot of sauce on his cuff. "On the other hand, Veber sells to us, and the mosque-rats will be very, very upset. I wouldn't like to be the target."

"How much ready cash is in the Knights account?"

"None."

How could that be? Zak did a run-down of credits. The Archbishop's collections alone were bringing in about twenty grand a month. Kurt was skimming?

As if reading his mind, Kurt added, "Don't forgot the forklift for the statue's installation, limo rental for the Bishop, concrete for the plinth, robes for the choir and honorarium for the artist."

"I'll check the spreadsheet." Zak ran his fingers through his hair. "If we can't buy off the Muslims—"

"Mosque-rats."

"The only thing left is to take the kid back. By force, if we have to. I'll send Bassem. Where's the kid at?

"Thought you'd ask me that. I think Veber stashed him in an abortion clinic somewhere near Antiquera. A fancy spa called Papillion, That's a French word."

"Don't patronize me."

"Veber's a genius. A phony spa that's really a medical set-up he runs under the radar."

"Where to find it?"

Kurt shrugged. "As if I should know." Then came a sly smile. "Idea. Tell that bimbo you're hiding in your boat you want a family. She starts in on making one, and you change your mind and ask around for a friendly doctor." Weber leaned back and laughed, cracked narrow lips, small yellow teeth.

Zak picked up the check. "You're so sick, you make me sick."

12

Tony started to say something, then fell quiet as he maneuvered the tiny Seat

Panda around a hairpin curve. "You're acting dodgy, Paige."

Irritable, fighting a sense of futility, I braced myself with a hand on the dashboard. "This whole trip's a waste. We'll never find Hamid."

Tony downshifted.

"I wish you had a GPS," I said.

"I told you, it doesn't work. Just follow the map on your phone."

"I throw up if I read in cars. Even if we find this Papillion place, for all we know the bad guys could have moved Hamid." A flash of the woman's remains on the beach. "Or even beheaded him."

"Tricky, love, with a baby. They wiggle and squirm.'

"Not funny."

Anxiety can be a physical state as well as a state of mind. My stomach fluttered, and my nerves were strung tight as guitar strings. "This Papillion spa, I'm wondering—" I half-turned to Tony, "why the Muslims didn't deliver the kid directly to his father? The big-shot, Tariq?"

"Simple. The little nipper's sick. The soldiers took him to be treated."

"Assuming spas have nurses. And what if the staff won't tell us if the kid's there. Or they lie."

Tony reached across the console and patted my hand.

Tony the rescuer. A label for me as well? I looked out at the forest rolling by the window, as if the trees answered the questions I asked myself. If not a rescuer, what was I doing in this underpowered kiddy-car, chasing across Spain, risking being done-in by jihadists, rescuing a child I didn't even know, but whose life I was hell-bent to save? You'd think years of clinical practice would put a dent in my urge to throw my arms around the addicted teen, the battered wife, the alcoholic retiree. Not that I ever did in fact. But maybe should have. Perhaps I should have used my arms to shield my husband from an inner demon he hated and feared.

So many times, I'd held Grant as he lay on the sofa berating himself, saying he was a failure, inadequate, useless. As if his brilliance belonged to a superior being inside him whom he had to destroy. And because Grant was a competent thirty-seven-year-old neurologist, he knew the exact dosage of barbiturates to do the job. Of course, I understood despair can lead to suicide. What I could never accept was my own failure to protect Grant from himself.

"Lost in thought?" Tony asked,

"Something bad's about to happen. I feel it."

"Nonsense." Tony squeezed my hand and turned his attention back to the wheel.

"And you'll know what to do after we find—if we find—Hamid?" I asked.

"I told you, I'll follow through."

As a doctor, it would be easy for Tony to contact local adoption agencies, have the child placed in a Spanish home after we found him. At first rescuing, Hamid seemed so simple. Reality hit last night that it would take two people, one to manage Hamid, the other to make a quick getaway from the Papillion, assuming the spa I brought up on the Net was the right place. I needed help. Zak was my choice until I thought of his quick temper and decided he was too volatile. Casey's connection to the Foreign Office might keep him from anything bordering on illegal, assuming re-kidnapping a kidnap victim was a crime. The solution was calm, sensible Tony.

My eyes followed the dense pines along the road until they became a blur.

"So quiet. Your broken bones kicking up?"

"Along with everything else, I worry about the emotional damage done to kids who've been biffed around. Like Hamid."

Tony glanced over at me. "He'll survive. Others have it much worse."

"You're an internist. I deal with the after-effects of trauma: Post Traumatic Stress, Major

Depression, suicidal ideation: I see them every day."

"Children transcend. We, my grandparents, that is, came through the London blitz, the Luftwaffe strafing the roof, my granddad outrunning bullets."

"Did he make it?"

"We all came through." The Panda bumped over a railroad crossing. "Family stability's the key. When I think of the stories about Gram's Christmas tree in the underground bunker and how she always fixed Sunday roast whenever she got her hands-on meat."

I studied his profile, sturdy cheekbones and jaw, weathered ruddy skin. On the surface, Brits and Americans look alike. But the profound differences in family narratives shaped profound differences in character. Take my anxiety, Tony's stoicism. Except for low-carb diets, my parents had never known hunger, nor life under siege. Americas forget that humans not only survive, but thrive in adversity.

A blown truck tire blocked the center of the narrow road. "What in bloody hell was a lorry doing way out here?" Tony said. "Getting back to kids' resiliency, I believe there's a link between a child's stability and his ego strength as an adult. The sooner we get Hamid to his dad, the better."

"Dad? What dad?" I leaned forward, closed my eyes, wanting to reject what I sensed was coming. "The imam dad? Tariq as dad?"

"So right. His family." Tony glanced over at me. "I say something wrong?"

It never occurred to me Tony would see Hamid as a Muslim. Or, rather, that Tony didn't see Hamid through my eyes, as a child yet to be exposed to violence, fanatism. "We don't know how Hamid will be raised and educated with his real family. We don't even know where Tariq lives."

What was I thinking? Of course, Tony would turn Hamid over to the police. What any normal law-abiding person would do. Like a fool, I'd assumed he'd get Hamid to a Spanish adoption agency. My heart, brain, and even my gut rebelled. "Let me get this straight. You want to add one more terrorist to the universal supply. You don't see anything wrong with him sitting cross-legged in a madrassa memorizing the Koran? No play, no music? As a teenager blowing himself up in a suicide bomb? I won't allow it. No way."

"You mean, your way."

"He has to listen to rap music, dance, chase girls and sing," I said.

"How sweet." Tony turned to me. "Don't take this the wrong way. But he's not your kid."

"Watch the road," I snapped.

Tony and I clearly reading from different scripts. My mind raced as I pretended to change it. I should not alienate Tony. I needed a plan B, and he might have to help. "Maybe you have a point," I said.

A mistake choosing Tony. If I wanted to rescue Hamid from his own people, a justifiable, but arrogant act if there were ever one, I should have called Zak. Whether a member of the screwball Catholics or not, as a Spanish Christian he'd be on my side.

We crested a hill overlooking miles of silvery olive trees. In the distance, the sea was a long gray snake stretched across the horizon. At a crossroad, Tony slowed at the faded sign marking the C2344. "Turn here?" I said. "If I'm reading the map right."

"You're sure this spa's the Papillion the soldier mentioned?"

"Has to be. The only thing like it north of Malaga. I think it's a covert abortion clinic. The website pitches it as a trendy beauty retreat for Tangier's society ladies. But between the lines, I picked up off-kilter references— confidentiality, pain management and a give-away phrase, maternity solutions. Geez, maternity solutions, what a spin on reality."

"Hey." Tony pointed ahead to a grove of striped umbrellas. "Food and petrol. Would you believe?"

"We don't have time."

"Except a loo and a cuppa would be spot on."

Before I could argue, he pulled up near the terrace café and got out. "Back in a sec." He trotted off toward the caballeros' sign. No other customers, and I pulled out a chair and reached for a menu in the grip of a chrome holder. An orange cat wove around the table legs.

"He's a sucker for attention." The waiter wore a green apron over a black tee-shirt and shorts. "You're a UK-er?" he asked. "Or speako de Deutch?"

"American."

"Seriously?" His smile revealed brown rotting teeth. Moustache seedlings failed to hide the acne on his upper lip. "I'm from Monroe. Ever heard of Loosianna.? Where y'all from?"

"Texas."

"Oh, wow. The first non-Brit I seen here."

My saying, "You're a long way from home," triggered his volley of unasked for self-disclosure.

"A bunch of us came to do Pamplona until Jamie got sick. I guess you wouldn't know Jamie. But being from Texas, you never can tell. Me?" He tapped his chest with his thumb. "They call me Kevin after my old man." He smiled with his hand half over his mouth, as if trying to hide his blackened teeth.

I tuned him out. Studied the menu marveling not at the exorbitant prices, but at the tragedy of methamphetamines, a home-cooked drug able to totally devastate teeth, judgment, and lives.

Tony returned and nodded to Kevin, who was now complaining about work visas." You from Texas, same as her?" Kevin asked.

Tony lifted a menu. "Earl Grey, please. And we need to double-check directions if you know the area. My GPS is on the fritz."

Why on earth was Tony asking this deadbeat anything? On the other hand, the kid was probably an expert on local low life.

Tony explained where we were headed, and added, "I understand this Papillion's a posh place."

Kevin looked up at the racing clouds competing with his thought process. "Yeah, run by Parisians from Paris." Staring pointedly at my waistline, he grinned. "I know where you're coming from, and why you're off to where you're going."

I pulled in my stomach and drew in a breath to tell the creep no, I wasn't pregnant, I was a doctor whose office overlooked the Gulf of Mexico and my income usually—I brought myself up short. My God, how pathetic could I get? Trying to impress this creep to offset humiliation? This was where feeling cheap lead.

Tony and Kevin huddled over the map, while I reflected on the word cheap, meaning of no value, temporary, a throwaway. The teenaged girls in the psychiatric service recovering from overdoses and motorcycle spills. A girl with tattooed breasts who was ashamed of the refrigerator in the front yard, and if she had a father, her dad's dirty mouth and hands. My upbringing and education were far too expensive for me to feel cheap. Until now.

"You ready to move on?" Tony said to me and turned to Kevin. "We'll find it."

I picked up my bag.

"Have a good one," Kevin said as we passed him on our way to the parking lot.

Was his wink real? Or imagined?

Tony was smiling as he turned the key in the engine. I spoke through gritted teeth. "You thought his thinking I'm pregnant was funny."

"You must admit the conclusion's logical."

"That wasn't a smile on your face. It was a smirk."

"I have never smirked in my life." Tony put the car in reverse.

"Furthermore," I said, "his directions will be as inept as he is."

"Stop picking on the lad. He knew all about the Arab's place, and we're almost there."

As if by magic the instant we turned onto the grounds of Le Papillon, the sky changed from the work-a-day washed-out azure of the coast to magnificent cerulean blue. I struggled from the cramped passenger seat and gazed at the white palace with its spires and fluted columns, its narrow reflecting pool flanked by Italian cypress and the Oleander nodding magenta heads over pink roses. Bougainville tumbled from marble urns. The air smelled of the jasmine tangled in a three-board fence.

Tony came up beside me. "In Xanadu did Kublai Khan," I recalled the words as he went along. "A stately pleasure-dome decreed, Where Arp the sacred river ran—

"Alph," I said. "Alph, Alph the sacred river ran."

"Arp, Tony said, locking the door. He shifted his briefcase from one hand to the other and shielded his eyes from the sun. "Two more minarets and Papillion would be the Taj Mahal."

"Except the architecture's Moroccan, not Mughal. Lovely," I said. "As its name, butterfly, right?"

"Morocco's French, or used to be."

"What a gold mine," I said, scanning the grounds. "Anything money can buy, abortions, liposuction, massage and pore-tightening facials with mud from the Dead Sea."

"Better be from the Jordanian side."

"Bus in the rich Arab ladies,"" I went on. "Imam-vetted staff. Swimming pools uncontaminated by infidels—what's in that briefcase?"

"Every ID in my arsenal."

"Good idea. We'll need it."

Our cover was hardly bulletproof. We decided Tony would explain he had been the attending when the child, Hamid—no record of the last name—was admitted to Marbella General's emergency room. Coincidently, a Nigerian with Ebola, was admitted the same day. By current Spanish policy, everyone exposed to Ebola was to be examined and referred for follow-up. Tony was here for a hands-on check of Hamid. The story shot through with inaccuracies, but plausible—providing no screw-ups. A doorman in pantaloons and red tarboosh guarded the entrance. He bowed as I proceeded Tony through the doorway into a lobby the size of an airport hangar. "I'll do all the talking," Tony said. "Only because you don't speak French."

The scent of cardamom floated on the air. In the center of the room, marble nymphs spilled water from amphorae into a lily-pond. A sharp chill almost sent me back for my windbreaker until a glance at the Louis XV furniture warned I would be even more underdressed than I already was, my jeans and tee-shirt probably threatening to give the doorman an embolism. Two well-fed ladies in glittering robes sailed across the room, as elegant as Viking ships. A uniformed cleaning lady—black burka and veil with an eye-screen, bent over a dustpan.

Tony headed to a granite counter that ran along a wall. A receptionist looked up from her computer. To me Tony's French sounded impressive until the woman winced at his pronunciation of "*Merce.*" She reached for her phone.

"Paging the Medical Director," Tony explained.

The physician in street clothes who emerged from a door behind the counter could have posed for a Louis Vuitton ad. Strategically placed silver strands in her short dark hair, and a splendid shantung jacket hung open over a white silk shirt. Wire-rimmed glasses were an unexpected touch that would be dated on anyone but Doctor Ollu.

Tony launched into a complex explanation ending with, "Ebola," and a sweeping gesture.

She frowned.

Why not agree? Who would want to risk not being vaccinated?

Ollu seemed to not notice me. I stood aside as Tony opened the briefcase and spread his credentials over the counter. A faint trilling from my bag and I took out my phone. A US area code with a familiar number. "Back in a minute," I said, heading toward the glass doors opening onto a flagstone patio.

Jason Ventura, my lawyer in Houston, must have been mufti-tasking again, for as usual, his voice sounded harried and distracted. "The Board agreed to a postponement. They'll schedule a new date next week."

Continuing fallout from a misjudgment of character on my part. I had made a referral to a colleague I had known since my residency in Baltimore. I thought Gary was competent—he was, after all, widely published, his name well-known. One would assume he was a trustworthy clinician. I was wrong. He prescribed opioids to my fifty-four-year-old patient. Worse, with no medical work-up. The patient wound up in rehab, and her husband went to the board of licensure, naming me along with every other provider involved in her treatment.

"Reinstating your license wouldn't be problematic, if we weren't in the middle of this opioid crisis," Johnathon said.

"Problematic?"

"We'll see what happens."

"Do they have cause?"

"Far as I can see, absolutely not."

"So, you're saying I should not sell my practice," I said lightly, testing the waters. I waited for his laugh. Instead, I listened to a prolonged silence.

"We'll know more after the hearing," Jay finally said.

"Remember, I'm in Spain, and—"

A woman's voice in the background brought Jay's muffled reply, "Tell him to wait." Then to me, "Gotta' run."

Through the glass in the French doors, I watched Tony follow Ollu across the lobby. Despite my resolve to kick the habit, I'd have killed for a cigarette. I dug in my bag for a Valium and pressed a pill through the blister-pack. Waiting for the euphoria to bloom, I circled the terrace, hardly seeing the gigantic pots of hibiscus and bougainvillea trailing from baskets overhead.

I turned into a narrow passageway that would take me back to the lobby. Midway along the corridor, a wide doorway was open to reveal a laundry room where wire carts held mountains of soiled sheets and towels. I stopped. Something a familiar blue in there. A blanket with teddy bears wearing red kerchiefs lay on the floor. I went in and slid the blanket toward me with my toe. The brown stain from the grandmother's medicine was still there, as was the tear in the binding. Next to the blanket lay a bib crusted with egg yolk and a rolled-up crib sheet. I looked up and down the hallway. All other doors closed. But for sure Hamid was behind one of them. Was he okay? I lifted the bib. Still moist, there was egg yolk on my finger. My first thought was to get to Tony. On second thought, get to Zak.

In the lobby, Tony rose from a gilt love seat as I approached. "Ollu swore there's no baby here," he said. "Where've you been?"

"Tell you later."

An elderly man in a kaftan escorting a veiled woman passed us on their way to the counter. When they were beyond earshot, Tony went on, "Ollu said she hadn't heard of Ebola in Spain, and no child was here, nor ever would be because the place isn't licensed for pediatrics. I came on strong. She stuck to her guns. I asked for a tour and got a condensed version—two beds occupied, one post-liposuction, the other with an amoxicillin IV. Ollu wouldn't explain. Possibly a botched abortion, but that's none of our business. No baby."

I faked disappointment. "We're in the wrong place. Let's get out of here."

"Back on the road," Tony said.

The receptionist shot us an 'are you still here?' look.

On our way out, I paused at a Botox ad on an easel. No ads for Juvéderm, of course. Wrinkles hidden behind black cloth. Let's hear it for veils.

Tony's voice carried from the entrance. "Are you coming?"

I caught up with him on the portico. The guy in the slave suit bowed with his hand on his heart.

In the parking lot, Tony opened the passenger door for me and said, "Back to Kevin for more ideas." I stopped his arm from closing the door. "If for one minute you think I'm facing that awful creep, you're crazy."

"Calm down."

I had to get to Zak. Quick, before someone decided to do something with, or to, the baby. "Hamid's okay even we don't know where he is." I said, trying to reassure myself as well as Tony.

"Are you daft?"

"Just because we didn't find him, doesn't mean he's at risk."

"Bollocks. Indeed, you are daft. For all we know right now they're chopping off the kid's head.

13

Six hours in Tony's rust-bucket Panda turned my vertebrae into teeth chewing the nerves of my spine. My back was killing me. If that weren't enough, the strain of keeping up the pretense with Tony that we had to find Hamid, took its toll.

"The next Papillion's sure to be it." Tony would repeat. He actually listened to the creepy waiter, Kevin, who suggested two other possibilities with the same name. One turned out to be the Papillion Thai massage parlor, the other a Vietnamese manicurist. All I wanted to do was get to Zak

Finally, home, my call to him went straight to voice mail. He'd mentioned spending every weekend on his sloop, and since the marina was only a twenty-minute walk down the esplanade, I figured, why not? The exercise would burn off some of Mozart's energy. What was it Zak said? His slip was the one nearest the harbormaster? Or did he say, farthest?

The minute I reached for the leash Mozart leaped from his cot, galloped around the kitchen and overturned the garbage; two empty mackerel cans, last December's LANCET, shreds of my half-written article on medication-averse patients and an expired Cascade coupon. So much for the floor I'd mopped yesterday. I went to the pantry for the broom before remembering I'd pitched it after Mozart tore out the straws. When he skidded into the kitchen, I grabbed his collar. Panting, he sat with his tongue dripping while I clipped on the lead.

Out of the apartment and in the hallway, one look at the stairs challenged my tolerance for aggravation. I dragged Mozart into the elevator, feeling like a Nazi while he trembled and whined all the way down to the lobby.

The usual Saturday night crowd on the promenade. Sunburned golfers, rowdy weekenders from Dublin and Spaniards down from Madrid for a day on the sand. The restaurants and bars were in full swing. But the shops were wrapping it up. The After-Beach Boutique had a good-looking sweater in the window. Easy to resist. Even this time of night, the temperature hung in the eighties. An African peddler approached offering me a Michael Kors knockoff.

"No."

He held up a lovely Furla bag, a remarkably good fake. "No," I said no too sharply, and he slunk away muttering in French. A twinge of anxiety he'd come after me for revenge. All the purse sellers knew where all the tenants lived. A ridiculous fear, totally unfounded making me think how easy it was to descend into paranoia.

I headed to the row of iron chairs facing the sea. One good thing about Spain, there were plenty of places to sit; enough seats in the mall restaurants, benches in the parks, sidewalk cafes where you can watch people or check email. Mozart flopped at my feet. The strolling accordionist swung into a waltz drowning the preferable sound of the waves lapping the jetty. Green running-lights shone from either a fishing boat or a fresh load of African refugees. I looked up at the sky-a Turkish flag of a sky—the crescent moon curved around a star, and I wondered if the Turks thought of themselves as the moon? Or the star.

Ahead I made out the cluster of tall masts swaying above the pier, Zak's sloop somewhere among them. Was it reasonable to assume he would take responsibility for Hamid? Keep him safe from the guys with the guns?

Should I trust Zak? How well did I know him? His English was perfected in the States where he got an engineering degree. He told me he'd returned to Spain with his American wife, a chemist who dumped him, he said, for a job back in New York. His version of the divorce. Be interesting to hear her side. As a flaming narcissist, Zak would be hell to live with.

But my gut told me when it came to rescuing Hamid, Zak would step up to the plate. The key question was, why did I care? Let the world have one more kid to blow up another Bamiyan, or an Israeli bus. Did one more jihadist matter? Maybe I was putting too much weight on the importance of one individual. Me, the rescuer. At any rate, maybe it was a conceit on my part to assume my saving Hamid would be moving humanity forward along the evolutionary path. One step for mankind. As if my idealism would improve the world. On the other hand, maybe it would. Each individual's effort mattered. If Mother Teresa mattered, so did Hamid.

I wondered if Zak felt the same way. I read the subtle clues. The flush of Zak's skin when he said, "Muslims." Or his hand in a fist at the name "Syria," Or the lift of his chin when he said, "Christian." I would not be surprised if he was a Knight. Considering they originally kidnapped Hamid, it stood to reason Zak would want him back.

I wrested an empty Styrofoam cup from Mozart's mouth. "Give me that." I got up, and we continued toward the forest of masts.

The marina was arranged according to Spanish social hierarchy. Runabouts—the peasants, tied up at the half-rotten docks beyond the jetty. The sportfishing boats of the bourgeoisie closer in. Then nobility, the sleek Windjammers, Magellan, and the Cortez 50 next to the harbormaster. Zak's sloop, Strega, was a 36 foot, high-freeboard beauty of teak and bright brass work rocking in its slip. The cabin light was on. Boat etiquette—one never boards unless invited. "Anyone home?"

Zak appeared at the entrance of the hatch.

"Permission to come aboard?" I asked.

"Paige, what the hell—?"

Not much of a welcome. "I can leave."

"Don't be silly." He crossed the open deck and reached for the leash. Mozart jumped the stern and began sniffing the planks. Zak wrapped the lead around a winch and held out his hand to help me off the dock. "I don't have Malaga, but there's dry red. Come inside."

Thinking about the humiliating tryst on my sofa the other night, I said, "I can't stay," and moved to the built-in bench along the bulwarks. "Here's more comfortable."

As usual, Zak was sartorially correct. White pants, rubber-grip sandals, a striped blue, and white Polo shirt, topped off with a red kerchief at the throat. The breeze ruffled his black hair.

I propped a life preserver cushion against the back of the bench.

"You like tostadas?" He asked.

"You have any?"

Zak disappeared into the galley and emerged with two filled glasses.

"One more minute." He disappeared again and returned with a box of Cordoba Tostados, the god-awful cheap ones, sugar baked with sawdust. He sat beside me, and I moved the glasses between us.

"This is serious," I said. "We have to talk."

He studied my face. I should have put on eye shadow. Then I recalled I hadn't brought any from Texas.

"Are you angry at me?" he asked.

I dropped a tostado on the deck for Mozart. "It's not about you."

He raised his eyebrows as if surprised there could be anything else.

"You know the hostage, the baby the Knights kidnapped?"

"Of course."

I took it from the top. The church, the grandmother, Tony, Casey and I present when the Jihadists abducted the kid. Now and then I passed Mozart a tostado.

I stopped for breath. The pale moon had risen above the dark sea. Zak rubbed the base of a winch and examined his thumb. "Tarnish," he said.

"Have you been listening?"

"Keep going."

I got the feeling he knew the story I was trying to tell. I plowed ahead anyway. I told him about Hamid in the Papillion and wound up with, "I'm asking you to get him out. I believe you will, because—I mean—you're committed to, let's say," I groped for a word. "Tradition."

A slow blink of the eyes. "Tradition?"

"Don't act cute."

He rose, turned, and went over to rest his elbows on the teak rail. "Come see the boats out there."

I joined him and said, "I think you're in sympathy with the revisionist Catholics."

He shaded his eyes as if there were sunlight on the waves. "Green running-lights. Going East."

"I'm talking to you."

"Toward Valencia where the catch brings a higher price."

My voice went up an octave. "You're always going on about a Muslim invasion. You've even made noises about the good old days of Franco. Then there's that wily German, Kurt something, who follows you like a Doberman. Now and then you say something about your being the Bishop's friend. Zak, look at me."

He stared straight ahead. "You are so typical. So American. Only the facts. Compiling evidence when you could just ask," he said.

"Are you in the Knights?"

"Yes."

"Why?"

He turned away from me and after a long pause, said, "To cut the loss, I suppose."

Laughter and the smell of grilled meat drifted from a few boats away. An insomniac gull crossed the beam of revolving light from the harbormaster's dome.

"The loss of our dignity the monarchy used to represent," He said slowly. "The loss of our self-respect when lost our empire, the loss of the wonderful orderly world that Franco imposed."

"Oh, come on."

"That's all changed. Franco gone, we went wild. The truth is, Spaniards need the Church," he said into the wind. He motioned to the roiling surf. "Like the ocean, it's feisty, then calm. The Church always changing and always the same." He nodded and addressed the night. "The duty, the demands of the faith, yet our irrational love of it." He turned to face me.

"You'd kill for God?"

He turned back to the sea.

"Exactly what the jihadists do," I said after a minute.

"Except they're wrong."

A sudden drop in temperature and I buttoned my summer sweater. "Getting back to Hamid."

Zak shook his head as if waking from a dream. "Where'd I leave my drink?"

"On the edge of the bench."

"I see it." He went over, sat, stretched out his long legs, and crossed his feet at his ankles. "I can get together five men, counting me. And check out an order of nuns who run a nursing home where we can stash the boy."

"The Papillion isn't hard to find," I said and started to give him directions.

"I have a GPS." He swung forward. You haven't touched your wine. Something wrong with it?" Without waiting for an answer, he rose and took his empty glass into the cabin, and returned with it filled.

The wind stiffened. Clouds rolled over the moon. The boat rocked, and I felt an odd bulge under the seat. I got up, lifted the bottom cushion, and drew out a crumpled tee-shirt. A faint smell of lilacs when I shook the thing out. Nebraska Is Corny written across the front. "I thought you went to Duke," I said.

"I did." He paused to down half the glass of wine, then moved toward me. "The shirt isn't mine."

Light brown makeup rimmed the shirt's collar. I smiled. "What's her name?"

Zak winced and closed his eyes. "Candy," he said quickly, then added, "Feel the wind? Looks like mother nature will be kicking up."

"Looks like she already has," I said.

14

The backhoe teetered on the brink off a limestone outcrop, its engine a high-pitched whine, the cheapest machine Kurt could rent. Instead of a factory-installed cab, a make-shift canvas canopy protected the driver from the fierce sun. The giant tires had the traction of eggshells, and rust flaked from the boom like red dandruff. A closer look revealed patches of gray where the broken stabilizer legs had been welded back together, a reminder you get what you pay for. Kurt held his breath as the Bobcat rocked back and forth, then gathered its breath like a sprinter taking a hill. "Stay between the flags, you fucking idiot," Kurt yelled. His Spanish wasn't the best, but the guys seemed to understand him. He turned to Bassem, who was polishing his sunglasses on his sleeve. "The dickhead will run it over the cliff."

Earlier that morning, Kurt and Bassem set out fluorescent flags to mark the grounds where the statue of Our Lady of Tarifa would be installed, God willing. Or inshallah, as the Mosque-rats say, but my God's real, Kurt thought. By mid-week the courtyard will be paved in marble, the gravel raked smooth, the scarlet lantana shining with watered foliage—provided the landscaper shows up. The Bishop was slated to unveil the statue strategically placed to face North Africa, Her stony eyes on the Moroccans across the Straits of Gibraltar. Kurt glanced at the dark stripe of the horizon and imagined Arabs crouching under date palms with binoculars scanning the Spanish coast for a vulnerable point to attack. "Take a good look, mosque-rats," Kurt said under his breath. "This is close as you'll get.

"I can't hear you," Bassem shouted.

"Pay attention to the backhoe."

Kurt turned from the sea to the town of Molina on the slope of the hill.

The overgrown village lay on the southern-most tip of Europe a half-mile from Tarifa where the Mediterranean joins the Atlantic. To Kurt's disgust at the erosion of civilization, the coast had become one more haven for crack-heads, pot-heads and other low-life's with needle tracks running through their tattoos. Losers like that dare-devil wind-surfer out there now, about to go down under. Serves him right. Any minute busloads of tourists would pull up to Molino's gate. Fools armed with sunscreen and cameras scrambling over the ramparts and video-taping a watchtower that never moved. A waste of film. Always the pictures. Can't the assholes remember anything? In the harbor, the Trans-Mediterranean ferry was about to cast off on its morning run to Tangier. An attendant in a white djellaba scurried around the deck organizing the lineup of cars.

Kurt drew a handkerchief from his hip pocket and wiped his brow. Another glance at the opposite shore and the golden glow over the Rif Mountains.

Bassem straightened his baseball cap. "Hard for the backhoe guy to finish in the heat." He smiled, strong teeth bright against his bronze skin.

"Wipe that silly grin off your face."

Bassam's perpetual smile drove Kurt crazy. Not to mention the incessant humming as he worked on the songs he wrote. Goofy, senseless song. In the middle of an earthquake, the guy would hum and laugh like a fool. A good foot soldier, but otherwise, a colossal pain the ass. Take this morning's drive to the site when he whined until Kurt pulled off the interstate at the McAuto so Bassem could get a latte. Couldn't live without it. Then he left the drink untouched in the cupholder. The Egyptian was unhinged, Kurt decided. Driven barking mad by his cock-a-mammie conviction the American woman would get him thrown in jail. How many times had Kurt told him, "Look, just because you and the American were on the beach at the same time doesn't mean she'd assume you'd chopped off the Berber girl's head. Think about it. If the American lady saw you, she would have run away, yelled, followed you to your car or called the Guardia Civil right then and there."

"Easy for you to say."

Kurt knew better than to argue with an Egyptian, all of them hysterical, overwrought, and contaminated by imagination. Kurt played around with a metaphor about turning anthills into pyramids, but couldn't quite work it out. He leaned to brush sand from his starched chinos he'd pressed last night, the crease razor-sharp despite the wind plastering the cloth to his knees. He straightened and shouted as the tractor churned past. "We need it leveled by noon." The driver waved and aimed the bucket at a tree stump. Kurt turned to Bassem. "Figure the concrete needs twenty-four hours to set, and allowing another two days for the plinth, plus a whole day to haul the statue from Genil providing you, meaning you, Bassem, get the forklift."

"I can't. I'll be a prisoner."

Kurt closed his eyes. "What part of 'she didn't see you' don't you understand?"

Bassem touched his head. "It's not in here." He tapped his heart. "In here says she told the Guardia Civil she saw me murder the kid's mother."

"For Christ's sake, you didn't murder anyone, and she didn't see anything."

Bassem's face flushed. "There'll be a Spanish judge, a Spanish court, and there's me, a small little Arab."

"Small as an ox."

"With no papers. No money. Spaniards hate Egyptians because our history has better buildings."

"Then get out of Spain," Kurt said.

"Why? I didn't do anything."

Kurt slapped his forehead with the heel of his hand. "Of course, you did, you moron, you felt sorry for that weepy Arab woman. If you're this worried, lawyer up."

Bassem's eyes followed the tractor as the driver scooped up a sapling and hold the loader high in the air. Roots dangled from the sides.

"There's a cheaper solution," Bassem said.

"Go for it."

His eyes following the backhoe, Bassem said, "Juan's supposed to take the American doctor-woman to Rocio to buy a picture from Alfonso."

Kurt had to think a minute before he remembered he was the one who suggested original art over the fireplace would help sell the house. "Tell Juan to not let her buy one of Afonso's Picasso knock-offs," Kurt said. "The blue robots."

"You made me lose my train of thought." Bassem eased up his baseball cap and scratched the back of his head. "Where was I? Oh, yeah, Zak told me the American's nervous about driving on the Autopista. Since the American woman saw me at the restaurant with the kid's mother, Zak ordered Juan to be the chauffeur."

Kurt backed away from Bassam's garlicky breath.

"To drop her off at Alfonso's house he calls his studio," Bassem said. "Then Juan will make an excuse to leave. Maybe he has a cousin nearby, a friend, whatever, leaving the American alone with Alfonso. When Juan comes back Alfonso will tell him she decided to take the overnight swamp-buggy tour and Zak will pick her up the next day. Juan doesn't know or suspect anything's fishy. But Alfonso will make sure she's gone for good. No person. No problem, I always say. "

"Gone where?"

"You shouldn't ask."

"The police will."

"Who's to ask Alfonso anything? Not all the pigeons are in the barn." Bassem tapped his head. "I, myself, will haul the lady's stuff from her apartment. No rent comes next month, her landlord finds the place empty and thinks she's back in the States. No one could connect an American doctor with a crazy artist in Rocio three hundred kilometers away."

"Let me get this straight. You set it up for Alfonso to kill someone just because you think—think, not know—the person witnessed something you didn't do." One look at the set of Bassem's chin beneath the stupid grin said it all. This was serious. Furthermore, Kurt suddenly realized he knew more than he wanted to know. "Why are you telling me?"

"I need the keys to your boat because Alfonso's borrowing it."

Kurt got the picture. "No, he isn't."

"Yes, he is."

"I'll get the Guardia Civil."

"I think you'll think again." Bassem turned back to the tractor, then as if making a decision, spun around to face Kurt. "Because why? Juan's a computer geek, and you're the accountant. He hacked into our books and showed me the spread-sheets the audit people will never see. He printed it out, and man, if you saw the numbers."

I earned it, Kurt almost said.

"The huge deposits in your pocket. The buyers' payments on condos under construction *Señor* Zak sells on spec."

"Impossible. The Excel sheets are encrypted and password protected."

"We knew that." Bassem beamed.

The backhoe lurched from a copse of trees and roared toward a boulder a stone's throw from where Kurt and Bassem stood. Kurt leaned to hear what Bassem was explaining. "... boat for one day... garbage bag... hauling away old furniture and tires." The motor stopped, catching Bassem in mid-shout. "The neighbors are happy. No more trash in Alfonso's yard."

"If murder were as easy as you make out, there would be no one alive on the planet," Kurt said. "What about blackmail? Alfonso holds this over your head."

"He's too crazy. He talks to the television set and thinks he has a black parrot he's teaching to count. The birdcage is empty."

Kurt nodded slowly.

"A worker from a mental health clinic stops by with pills that Alfonso feeds to his cat. The pills don't work, the cat's crazier than he is."

"And you trust him?"

The driver of the tractor put the machine in neutral while he lit a cigarette.

"Alfonso listens to me because I listen to him," Bassem said. "The American lady-doctor will wind up in the Guadalquivir that's already full of dead drug dealers, and dead mayors." Bassem laughed. "And enough dead Russians to make another Moscow."

"What about the dog.?" Kurt said.

"What dog?"

"That the American keeps in the apartment."

Bassam made a gun with his thumb and index finger.

The driver engaged the backhoe and headed toward the pile of debris at the edge of the clearing. Kurt shook his head as if to loosen the words inside it. "What does Zak say about all this?

"He doesn't know."

"You do remember he's seeing the woman."

Bassam's grin morphed into a leer. "A love is only love," he sang.

Kurt interrupted before Bassem could move on to the next stanza. "Don't do this to the American," Kurt said, surprised at the sharp pang of regret he felt. He, himself, was attracted to the pretty little lady who liked Bach. She was smart, too, the only woman Kurt knew who understood drywall. "You and Alfonso could get in very deep shit."

Kurt sighed, drew out his Marlboros, and said he needed a cigarette, when what he really needed was a break from Bassem, the little shit. "Watch the driver doesn't plow into that tree."

Kurt walked back to the Great Estate's Jeep, climbed inside, and turned on the air conditioner. He tapped out a Marlboro while thinking, suppose tourists on a guided swamp tour see a man slide a human-sized bag over the stern. Or the body washes up too soon, instantly recognizable. Or Alfonso blabs to his health aide.

One screw up and the plan goes splat like an egg dropped on tile.

What if the police discover the owner of the boat? I'm a co-conspirator, Kurt thought. Or an accomplice, or whatever they call them on TV's "Crime Beat." He felt for his lighter that must be somewhere in an inside pocket.

If the Guardia Civil came around to investigate, it was critical that he and Zak stay on the same sheet of music. Zak had to understand Bassem was behind all of it. Like any right-hand man, Kurt knew more of the rank and file employees than the boss himself. For instance, Kurt knew Bassem's father was a well-respected Coptic Christian, why the Muslim Brotherhood fire-bombed their house in Cairo. Bassem confessed to Kurt that he had found an upscale trafficker who ran a cabin cruiser to Spain from Libya to Malaga via Tangier. Kurt wanted the trafficker's name. You never knew, he thought, when that information could come in handy, Bassem wouldn't say. He did tell Kurt about the two other passengers aboard, three, if you counted the infant. There was Tariq, an imam, his sexy Berber wife, and their baby. According to Bassem, at sea he and Tariq killed time debating Knights versus the Emir's Army. Some argument that must have been, Kurt thought.

Safe in Spain, Bassem, the rat, was the one who suggested the Knights kidnap Tariq's kid as collateral to assure the Muslims would leave the statue alone. This was no problem. Bassem told Kurt the child was snatched while the sexy mom was hanging clothes on the roof. As Tariq's friend, Bassem had offered useless advice and sympathy along with hints to the mother that he could help. She begged him to take her to her baby. In his rented room she gave him anything, everything. And everything would have worked out just fine, had the Emir's men not caught up with her and Bassem and run them off the road. The little shit Bassem, Kurt thought, probably pushed her from the car. He knew what the Army of the Emir does to guys who mess with their women. Next day the shit remembered he lost his money clip. Where was it?

Kurt lit his cigarette, exhaled, and watched the smoke curl toward the pines. But the next morning instead of the money clip, what does Bassem find? The remains. Now the idiot believed the only way out was to take out the American. Where I come in, Kurt thought. If the police ask about the boat? Kurt studied the tip of the Marlboro. He'd say he'd loaned Bassem his keys to the office, forgetting a duplicate car, house and boat key were on the ring. Never mind his statement would kick Bassem under the bus. As they say, "Inshallah."

15

The fender of the Great Estates Jeep was scraped like every fender in Spain is scarred by the walls of the narrow village streets, and the tunnels leading to the crypts they call underground garages. After a cursory good morning to Juan, I tossed my bag in the car and climbed into the passenger seat. "Does Alfonso know we're coming?"

"Who knows what's in that crazy brain?" Juan laughed and added, "You bought doughnuts for me?" I fussed with my seatbelt, unwilling to share my one cheese Danish.

Juan patted his stomach. "As if I need them." He laughed and backed out of the parking lot.

Juan was fat. Not muscle heavy, but roly-poly fat with plump cheeks and pudgy fingers wrapped around the wheel. Eight in the morning and already his jolly good humor was getting on my nerves. Phony, I suspected. Not surprising. Zak said before Juan came to work for Great Estates and the Knights, he trained as a dental assistant. Maybe his was the voice that said, "You may experience discomfort," while lighting a fire in a mosque.

The original plan was for Zak to drive me to Rocio. Instead, he foisted me off on an employee. Maybe avoiding the hours in the car when I might ask, "Were your Catholic colleagues responsible for the mosque bombings? Shooting refugees wading in from shore?"

On the other hand, maybe Zak actually did have a property closing in Marbella.

The traffic was light, and Juan sailed through the roundabout. Making small talk, I asked, "You mentioned you knew Zak since he was a kid."

Juan began in his excellent English. "My great grandmother's aunt married this soldier from Cadiz, who was Zak's great someone."

"His mom and dad still alive?"

"Alive? Yes. His dad, Emil, bought a place in Mijas after he signed over Great Estates to Zak. Emil might even like Mijas if he didn't hate the neighbors so much. Can you imagine being the only card-carrying commie in a gated community?"

"The party still gives out cards? Interesting," I said. "Leftist father, right-wing son. Polar opposites."

"Wrong." Juan looked in the rear-view mirror and accelerated. "Not opposites, both hot-tempered like all men of serious convictions."

"Fanatics," I said.

Juan laughed softly. "If you knew how he takes care of his family. Supports Alfonso since he went bonkers in the army. Even rented the exhibition Center in Marbella thinking an art show would make Alfonso famous. Can you imagine?" Juan continued, "I'll never forget how he dragged us to see "The Obama Triptych. To me it looked like three sticks. But what do I know? After the show, his sales took off. Then—" Juan gave a thumbs-down.

I braced myself for an afternoon of awful art. "I just need something pretty for over a fireplace."

I half dozed, and half followed the landscape as it rolled past. Bach's Brandenburg on the CD played to the dressage horses grazing under the rosy sun. Steam curled from a glassy lake, its surface reflecting a single chubby cloud. A castle loomed over the valley. Approaching Seville, we crossed the Guadalquivir. West of the city, the fields of sunflowers gave way to scrubby undergrowth. A few miles farther, strange pines appeared. Their trunks smooth poles that rose to hold perfectly round globes of needles on top. Sticks balancing green balls. Lollipop trees in a fairy-tale world.

A sun-bleached wooden arrow pointed to an unpaved track. After bumping over exposed stone, we entered a landscape that could have been Mars. Ochre sand covered the road. "Why no paving?" I asked.

"They keep it soft for the horses' hooves." Juan said, plowing steadily ahead.

Relentless wind stirred gritty clouds over the hood. Metallic grains forced their way between my teeth. The Jeep slid into gullies between low dunes and rose to crest the next mound. The most bizarre town I'd ever seen gradually emerged through the tawny dust. Wide streets flanked by pink, yellow, and blue adobe buildings. Over each entrance, a sign read, Hermandades, then the name of a city.

"Brotherhoods," Juan said. "Clubs that fix up the floats for the procession. Ever hear of New Orleans?"

"Vaguely," I said with a smile.

"Hermandades are like the Mardi Gras's Krews. Same idea."

We passed Hermandades Madrid, Hermandades Barcelona, and Hermandades Burgos. A two-wheeled trailer was parked in front of the Hermandades Salamanca. Orange and pink paper flowers covered the entire vehicle. Why the wind didn't blow the flowers clear to Portugal was beyond me.

"Leftover from the procession." Juan pulled into a vast square, turned off the engine, and pointed to the cathedral. "Rebuilt in the Sixties after the earthquake." The church was a mish-mosh of Mudejar towers, iron crosses, and gothic flourishes like the seashell patterned plaster over the entrance. The church too pretentious for this wild west of a town.

"It doesn't fit," I said. "The imitation Gothic and fake Mudejar in these rough and tumble streets.

Juan's mouth tightened as he started the engine. "It's perfectly normal." After a minute of thought, he brightened. "You should come during the procession. It starts here and goes all the way to—I forget where. Hey, look at that guy."

A caballero wearing a tight embroidered vest and round flat hat sat on a magnificent stallion. The horse pranced in place. The animal's arched neck was held on a tight rein attached to a savage bit. I couldn't look. A fairy tale world all right, where frightened children are lost in an evil forest. An unreasonable feeling of wanting to get out of here swept over me. We passed a raised wooden walkway of shops selling flamenco costumes and resin Virgins with plastic halos. A farrier's workshop marked the entrance to a park on the shore of a lagoon. Startled birds flapped up from the reeds. The beady heads of pink Flamingoes bobbed up and down as they fished in the algae. Juan turned onto a trail leading deeper into the lollipop forest.

"I should give Alfonso a heads-up. But no cell coverage out here."

Maybe it was the howling wind. Or the sun glowering down at the cathedral. The place felt menacing. As if the grains of sand were the eyes of hungry insects. The word predatory made no sense. It took a minute to recall the last time I felt such a nameless anxiety.

Two in the morning after a twelve-hour stretch in the emergency room, I took the underground tunnel between Houston General and the parking lot. Midway through the passageway, the overhead fluorescent tubes went out. I move to the side of the cat-walk and keeping my hand on the rough cement wall, made my way through the tunnel with no light at the end. Footsteps clicked behind me, tap shoes on the heels of my steps. I stopped; the clicks stopped. I turn. No one there. I resumed. The clicks resumed. Muscle memory led my hand to the cell phone in my bag. No signal. The clicks become the heartbeats of the walls breathing in, breathing out. A faint glow ahead. I ran. My fear reached for the ray of light as a swimmer reaches for the raft. Safe under the lot's halogen lamps, I looked behind me. No one. I fumbled with the car door, and although it was winter, my palms were slippery with sweat.

Get a painting and get out of Rocio.

The combative sun had turned the exterior of Alfonzo's cottage to chalk. A palm with shaggy dead leaves leaned over the roof. Branches of a wily shrub groped for the door. Despite the dappled light filtering through the pines and the pleasant scent of rosemary, I resisted leaving the safety of the car. Juan rummaged around in the trunk for the bottle of Manzanilla he'd brought as a gift. I followed him up the path.

Alfonso must have heard the car for he waited for us in the doorway.

You can spot psychosis by the quivering hands, glassy stare, sunken cheeks and disheveled clothing of its hosts. Paint-smeared jeans rode low on Alfonzo's hips. Despite the heat, the sleeves his filthy jersey hung to his wrists. The angled ropes of gray dangled to his shoulders; threads of a beard drifted down his chest. Skinny arms, skinny legs—the guy was a spider.

He rubbed his palms together, then held one out to me. "You here to buy?"

"Maybe." I shook his scaly hand.

A quick Spanish style embrace with Juan, and Alfonso ushered us into a stadium of a room where sunbeams glowered through the skylights. White chairs circled a white table, and canvasses, everywhere, rested against whitewashed walls. Fencing foils hung over a mattress on the floor, and on a coffee table next to the mattress, a handgun lay atop a map of Spain. The air smelled of linseed oil with a turpentine kick.

"You want to talk Spanish or English?" Alfonso asked.

"Her Spanish is hopeless," Juan said.

Alfonso drew out a chair and with sweeping gestures, cleared the seat of imaginary dust.

I lowered my bag onto an empty chair. "Juan mentioned you studied design in New York," I said.

"Hey, Juanito, you told her everything?" Alfonso turned from Juan and leaned over me. His warm breath smelled of yeast. "He tells you what I do with my sword?" His laugh a soft cackle. "Get it? Sword?"

"Cool it, 'Fonze." Juan set the wine on the table. "Go get your sherry glasses."

Alfonso motioned to a cardboard box beside the two-burner stove. "Help yourself."

Juan looked down into the box. "I've been telling you for years, Fonze, buy some god damned furniture."

"Who needs it?"

"You always say that," Juan grumbled.

Juan held up a wine-stained paper cup. "No glass-glasses?"

"They were spies, and I killed them," Alfonse said.

Alfonso drew an imaginary vertical line on the table. "Call this the Pope." He drew another line parallel to the first one. "There's Obama." His finger zig-zagged between the lines. "Here's me, stuck in the middle."

Juan rolled his eyes.

Alfonzo's delusion of importance. A delusion that could twist around the mind like a boa constrictor wraps itself around a tree. Arguing with him would make the problem worse, for in the process of defending the delusion Alfonzo would just dig in deeper. If I could reduce the underlying anxiety, the problem would resolve itself.

I smiled at Alfonso. "Paper cups are a good idea. No dishes to wash."

He held up his cup. "Here's to money." He wiped his mouth on his sleeve and poured a refill. Then he strolled to the refrigerator, opened it and took out a bottle of Hennessey. "Let's get stronger."

I covered my cup with my hand.

Juan shook his head no, his cup still half-filled with sherry. Alfonso topped his own with brandy.

"What kind of painting would you like?"

"Something for over a fireplace."

Alfonso winced as if irritated, and I realized I had trivialized his art. He glanced at the ceiling as if for inspiration, got up and began sorting through the canvasses propped against the wall. He pulled out an oil of a cockroach in a woman's fist.

I pretended to admire it. "Not quite what I had in mind."

He set the work aside and resumed flipping through the stack, one picture after another. The window air conditioner exhaled icy breath and shivering, I wished I had worn something heavier than a cotton shirt.

Alfonso slowly considered each canvas. Some were of abstract designs in primary colors. Others black and white streaks. His only way of communicating, I thought, with a wave of empathy. He expressed ideas he could not explain in words. An isolation that would be painful, complete, and oh, so lonely.

A spasm that lasted only an instant shook his entire body, most likely a reaction to antipsychotic drugs. I wondered what he'd been prescribed.

"You okay?" Juan asked from where he sat at the kitchen table.

"Don't ask," Alfonso said, his eyes fixed on the canvas in front of him.

"Do you have a landscape? I asked. I heard the jingle of keys and spun around to see Juan toying with a keyring.

Startled, I asked, "We're leaving?"

"I have to get with a guy in town."

"You're leaving me here?" My skin crawled as if a tarantula climbed my spine. "I'll come with you."

He stepped away. "This is personal."

"Wait," I called and followed him through the entrance to the landing outside. Not wanting to be overheard, I closed the front door. "The man's a time bomb. Paranoid as hell and dangerous if he decides I'm the enemy. "

Juan started down the path. "Oh, come on," he said over his shoulder. "He's a bit off, is all."

"You see the gun on the coffee table?"

"Only one." Juan faced me. "Look, you're a doctor for crazy people," he said. "Which explains why you see crazy everywhere." His boots crunched in the gravel driveway on his way to the car. He unlocked the driver's side, slid into the seat and thrust the key in the ignition. "Just don't get him excited," he said above the rattle of the engine.

I was being set up. I went inside to join Alfonso. While pretending to be absorbed in the roach picture, I searched for clues for what was going on. The chronology. First, Zak insists I go all the way to Rocio to buy a picture when there are galleries up the kazoo in Marbella, some even selling Alfonso's stuff. Then Zak reneges on being alone with me in the car. Finally, Juan splits and leaves me with an armed schizophrenic.

"Let's see another," I said.

Alfonso presented an oil of a stork inside a Coca-Cola can. "I call it, 'Flight in America.'"

I smiled and in a teasing tone said, "A shame America doesn't have storks."

He lifted the painting higher. "Buy this for a reminder for the storks you never had and lost."

"I'm really not fond of storks."

"Then look around for a picture of something else you didn't have."

The sun dropped toward the rim of the world. The rosy light slid to the floor. Alfonso held up a canvas depicting knives raining from clouds.

Knives I didn't need. "Let's go back to what I never had," I said. "What's the asking price for the stork?"

Alfonso gazed at the floor, either calculating the cost or deciding how much the traffic would bear. He looked up. "Ten."

"Dollars?"

"Ten one-hundred euros, please."

"A thousand?" I shook my head. "No can do."

He drew himself to full height. "You don't like my work." He slammed the canvas against the stack.

One look at his flushed face curdled whatever was in my stomach. The air conditioner was taking a brief rest, but goosebumps rode my skin.

Without warning Alfonso crossed the room, reached under the mattress, drew out a pack of Ducados, and sat with his legs crossed. In an abrupt change of mood, he said, "You'd be pretty if you fixed your hair."

Anger chasing peace through his brain, then a turnaround with peace in hot pursuit.

Squinting through the cigarette smoke, Alfonso studied me. "Shorter hair with the front cut on a slant." he drew a diagonal line across his forehead. "French-people style. For the face, you'll want more color, lipstick. I like lipstick. Cadmium red—you'll need a lot. Juan tells me you're a spy."

I kept my breath steady. "I'm wondering what painting to take home. So many beautiful choices."

"Juan said you work for the ocean police."

"Why would I do that?"

He winked at me as if saying, we both know why. When he refilled his paper cup with Hennessey and polished it off, it occurred to me that with drugs and alcohol he was well on his way to a blackout, and if he passed out, I could escape. I lifted the bottle, poured, and looked up at the gun aimed at my head.

The pistol was snub-nosed and matte-black. I don't know squat about weapons but judging from the trembling in his hand, it must have been heavy. I slowly set the brandy and paper cup on the coffee table. Don't get him excited. I held out the cup that was filled to the brim. He shifted the weapon to his left hand and lifted the drink with his right.

I motioned to the mattress. "May I sit beside you?" Quickly, before he caught the shaking of my knees, I sat and crossed my legs to mirror his position. He drained the cup and lowered it to the floor.

Just as I leaned to pick it up, the shot split the air. Glass shattered behind me. Splinters of sound crashed through my brain, proof I was still alive. My bones went soft, everything limp except my jaw holding my chattering teeth. Alfonso stared at the gun as if amazed it worked.

Then he burst out laughing, rocked back and forth tossing his ropy hair. He closed his eyes, opened them only long enough to gasp, "You should see yourself," and went off again.

A buzzard's laugh would sound like this.

Watching him wipe his eyes on the hem of his sweatshirt, I ran down my options. Pounce and grab for the gun, and I'd get it in the chest. Or dash for the door and get it in the back.

He pulled himself together and sat upright. The dying light in the room cast a ruddy glow to his features, He nodded to the TV and spoke to the dark screen. "Hey, Samsung, don't look at me like that. I'm only teasing."

"What does the screen say back?"

The bitterness in his eyes told me my attempt to play along fell flat.

He raised the pistol. "Don't humor me. Are you buying my stork piece or not? I'll do you a one, two, three to make up your mind. One comes first."

I swallowed the dry saliva in my throat. I'd told myself when the time of my death came, I would not cringe. Tell that to every nerve in my body, each cringing like a child waiting for an injection.

A last-ditch effort. "Get real, Alfonso. No one carries around a thousand euros. I have a hundred on me you can have."

"Yeah?" His voice soft. The room was in twilight but for the glint of the white furniture gleaming like wicker bones. Alfonso's words came as the sound of the night itself. "Show me."

"After you give me the gun."

Silence.

Taking a chance, I reached and put my hand over his hand holding the weapon. The warmth of his dry skin radiated from his flesh to mine. The muscle quivered as he tightened his grip. I stroked his wrist. The soft hairs atop the bone.

"Your work speaks to me." A partial truth.

He hesitated, then quickly, as if acting without thought, passed me the gun. The corrugated handle was damp from the slime of his palm. My spine loosened from the knot my terror had tied. The gun was indeed heavy, and I looked around for a place to put it.

I got up, went to the kitchen, and groped for the light switch over the counter. How normal the cottage became under the overhead fixture? A toaster, a clock.

I dropped the gun in a side pocket of my carryall and zipped the top closed. Then I dug through the center compartment for my wallet. A creak of the front door and I heard Juan's voice.

"I'm back." Juan's eyes moved from Alfonso to me, to the coffee table where the gun had been, then back to me. "Why aren't you with the tourist tour? Bassem said—" Juan stopped himself. "I mean, I thought you would be gone somewhere else."

"Somewhere where?"

Ignoring my question, Juan went to the painting of the stork. "This the one you picked?"

"Juan, where did you go?"

"I'll explain in the car, later."

Fat chance.

"We need to start back," I said. "We can put the painting in the trunk."

All at once, I wanted no reminder of Alfonso, Juan, Rocio, none of them. "Forget it. I'm not buying anything."

Juan shrugged. He and Alfonso exchanged a few words in Spanish, and anxious to get away I hurried to the door. Halfway down the walk I realized something needed to be rectified, and not allowing myself to dwell on what I was doing, or why, I returned to the house, passed Alfonso in the doorway, and lay the hundred euros on the kitchen table. Alfonso's eyes were impassive. In them, I saw the same indifference I saw in the metal toaster, the Formica table, and the TV set in the corner with no reception and its brain turned off.

16

Whenever Zak stood before a work of art, he imagined instead of him admiring the object, the object was admiring him. Take the fountain in front of him that was carved by Lalagos, the sixteenth-century genius whose statue of an angel brandishing a spear presided over the square in Malaga. Zak distinctly saw her lips part and heard her say, "Go."

I'm trying, I'm trying, Zak thought. But, as Chairman Mao said, it's a protracted struggle. Despite what the media said, in Zak's opinion, the Sons of the Emir were not entering Spain seeking freedom, justice, or opportunity. They wanted his stuff.

He looked around the square for his crew and spotted them in the corner café. He crossed the flagstone and waved to Antonio, Juan, and Carlos who were grouped along one side of the table, then to Bassem who sat alone on the other. He pulled out the empty chair next to his for Zak.

"The barbarians are at the gate," Zak said, reaching for a menu. "Who was it said that?"

Bassem tore open a packet of sugar. "You just did."

"I mean," Zak said, "someone like Cicero or Homer."

"Don't know either guy."

Fair enough, for how would Bassem know history? Toughened in the streets of Cairo, he was one of the Knight's best. His jacket hung aslant as if his body was trying to adjust to European styles after years of wearing a kaftan.

Today all the men wore black tee-shirts and jeans. Antonio was the only one with a hat. A John Deere baseball cap worn backward.

"Get that fucking thing off your head," Zak snapped.

Antonio jammed the cap in his pocket.

Zak studied his team. Good Catholic men, Zak thought with pride, men who put bread on the table, drove their grandmothers to mass and would kill for the church. Zak's title, conferred by the Archbishop, was Commandant of Andalucía. Appointed, mind you, not elected. "Democracy is for peasants," the Archbishop said. "Everyone knows peasants can't manage fiscal affairs. So how can they choose a leader?" At first, Zak found the reasoning overly judgmental. Until he got to thinking about it. It was true, he decided: the distinguishing characteristic of the poor was their inability to acquire or retain money. Successful political movements needed creative fiscal management to survive.

The Knights were supported by the Diocese, by contributions, and by grants from provincial governments who knew full well they were funding a terrorist outfit, but disguised the purpose of the awards with vague goals like, 'strengthening the infrastructure.' They funded work-scopes with enough wiggle room to permit anything, including stock-piling weapons and training volunteer militia. The Knights, as an organization, was beginning to come together. Zak believed not only Spain, but he himself on the brink of a new era of discipline, duty and love. Duty, he knew. Love? He was working on it.

A waiter approached, and Zak ordered coffee. The guy tucked the menu under his arm and drifted away. All eyes around the table were following a woman in shorts pushing a baby carriage across the square. When she disappeared behind the fountain, Antonio leaned across the table. "How far are we going?"

"Antiquera," Zak replied.

Busy brushing crumbs from his tee-shirt, Carolos said, "Juan, why don't you drive?"

Juan lowered his newspaper. "Don't look at me. I'm here to deal with the kid."

Bassem shot Zak a significant glance and unzipped his nylon jacket to reveal the butt of a Beretta

"Not unless we need it," Zak said.

"Or want to." Bassem flashed him a grin. "Tell me, *Senor* Zuko, who tipped us off where the kid is?"

Zak would never even think of going into the discussion he had with Paige. "Forget it,"

He got to his feet and waited for the group's attention. "Listen up. Everyone has a hood?"

A few shook their heads no, and Carlos drew a handful of balaclavas from a Carrefour's shopping bag.

"Remember I'm the only one to deal with whoever's in charge," Zak continued. "You—Juan, Antonio, and Bassem, back me up. Carlos, you park at the emergency exit and stay Our partners from Fidelity Teleco did a super reconnaissance and timed out the site's interconnectivity, so no worries on that score. with the car. Keep it running. No security was seen when the techs were there, but don't think we're home free. I was told to expect a French doctor, a receptionist, and possibly clients, or patrons, whatever they're called." Zak looked directly at Juan. "Be sure to get all the medical shit that comes with the kid."

"What if he's just had surgery? Or is intubated?" Juan asked.

Zak closed his eyes, opened them. "That's why you're here."

"I assume there'll be docs at the nuns nursing home where we're taking him," Juan said.

"Don't assume anything."

The scrape of chair legs on flagstone as the men rose, folded newspapers and tossed napkins into a bin. Zak dropped euros on the table and with the flourish of a matador, draped his linen jacket over his shoulders as if it were a cape.

Bassem gave a remaining croissant a wistful look.

"Wrap it in a napkin. I paid for it," Zak said over his shoulder as he wove around the tables toward the car park.

They clambered into the BMW SUV. As soon as Carlos convinced the others to fasten seat belts, he accelerated onto the A 20 without checking the mirrors. Carlos shouted above the roar of a passing truck. "You said the spa people on the phone told our contact the baby wasn't there."

Zak pushed the cigarette lighter into its charger. "Because people hiding a kidnapped hostage don't always tell the truth?" The lighter sprang from the socket and Zak lit a Marlboro.

"Does that make us re-kidnappers?" came from behind.

Zak turned to Bassem in the back seat. "Don't stir shit." Zak groped around the floor for a McAuto cup for an ashtray, then once more faced the rear seats. "Antonio, you remembered the wire cutters?"

Antonio nodded.

The SUV climbed the mountains north of Malaga. Miles of hairpin curves, At the turnoff onto the secondary road, Carlos slowed as they approached a petrol station. He looked at the instrument panel. "Could use gas."

"We can't stop here," Zak said. "We'd be remembered. Too conspicuous. Can we hold out until the Interstate on the way back?"

"I'll try."

A few kilometers farther, the Papillion sat in all its splendor, as grand as Paige described.

Carlos whistled.

"Quite a spread," Zak agreed. "My contact guessed there would only be a skeleton staff on Sunday."

Carolos pulled up under the portico. One glance through the window of the vehicle and a doorman in white pantaloons and red tarboosh spun and hurried into the building.

"Out. Antonio, you first." Zak ordered.

Antonio adjusted his balaclava, slid from the seat, and took off.

Zak flung the door open into the afternoon glare.

The doorman returned followed by a woman in an ankle-length white coat. She stood with her arms crossed, blocking the entrance. A tag on her lapel read 'Doctor Mercedes Ollu, Jefe.' "You're bringing in a patient?" Her Spanish carried a French accent.

Zak stepped into the beam of the automatic doors. "We're here to retrieve the baby. Hamid's his name."

"We don't admit children," she said.

"Unless they're hostages," Zak said.

Ollu refused to budge. He moved toward her. The doorman lunged. Zak slammed him against the wall. The tarboosh tumbled to the ground and rolled into a bed of pansies.

Zak grabbed Ollu's wrist and twisted her arm up behind her back. "Move it," he ordered and force-stepped her through the entrance. The bareheaded doorman stood aside as Juan and Bassem passed in single file.

No customers in the lobby. Only the receptionist on her feet behind the counter. She swiped her cell phone, held it to her ear, looked at the device, and tipped it back and forth.

A blast of warm air, the fan's last gasp before the air conditioning conked out. The recessed lighting dead, pale rays from the skylights cast the room in twilight. Swinging the wire-cutters Antonio rounded the corner of a corridor and came up beside Zak. "Piece of cake, found the generator. "

Zak ratcheted up the tension on Ollu's arm.

"I told you we don't admit children," she gasped.

The arm went higher. She stifled a sob.

"Tell me what room and get it over with," Zak said. He imagined the quandary behind those wire-rimmed glasses. The kid goes missing on her watch, and payment's down the tubes. On the other hand, no amount of money was worth her life. The choice a no-brainer.

Ollu took a halting step forward.

The hallway floor was lit by square patches of light that streamed from windows high along the wall. Too women in flowered smocks and headscarves burst from behind swinging doors. They stopped.

"What's going on?" one said in English.

"Nothing. Go home," Ollu ordered. "Quickly."

The women bolted toward the lobby.

Zak marched Ollu past an alcove holding a copy machine, then a cafeteria empty except for a woman in a burka wiping a table. A push-broom leaned against a chair. Ollu nodded to an unmarked door.

The spotless room smelled of bleach and baby powder. Bassem aimed and shot out the overhead cameras, one, two, three. The ceiling rained shards.

Zak shouted at Bassem. "I told you not to use that. Put it away."

When the air cleared, Zak saw a cart laden with diapers, a bedside table, a few plastic chairs, and a crib on high wheels parked in the far end of the room. Plastic tubes and wires as intertwined as bougainvillea vines curled over and around the baby. An IV line tethered a bag of fluid to a needle in Hamid's bird's leg of an arm. The infant was shrieking, his hands in fists.

Juan examined the contents of the bag atop the pole. "Saline.".

Zak freed Ollu from his grip, and she rubbed her reddened wrist.

He glanced to see how Juan was progressing. "Why saline?"

"Ask our consulting pediatrician," she replied.

Juan monkeyed with the IV as the infant shrieked at the top of his lungs. Juan finally lifted the baby and held him against his chest with one hand, while the other picked up a prescription vial from the table. "Grab the rest of the medical shit," he shouted to Antonio.

"It's dangerous to move—" Ollu began.

An alarm siren howled through every orifice in the building, loud, louder.

"What the fuck?" Juan yelled.

"Our auxiliary back-up to the gendarmes." Ollu's tone triumphant.

"Haul ass," Zak said.

Juan circled the table on his way to the hall. Ollu grabbed the rail and with one mighty shove rammed the crib into his hip. Juan reeled, fought for balance, and gave 'way when Ollu kicked him in the groin. As he doubled over, she grabbed Hamid. Juan stumbled backward until he reached a chair that slid out from under him.

Zak and Antonio dashed to block Ollu's exit.

"You two steer clear," Bassem ordered, taking aim.

"Put that fucking thing down," Zak yelled.

The siren escalated to an ear-splitting crescendo.

"I said, no," Zak shouted as the gun went off.

Ollu slumped against the wall. Zak wrested the infant away just in time before she slid to the floor. Hamid kicked, his arms flailing with each scream. Zak thrust him toward Bassem "Get him out of here."

Zak saw that the bullet entered Ollu's shoulder. Was there an exit wound? No time to check.

Juan struggled to his feet.

"Can you make it to the car okay? Zak asked.

Juan nodded and limped from the room.

Zak went over to Ollu. The sleeve of her white coat dripped red. He drew her to her feet and supporting her weight, led her to a chair. She collapsed onto it, breathing hard. Her glasses must be somewhere on the floor. He found them under the cart and gently hooked the stems behind her ears.

"I wish you had cooperated."

He strode down the hall to the *salida* sign, then bore down on the bar across the door. Sunlight pierced his eyes, and it took a minute to make out Carlos behind the wheel.

"We all in?" Zak said, catching his breath.

"There's blood on your hands," Carlos said.

Zak wiped his palms on his slacks.

"Will the lady doctor be all right?" Bassem said from the rear seat.

"Shut up," Zak replied without turning around.

"Don't blame me. You saw I aimed past her," Bassem said. "A scare tactic."

Zak stared straight ahead.

Hamid organized his whimpers into a god-awful shriek.

"Mind if I strangle the fucking brat?" Antonio said.

The BMW churned through the gravel and bumped over a curb onto the cement driveway. A mile farther, Carlos swung onto the secondary road and gunned it. With Le Papillon receding in the distance, Carlos said, "Thank God the police didn't catch the alarm."

"Wrong. Coming up on your blind side," Bassem said. "A Guardia Civil Mini Cooper."

"A roach on wheels." Carlos laughed. "We'll outrun it in a heartbeat. If our gas holds out."

The khaki-colored Cooper raced along the shoulder and came up on the passenger side of the SUV

"They're gaining ground," Zak glimpsed a black beret and the glint of a weapon balanced on the frame of the back-passenger's window. Just as the mini drew abreast of the SUV, it gathered a second wind and soared ahead.

"How much gas do we have?" Zak said.

Carlos spoke through clenched teeth. "Fumes."

17

The day after Rocio, Zak was explaining the outcome of re-kidnapping Hamid, operation tot rescue, he called it. Talking non-stop he trailed me into the kitchen.

I finally got a word in edge-wise. "You're sure Hamid's okay?"

"The aide at the nursing home said no fever, and the lungs were clear."

"What about the police and running out of gas?" I handed him a bottle of rioja. "Can you open this?"

He took the wine and spoke over his shoulder while he picked at the seal. "Carlos swung into a village off the highway, and bam, a one-pump station."

The moan of a cello drifted from the radio on the countertop. I leaned to turn it off.

"DeFalla. Leave it on," Zak said.

I lowered the volume and ready for the kill, said, "Yesterday when I was at Alfonso's—you said you couldn't go with me because of a closing in Marbella. True?"

"The seller from hell." Zak wound off the seal and looked around for the trash can.

"It's under the sink."

He opened the lower cabinet. "A hysterical buyer waiting at the notaria's, and I'm cruising the alleys for a parking place in that damned town."

"You're sticking to your story."

"I saw my commission go down the tube when the seller—" He paused mid-sentence. "Why are you looking at me like that?"

"Alfonzo tried to kill me."

He lowered the bottle. "Holy shit."

"He shot his handgun over my head. God knows what if I hadn't talked him down."

"Where was Juan?"

"Off to wherever you told him to go."

In slow motion, Zak reached for the corkscrew.

"You set it up, didn't you?" I said. "Ordered Juan to leave me alone with an armed paranoid schizophrenic. How convenient for you, if the witness, meaning me, who saw you in the restaurant with the dead woman before she was dead, is out of the picture." I raised my hand, and with a flick of the wrist said, "Poof."

My harsh breath was the only sound in the room.

"You're wrong." He sounded hurt. "I did not set you up." He twisted the screw into the cork: his hand stopped. "Wait. A gun? With his diagnosis, the mental health people won't let 'Fonze have one. What the hell's this all about?"

I kept it short. He stared at me as if stunned, and I almost believed his bewilderment and outrage were genuine.

"Impossible," he muttered as he screwed the bit into the cork. "You think I'd kill you?"

"Exactly what I think." But now I wasn't sure. "Or I thought you tried to."

"You know me better than that."

Was I being conned?

Halfway out of the bottle, the cork fell apart. "Fuck." Zak unscrewed the bit, leaving the stump inside. "This pisses me off."

"I got the corkscrew from the Chinese outlet; you know the one near—"

"No, I'm pissed at you."

I wasn't surprised at his anger, just unprepared for the heat of it. "Maybe Alfonzo was exaggerating his craziness, a defense for his aggression, Patients will do that."

"He's not your patient."

"Could he be off his meds?"

Zak didn't answer. Silently we moved around each other, Zak arranging glasses on the table, me rummaging for spoons and knives. When the microwave pinged, I found a potholder, and trying to come off as matter-of-fact, said, "There's hot sauce." When I lowered the plate, I caught the look on his face.

"I thought you'd like tacos," I said. "Mexican."

"That's why I don't like them."

"I have paella in the freezer. One hundred percent *Español.*" My joke fell flat.

We avoided each other's eyes. He gave an exasperated sigh. "How can you believe... never mind." Once more, his hurt came through.

Tension hung in the kitchen like the acrid aftermath of a grease fire. My sixth sense said he was innocent. And my sixth sense was always on the mark. "I'm sorry. My suppositions aren't your fault."

Mozart crossed the room toward his bowl. He drank, raised his head, and with his tongue dripping a stream of water, he padded over and rested his muzzle on Zak's knee.

The air lightened. As if relieved, Zak said, "The nuns made a huge fuss over Hamid. Thanks to you telling me where the kid was."

"De nada." At the sink, I drew the paella from its plastic sleeve. "Just so he doesn't go back to the jihadists."

Zak fooled with the shred of cork, tapping it down into the wine and watching it bob to the surface. "Don't worry," he said. "Sunday he'll be safe enough."

My hands stopped. "That's not the deal. Not just Sunday. You promised you'd fix it with the church to get him adopted." The air thickened again.

"Only one problem." Zak fished out a shred of cork. "The Knights swore to return the kid to the Muslims when it's over." He examined his wet finger. "This is a mess."

"Damn straight."

He wiped his finger on a napkin.

I pulled out a chair opposite Zak's. "Choice. Break your commitment to the Muslims. Or break your commitment to me."

Zak tipped his glass in my direction. "All will be resolved. Trust me."

In the background, the jolly British announcer on Gibraltar Radio ran down the Costa del Sol's coming events. "For all you ex-pats out there looking for a taste of the real Spain, get yourselves to the festival in Molino. A stone's throw from Tarifa."

"That's us. Turn up," Zak said.

"*Entrada* free." The announcer chuckled at his own Spanish. "For the food, you're on your own. Sponsored by the Diocese of Cadiz, music by *España Antigua,* bring the nippers and you'll find plenty of parking. Parking? You heard me. Parking, spot on." The rest of the announcement was drowned in static.

"You're going?" Zak said.

"With the doctor with us when we found Hamid. Tony, remember?"

"I forgot."

Fifteen minutes later, I brought out the paella of prawns and chicken wings soaking in orange broth. "Turmeric," I said. "The poor man's saffron."

With Mozart snoring under the table, I explained my vision of the renovation of Dad's house. "Get rid of those fluorescent bulbs," I said.

A lull in the conversation. "Incredible," Zak said. "That you worry about latex paint and grout. That's what Great Estates is for: we'll do it right. I can't believe a woman like you—that any woman, but especially one as, well, as elegant as you can be concerned about trivia."

I didn't know where to look.

He lifted the rioja and held it in mid-air. "I mean, come on, you're a doctor, and much, much too—special, I should say, to get excited over latex paint." He refilled my glass.

"I never get excited."

"Never?"

How cute. A hidden meaning I pretended not to catch. I fingered the top button of my blouse.

His eyes moved from my neckline to somewhere beyond my shoulder. "You're afraid of getting close, to me, to anyone, aren't you?"

"I don't know you well enough,"

"That can change."

I thought for a minute. "But I can't."

True, I was afraid. Not necessarily of him, but of heading into a buzz saw of a relationship I couldn't handle.

"More rice?" I asked.

With his hands on the edge of the table, he leaned back with the chair resting on its hind legs. "More everything except rice."

My skin felt clammy. I rose to go to the door and let in the night breeze. Then I returned to my chair when I realized the door was already open. "Looking for fresh air." How stupid that sounded.

"Next week, let's go sailing." Zak swung forward bringing the chair to all fours. "We could overnight in Cadiz."

Casey's warning, 'he'll ply you with wine and get you in his boat.'

"Tempting, but I'm editing a paper on a deadline."

"Work can wait."

"I need the money."

Zak came over and cupped his hand over my shoulder. "What you really need is a man to take care of you." His palm inched up from my shoulder to the nape of my neck.

"I take care of myself, thank you very much."

Mozart let out a soft yip as he chased cats in a dog's dream.

Zak ran his fingers s around the rim of my ear. His touch was playful, warm. He loosened a few strands of hair and arranged them around my face, then stepped back to study the effect. "Hot."

My drink went down in one swallow.

He undid the top button of my blouse. "Better?" He worked on the next one. "Better yet." He undid the third. "What's this?"

"Called a slip."

"So that was the thing on my mother's clothesline." His finger outlined the lace. "This time we'll close the door. Not like when Mozart got sick all over your carpet and—"

"The kitchen doesn't have a door."

"The bedroom does," he said.

I should not have followed him. But I did. The breeze sailed through the open bedroom window, where the sheer curtain billowed like a spinnaker running a rough sea.

I reached for the zipper on my skirt. "Let me," Zak said.

I lay on the bed as he tossed his underwear into a corner. Cotton boxers, horses prancing on the seams.

Tell him to leave. Now. Charming as he was, he possibly tried to kill me. In fact, it could be this entire seduction was a ploy to get me on his side and shut me up. "It's no good," I said to answer a question he hadn't asked. His cool body eased over mine. The force, the pressure, the drive pinning me to the sheet.

"Your knee's in my way," he said.

"Sorry."

Dad on the grass with Doctor Castillo, the memory never far from my mind. Dad, eager to oblige. Subservient.

"So tight. Not many visitors." His voice low.

Outraged, I struggled to sit up. He forced me down.

His arms on each side of me, he raised his chest, his eyes never leaving mine, "You want me deeper. All of them do."

Kick this guy out.

With one deft motion, he flipped me onto my stomach. "Don't," I said in a voice heard only by myself. A rake inside of me tore at snarled weeds I hadn't known were there. I buried a scream in a pillow.

"Move with me," he gasped. "It won't hurt as bad,"

I gripped the edge of the mattress.

Strangling in my own breath, I fought for air until Zak collapsed. Finished. So was I, but in a different way.

I rolled to my side and said, "You have... power" was all I could think of.

"Oh, yeah?" he said as if eager to hear more.

My response was a glance at the pink stain on the sheet.

Zak followed my gaze. "I didn't mean to." Slowly he took my face in his hands and kissed my eyelids. We lay side by side, Zak running his hand over my stomach, back and forth, the way on that summer day Dad stroked Doctor Castillo's chest. Jorge Castillo watching me watch him with his leering eyes. Eyes can't leer. But Castillo's did.

"Stop it." I slid from his reach and swung out of bed. My slip lay crumpled on the floor. I shook out the wrinkles. My knees weak, I half-staggered to the bathroom. Something was wrong with the mirror. My face took up too much of it. Swollen? I splashed on cold water. Turning to leave, I saw a trace of my blood on the toilet seat. I'd investigate later.

Zak was rummaging in his jeans' pockets. "I only allow myself one cigarette, and that's only when I'm through with the you-know-what."

"Don't try to be clever," I said.

Zak lit a Marlboro and waved out the match, sat on the edge of the bed and watched me pull the skirt over my head. While the cigarette smoldered in the saucer on the nightstand, he smoothed the embroidery on the hem. "Reminds me of the Virgin's robe in Perragato's 'Women in Attendance.' Know what I'm talking about? The Madonna and the prostitute."

I nodded.

"Amazing," Zak said, "how he achieved the precise colors to capture the psyche of each character." He handed over the blouse.

As I buttoned the sleeve, a dangerous question crossed my mind. "What about me? Do you view me as the Madonna? Or the other one."

His burst of laughter was no answer.

After he left, I sat on the balcony. The moon was behind clouds, but light trod water on the sea. Light from stars, or maybe the low voltage bulbs along the dock. Mozart sprawled on the chaise lounge, and I drew up a chair to wait for the Valium to cauterize my self-loathing. Why had I allowed myself—not for the first time—to be humiliated. Grant needed to do a line before we got in bed. The guy from the offshore rig looking for only a romp in the hay. Now Zak. In all fairness, the problem was me, not them. My internal avoidance-of pain-detector that kept men who might have been emotionally significant, sufficiently insignificant. An intuitive reaction that began that night so long ago, when like an ostrich, I hid my face in a pillow so no one would find me.

The valium kicked in; my thoughts mellowed until a sudden beam of light shot from somewhere out at sea. It climbed the rail of the balcony and rested on the tangled wires overhead. Mozart scrambled from the chaise lounge. The harbormaster's searchlight? No, seemed to come from farther out. The beam moved down from the wires, low, lower until it found my eyes. Almost blinded I flung myself into the living room. The beam circled the chandelier, then disappeared.

I returned to the balcony door and double-checked the lock. Then crossed the living room and tested the dead-bolt. The room quiet now, so quiet—as if the light had been sound.

18

When I awoke the next morning, my first thought was, I'm tied to a stake while the crowd throws stones. The thugs in cop costumes, Alfonso with his gun, then some asshole with a spotlight. I went into the kitchen and filled the basket on the espresso machine Mozart licked the floor where I'd spilled coffee. "You'll be awake all day, kid." He then padded from the table to the refrigerator, then back to the table the way I paced last night. "You feel it too?" He stopped, looked up, then picked up his trajectory where he left off.

My ribcage was almost healed, but the pain was worse. Imagination gone somatic. I fought the urge to crawl back into bed. Wallow in unproductivity. Veg out. In bed, I Stare at the ceiling and waste just enough time to trigger more depression, more pain, and a greater need to bury my head under a pillow. Get out of the apartment. Go somewhere, anywhere. The beach a good place, its bright umbrellas and the smell of sun-screen. The good beach in front of my apartment. But a perverse curiosity drew me to the bad beach where I had found the head. Maybe I needed what they call closure. A stupid word for a stupid concept. That the memory of an event, feeling, or person can be sutured shut and locked like the front door when you leave the house. I was curious to see if the police found the remains and if so if anyone raked the bloodstains from the sand. A quick visit to the scene wouldn't hurt. I took Mozart's leash from the peg-board and with my cheer-leader chant that drove him wild—"Are you ready? Let's go,"—He jumped and spun in circles.

At the turnoff from the service road to the hard-packed dirt track, a flock of tourists with cameras milled around the concrete overlook. Jockeying for a good shot, the tourists aimed their lenses at Gibraltar.

The sun-bleached the world white. Objects appeared to break loose from their moorings and tremble in the creamy glare. The sun burned my skin through my thin cotton tee-shirt. Instead of denim, my skirt felt heavy as burlap. Mozart strained at the leash. "No way you're running loose."

The stalks of the pampas grass rustled in the breeze. A stork swooped gracefully onto the roof of the gas station across the highway, steadied itself on one leg, then folded its splendid wings. Atop a low dune, a teenaged couple sat on a blanket with an empty six-pack beside them. A tattooed lizard scuttled up the guy's arm.

"Hey look at the pretty Labrador Retriever," the girl called in English, the words diluted by Corona.

"Weimaraner," I said.

The guy cringed, and the girl laughed and said, "He's scared of dogs."

I dragged Mozart from the edge of their blanket and onto the trail that led to where I'd come upon the head. Beyond the low branches, the clearing was a trampled mass of cigarette butts, Hagen-Das wrappers, and corrugated footprints—probably from the boots of the Guardia Civil. I stared at the exact spot where the remains had been. The memory of the tattooed face and the cruel work of the blade brought a mix of anger and resignation.

Mozart stopped panting. I turned toward the hillock of low scrub. Halfway up the slope, a red rubber band caught my eye. Spaniards sell wonderful rubber bands, strong and with plenty of twang. I leaned and picked up a tightly bound wad of euros. I unrolled the pack. Three one-hundreds. I lifted my head and looked around. Did it belong to the kids on the blanket? Ask them, and it certainly would.

What do you do with money? I put it in my pocket.

19

The strains of Yo-Yo Ma's cello covered the hum of the vacuum I was running under the bed. It took a minute before I realized the music was also almost drowning the knock on the door. I turned off the motor. Probably Casey—who else eight at night?

I slid back the deadbolt and faced Zak holding Hamid in his arms. My first thought was that overnight Zak had aged. The tight black jersey bringing out the loose skin of his neck. My second thought was the memory of last night's tryst and my decision to keep all contacts with Zak strictly to business.

He looked down at Hamid, who was squirming and yawning. "Where can I put this little guy?"

"Why are you here? Why is he here?"

"Give me a minute."

I motioned to the sofa. "Make a cushion barricade so he won't roll off." I took a pillow from the easy chair. "Here, let me help. Why isn't he at Saint Elias's?"

Zak lowered Hamid onto the couch: then as if he were ninety years old, he straightened with his hand on the small of his back. "It's a long story."

Hamid sucked in his breath. His scream took decibel readings to a whole new scale. Zak lifted him halfway up, then laid him back down. "I've got diapers in the van. Stopped for a few things at Carrefour's. Keep an eye on him."

"Leave the latch off for when you come back," I called as he headed to the door. Leaning over the sofa, I ran my hands down Hamid's flannel sleeper to check for a rogue strip of Velcro or a loose button. His little body is solid and warm. The screams diminished to strangled gasps. I ran my finger around the top of the diaper. Zak was right. Mozart sniffed the blanket, then moved his nose along the baby's leg. "Knock it off." He drifted away, and a minute later I heard the clatter of dog tags against his steel bowl.

Weren't babies supposed to be in bed about now? Before an uneasy suspicion came

To rest, Zak called from the foyer, "I'm back." He swung the door closed. In one hand he held a shopping bag with a pack of Pampers on top. The other gripped a huge box by its plastic handle. "Would you believe they make folding cribs? Bet the instructions are in Chinese."

"St. Elias's doesn't have a crib?"

"Of course, they do—did." Zak set the bag on the desk and propped the box against the chair. "The center's run by the Sisters of Mercy, and—"

"Why's he here instead of there?"

Zak slipped off his nylon jacket and draped it on the back of the chair. "It started to rain just when I got to Carrefour's—"

"Don't change the subject."

He sat at the desk and drew a stuffed penguin from the bag. "Look at the crazy yellow feet." He balanced the bird on his knee, and with his index finger, flapped the beak up and down. "Anyway, the nuns' geriatric place isn't, well, ready you might say." He set the penguin on the floor and took out a package of teething rings. "Seems the diocese of Cadiz ran into a problem."

"Where are you taking him right this minute? Now?" As if I didn't know.

"Calm down."

"I'm calm."

"You're not listening."

"Oh, yes I am."

Zak took a deep breath. "A problem with contaminated water so since you're here with nothing to do except watch Kurt fix your dad's house—" He paused. "Before you say no—"

"No."

"Just until Sunday." Zak held his hands about three feet apart. "He's only this big."

"Fine. You take him."

"I live on a boat."

"Good for you," I snapped.

"You're a doctor and a woman."

"Therefore, can be foisted upon."

"I'm not foisting," he said.

"You're foisting."

Hamid whimpered, and Zak took the Carrefour's bag to the sofa. "Hold on pal, I didn't forget you." He slid the wall of cushions aside and unsnapped Hamid's pajamas.

"Let your lackey, Kurt, take him."

Zak looked up and snapped his fingers. "Great God, why didn't I think of that? An old German alcoholic caring for a baby. Perfect."

He resumed peeling the wet diaper from its Velcro. The sharp smell of ammonia stung my eyes, and I stepped back. Zak lowered his face until his nose touched the baby's forehead, and they both laughed. Impressed, I watched him inch the diaper out from under and slip it into a disposable bag.

"Where can I put this?" he asked

I took the bag into the kitchen and dropped it into the metal can, Mozart sniffed the lid. "Don't." With my foot, I shoved the can into the pantry and closed the door. When I got back, Zak was working on Hamid with a handful of baby-wipes.

He rummaged in the bag and came up with a can of talcum powder. "Hold this," he said while he reached for a clean diaper.

My heart softened as I saw how gently he lifted the tiny legs, restrained the waving arms.

"Ready for talcum," he said.

"Looks like you know what you're doing."

"With four younger brothers, you get the hang of it."

Why couldn't I get the hang of it? Take temporary care of Hamid? Chief reason was, I didn't want to. The mess, the noise, the responsibility, the disruption of my routine—Still, I needed a better rationale. The one I came up sounded feeble even to myself. "Problem is, I'm leaving Spain as soon as I get my passport," I said.

"Just keep the little fellow short-term while I find another solution." Zak glanced up, then resumed stuffing Hamid's arm through a sleeve.

"It's not, well, convenient. Besides, I don't want to. Let me explain. If men can be househusbands, and if people can marry same-sex other people, why can't some women refrain from going gaga over babies? I ask, because I'm one of them. The latter, I mean."

"Interesting." Zak's tone so polite. He put Hamid's clothing in order, gathered the used wipes, and took them to the kitchen. When he returned, he brought an opened bottle of rioja and two glasses which he placed on the desk. Some nerve, raiding my cupboard. Then I remembered this was the Navarro he bought.

With his thumb, he pried the cork from the bottle. "You're refusing because it's inconvenient. What about me? You hadn't told Tony where Hamid was because you don't want him turned over to the police. So instead, you got hold of me assuming, correctly, I was affiliated with the Knights, and we would want the kid back. I'm supposed to do the heavy lifting." He held the bottle over a glass. "Say when."

"More."

"And you would only tell me where the kid was on the condition, I figure out how to place the kid with a Spanish family—"

"Doesn't have to be Spanish."

"Hear me out. For you, I upset the entire original plan, which pissed off the Archbishop. I had to twist his arm to agree to place the boy when this is over."

I shrugged as if to say no big deal. Except it was, of course.

"When the kid isn't given back on Sunday, the Jihadists will go bat shit, and I'm on the receiving end."

Hamid lay on one end of the sofa gurgling softly. "Don't forget I did the Delegates a favor," I said. "They have their hostage back."

Zak agreed after a minute. "You're right. This isn't about a hostage. It's about protecting the faith."

"It is? Could have fooled me."

"Protecting the statue of the Virgin when it's unveiled. The statue is a symbol. It's, well, think of it as Spain's Statue of Liberty."

I sat back, amazed by his convoluted logic. "The Statue of Liberty's the exact opposite. It welcomes the world. The Knights' statue says, 'screw you if you're not Christian.'"

Zak nodded quickly. "Exactly why America has problems."

"You are making no sense at all."

Undeterred, he said, "When you told me where Hamid was, you, or some voice inside you took a stance. In effect, you joined the Knights."

"Oh, I did not."

"You, a psychiatrist, and that's all the insight you have?" He lifted his glass and rubbed the ring of moisture with the heel of his palm and set the glass on the same place. "I'm sticking my neck out for you." Then he added, "References to beheading explicitly intended."

The memory of the Berber woman's face, the ragged stump of severed spine... What if they find me with Hamid?

"Your refusal to take the kid has a name." Zak held up his index finger. "Altruism at someone else's expense. You do the verbal grandstanding about saving the kid from jihadists, while someone else—like me—does the work."

Ashamed of myself, I knew he was right. I began thinking out loud. "I'm the only American in this building. Easy for the jihadists to spot."

"Not an issue. The coast has hundreds of English-speaking ex-pats and the Emir's Army's headquartered in a strip mall fifty kilometers away."

"The owner of the Rabat Palace Bistro has the first-floor apartment. He sees a baby who popped up out of nowhere? Or spots me in Carrefour's buying diapers. And I don't mean the old-people kind."

Zak leaned and lifted one of Mozart's ears, dropped it, and scratched the dog under the collar. The ping of the elevator came from the hall. Somewhere a dog barked. "I thought you had guts," he said.

I'd been accused of nit-picking, perfectionism, and irritability, but never cowardice. The zone between courage and irresponsibility was a no man's land. I felt Zak was too cavalier about the Jihadist threat. "There's more to it. The creep in the weeds near the decapitated head might want to shut me up. Or if the jihadists find us, Hamid's the target, and I'm the collateral."

Zak resumed playing with Hamid's penguin. I turned to look through the glass door which I'd left open. Silver clouds tumbled over the moon and palms swayed and clattered in the stiff wind. Seemed like more sailors than usual were motoring into port seeking a safe harbor. Prudence? Or cowardice? Life was stacked against the living. Bacteria in every breath you breathe, the precancerous brown spot on your toe that won't wash off. Face it. The only safe harbor's a grave.

Before I knew what I was doing, I got to my feet. "Did the baby-bed from Carrefour's come with a mattress? If not, we can invent one."

It took Zak an hour to put the crib together, most of the time spent figuring out what to do with two leftover screws. "I give up. Here, save them."

We converted the bedroom to a nursery: assembled a jury-rigged mattress of towels and a terry cloth bathrobe. Organized the diapers, cotton swabs, wipes, talcum powder, bottles, something called a sippy cup, baby shampoo, baby oil, teething rings, booties and one-piece suits with zebras on the flannel—all on the dresser, my hairbrush shoved in a drawer. Hard to believe one small organism needed so much effluvia. What did cavewomen do?

After Zak left, I sat on the edge of my bed and looked at Hamid asleep, the penguin's beak flattened in the curve of his neck. Would sleep for how long? A tune ran through my mind, and I smiled at the memory. When had I last heard what my mother called the 'hostile rocking song?'

'This is the day we give babies away.
With a half a pound of tea.
If you know anybody
Who wants a baby?
Send them around to me.'

20

I held a pencil ready while Tony stretched a tape measure across the width of the front door. "Mark the center," he said.

I drew an X.

He dropped the tape measure in the top tray of the toolbox he'd set on a kitchen chair in the foyer. He was a perfectionist: look at the drill attachments lined up like soldiers and the cord bound neatly in a twist'em. His starched plaid shirt was tucked into jeans, his belt the same scarred Spanish leather of his calf-high boots. In the dim overhead light, it was hard to tell if those streaks in his thinning hair were gray, or just lighter strands of the overall ash-blond. I settled on gray.

Hamid's crib was parked in the living room where I could keep an eye on him. He'd tossed his penguin on the floor, grinning at me as I crossed the room and picked it up. I tucked it under Hamid's chin where the toy usually slept.

"Bollocks, where's my work gloves?" Tony said, then held them up. "Aha."

Standing beside him, I felt the reassurance of his presence. Not size nor strength, just the sheer comfort of nearby masculinity harbored in every woman's DNA. "Tony—" I tried for a steady voice but couldn't pull it off. "I'm scared out of my mind. That weird light I told you about? Then last night's sounds in the hall."

"Footsteps, you said, right? How long were they there?" The doctor in him replacing fear with fact.

"I heard rustling, then breathing before Mozart went nuts." I looked down at the dog who sat with his tongue dripping on my tennis shoe. "Yes, you." Then back to Tony, "When I opened the door, no one."

"No more opening without looking. That's what this peephole's for. Although anyone's who's jolly well determined to get you, will get you."

Anxiety had overcome my ability to handle breakfast, and Tony's warning stirred every acidic enzyme in my gut.

He turned to the array of tools. "Let's hope the midnight visitor was only a passing nutter. You see a brad-bit?" He found it and clicked it into the mouth of the drill. At the whine of the motor, Mozart slipped into the bedroom and Hamid's eyes opened. I braced myself for the wake-up scream. So far, so good. Tony positioned the drill and bore down on the X sending sawdust up and over the furniture. He withdrew the tool and blew the dust from the bit. "Tomorrow, love, take the nipper straight back to Zak and say sorry, mate, no go."

"Wonderful. Allow Hamid to be shipped to the Muslims."

"So what?" When I didn't answer, Tony added. "I'll tell you why so what. You're too pig-headed—"

"It's not that."

"Too pig-headed to admit you let yourself in for a giant cock-up. Why did you go along with such a stupid scheme?"

How could I say I wanted Hamid to be Christian without sounding like a born-again nut—nuttter—as Tony would put it. I kept it generic: "A feeling—irrational—I know. Plus, a bevy of personal reasons, that I don't have a clue as to what they are." I listened to myself, not making sense.

Tony shook his head slowly as if baffled until he finally took a deep breath and broke the silence. "If you're hell-bent on keeping the tyke, at least get that Welshman downstairs to babysit, give you a break." Running his fingers over the newly drilled hole, he said, "You look knackered as hell."

"Hamid screamed until four AM. And about Casey, I like his company but don't trust him. Always whining he's broke, and he goes and buys thirty-euro wine. Bragging about the big shots he knows, yet he's unemployed. Hamid's a hot item. If Casey knew he was here, he'd sell me out to impress—" It took me a minute to think of who he would want to impress and conclude I didn't know. "Whoever he thinks could do him some good. I'm really sorry he has access to the apartment."

"How the devil—"

"After the ribs disaster, I thought someone else should have a key."

"Get it back."

"I'd need a reason."

"Not if you get rid of the kid."

I handed Tony the bag he'd brought from the hardware store. "The Archbishop DeAlba himself is helping with a permanent placement."

"According to your friend Zak."

The peephole came in a kit packaged in a plastic case that required a linoleum knife to open. Tony took out the decorative back-plate and slid it over the hole. "Perfect." He stepped away. "Ready for a test run?"

Squinting into the opening, I made out the Picasso reproduction on the wall opposite my door.

From behind me, Tony asked, "Think I can wear shorts to that church-thing next Sunday?"

I turned to face him. "I've never been to a dedication. The Pope's coming in from Rome. The radio said the Musica Antigua will play—you'll like that." Wanting to remind him, but not wanting to be an alarmist, I said, "You're aware the Emir's Army threatened to cause trouble."

"Count on it."

Ignoring Tony, I leaned over the crib. Since Hamid had screamed all night, it was no wonder he was out like a light. I drew the summer blanket over his shoulders. "If the dedication comes off okay, Zak's supposed to hand this little guy over to the church. The local version of Associated Catholic Charities."

"This whole production is absolutely daft. You believe Tariq won't bomb the place? Will honor a deal? Let me lay it out. When I was with Medicines Sans—sorry, Doctors Without Borders—we tangled with Boko Haram, and I'm warning you, prepare for the Emir's chaps to come roaring in on motorcycles with all guns blazing."

"Not while the Catholics have Hamid."

Tony touched his forehead with the heel of his hand. "You're in La-La land. They don't care."

"Remember, Hamid's the imam's son."

"Like the daughter whose throat he's ready to cut if she looks at a boy sideways."

I wanted to convince myself Tony was overreacting. "We don't have to stay long." I moved to the sofa and sat with my foot on the crib, rolling it back and forth.

Busy putting away his tools, Tony said, "Don't think the Muslims are ordinary people in funny costumes, like the goblins in Disneyworld." He looked up. "Hey, good idea: a jihadist theme park. Re-enactments. Their ads can say, 'Holiday coming up? Take the nippers to simulated beheadings, to the live amputation exhibit, the gift shop for plastic rocks made like the real ones used to stone your neighborhood adulterer.'"

"Spoken like a true Islamaphobe."

"Think so? Wait until the Army cuts off your head."

Tony closed his toolbox with a click and returned the chair to the kitchen. He came into the living room and stood over me. I caught a whiff of Ralph Lauren's aftershave. Gently he lifted my chin with his index finger. "If they hunt you down, you'll be lucky if they kill you before the rape."

I swallowed hard.

A light pat on my cheek and he took the other end of the sofa and stretched his long legs under the coffee table.

"Tony, let me run this by you. I've been thinking that I should get out of here." My voice came out strangled. "There's my dad's place." A vague plan organized itself as I talked it through. "The electricity's working there, and the water's on. The workmen won't bother me, they're just starting on the roof. Only what if the jihadists know my car..."

"Not if we're in mime," Tony said. "Tomorrow morning, I take Hamid back to where he came from, to Zak's office, you'll tell me where. Then I take you to your dad's, and the next day we go to the embassy in Madrid and get your passport."

"The Guardia Civil has it right here."

"Madrid doesn't know that."

It took a minute for the fact to sink in.

He went on. "Embassies routinely issue replacements if you tell them one's lost. You fill out a form. A clerk fusses around, and Bob's your uncle."

"But it isn't lost."

Tony brushed the truth aside. "Spaniard's aren't all that efficient. If a lowly constable in

Andalusia confiscates a passport, and from what you said, I bet he did it without proper procedures or authority. Did you get a receipt?"

"Come to think of it, no."

"You really believe a local copper would take it upon himself to call the American Embassy? Come on, love, you know how the world works."

Of course, I did. Or thought I did. How on earth did the obvious shoot right past? I cut myself some slack. I'd had been so flummoxed by the foreign police and rattled by the crime, I'd forgotten Dad's famous Occam's razor. Keep it simple.

"Suppose Madrid checks."

"Spot on. You believe the embassy routinely calls every provincial police officer to ask if they happen to be illegally holding an American's passport? Worst case scenario, Robert, friend of mine, the Doc's without borders own visa and work-permit-paper pusher, might go to bat for you. He eats bureaucrats for lunch."

"He doesn't know me from Adam."

"He'll know you're an American psychiatrist who's in the process of signing on as a volunteer."

"But I'm not."

He frowned as if in thought. "Or she could be."

Before I could argue, Tony got to his feet. "Throw some things in a bag. Madrid's an overnight."

I looked down at Mozart, chewing a rawhide bone.

"He goes to La Casa Perro," Tony said. "They're super nice with my Spider, the barmiest Siamese ever born, the damn cat never shuts up." Tony's cell phone went off, and he checked the sender. "The clinic." He stepped into the bedroom to take the call, returned and said, "I've got to go. Tomorrow, eleven sharp. You'll be okay? Lock the doors. Stay inside. You have my number."

He closed the door behind him. The peephole revealed plaid moving along the green paint of the hallway wall. After sliding the deadbolt in place, I returned to the living room that would have been empty were it not for the motes of danger hovering in the air. Hamid was batting the mobile over his head. I lifted him from the crib, bouncing him up and down on our way to the glass door. "See the pretty boats on the pretty water?"

Along the shore, dirty surf tossed ragged debris on the sand. The dingy whitecaps were not white at all. The sea was in a terrible mood. But Hamid had to learn to face down fear. So did I.

Holding the warm body close, I told him about the seagull who lived on the South Pole, about Rainbow Whale who took all little boys who don't scream, on rides through the clouds. I turned to shield his eyes from the advancing tide lashing the black pilings of the pier and shield my own eyes from the angry waves foaming at the mouth.

21

Tony ran the long black scarf between his hands. "Silk?" Before the saleswoman could reply, he read the label aloud. "*Seda, hecho Barcelona.* Wrap it up."

"A gift?"

Startled by the question in English, he said, "Why not?" After which the clerk disappeared and returned with a box, gold paper, and red ribbon. Like all saleswomen at Corte Ingles, she wore the uniform of black skirt and white blouse. Tony liked that. He'd set up his low-fee clinic in Spain to recover from four years with Medicines Sans Frontieras. He liked the nononsense Spaniards and their vestiges of European old-world gentility. A civilized place to heal third-world burn-out. No country's perfect, but at least Spain's parliament gave lip service to the rule of law, lawlessness being the Achilles heel of emerging nations and Tony was sick of emerging nations. His last Medecines post had been on the horn of Africa where typhoid, cholera, and parasites with unbelievably exotic lifestyles sent his tolerance for discomfort over the top. How in God's hell could there be starvation amid all that garbage? Only the flies ate.

The sales Tony woman held up the package for Tony's approval before she accepted payment. Tony liked that, too.

To throw off the creep who might be watching Paige's apartment, he parked half a kilometer from her building. At ten in the morning, the shops along the esplanade bustled with activity that would continue until siestatime at one. Theoretically, commerce would resume at four: and for a few businesses, it actually did.

The wind too brisk for recreational sailing, only the fishing fleet braved the whitecaps. Tony's imagination saw far beyond his eyes: saw the boats' peeling hulls, the seaweed caught on the sheets and the weathered skin of the sailors—perhaps the very same sailors who'd been plying these waters since Neanderthals roamed Marbella before it was, well, Marbella. Tony smiled at his own whimsy. Possibly Paige's flights of fancy, as he called them, were rubbing off. God forbid he should acquire her fervent Catholicism. Fervent to the point of being daft. Her insistence on harboring that baby was beyond comprehension. Wanted the boy raised in the church, she said, whatever that meant. On second thought, maybe she wasn't all that daft. Every blooming Sunday his own mum had dragged him to Bible school where the jolly Anglican chap drummed the gospel into the skulls of the restless nippers wiggling around. A smattering of religious fervor was probably perfectly harmless. It's just that Paige's adamant Christianity was so—what was the right word? Common, he decided.

On the sea to Tony's right, a tanker flying the Union Jack rounded the buoy. A few miles down the coast lay the broken stones of forgotten conquerors. Phoenician, Roman, Visigoth... Of all the invaders, Tony found the current tourists the most despicable. Packaged tours and teenaged brat-packers brought no art, architecture, nor artifacts—just rubbish-strewn beaches and yogurt thickened with gelatin.

Tony made his way past a gang of tattooed Swedes and a German bicyclist who whizzed around an elderly Spanish couple without slowing down. Tony nodded politely as he crossed the couple's path on his way to Paige's building.

As soon as she opened her door, Tony stepped back overwhelmed by the smell of scorched milk and urine. Hamid kicked and screamed under her arm. "He's been like this all morning," she said.

"How totally awful," Tony followed her into the kitchen. The crib sat beside the table. Paige lowered Hamid into it and wiped her brow with her sleeve. The sobs quieted. "Finally." She slumped onto a chair and put her head in her hands.

Usually, Paige could have stepped out of an ad in "Elle." Look at her now, Tony thought. A crust of dried milk on her jeans. Strands of unwashed hair plastered in the sweat on the back of her neck.

"Your shirt's buttoned wrong," he said.

She glanced down as if wondering what a shirt was.

"Had breakfast?" he asked.

She raised her head and studied Tony as if he were from Mars, and said in a hoarse voice, "A walk to the corner grocery and Hamid's howling in his stroller and Mozart's straining on the leash and I'm juggling a six-pack of Coke, and since the damn dog won't use the elevator, I'm dragging a baby, a stroller, a bag, and a dog up three flights."

"Why go out at all?"

"Ever been cooped up in hell?"

Tony hesitated, then reached over and stroked her hair. "Mustn't grumble. What my grandmother said to get her through the Blitz."

"She hadn't met Hamid," Paige said with a weak smile.

Tony lay the Corte Ingles bag on the table. "You're still gung-ho on keeping him?"

She took a deep breath. "I meant every single word I said on the phone. You're not giving him to Zak until I know there's a permanent placement. End of conversation."

"Have it your way," he said after a minute of silence. "Meanwhile let's get cracking. Mozart's off to the kennel, and you're off to your Dad's."

"A jihadist might spot us leaving the building."

"Aha. Thought of that." Tony brightened. Dealing with logistics so much easier than dealing with feelings. "He won't be looking for a Mid-East twosome. We fit you out in whatever long black things you have and act like I'm the Brit who married a Turk, or a Jordanian. Hamid's the family kid."

"Not a bad idea."

He looked from the crib to Mozart. "I'll manage these fellows while you turn yourself into a Muslim housewife."

She went to the bedroom, and he heard the thrum of the shower. He opened a can of Lavazza and filled the coffee holder of the espresso machine. He groped for the button on the back panel. "Why do manufactures resist putting controls in plain sight?" he grumbled aloud. Aesthetics? Hostility? Hamid wiggled and tossed in the crib, tiny bubbles ballooning on his lips and bursting, the saliva running down his chin. He let out a short cry. "Don't you dare tell me nappy." Hamid quieted, and Tony sighed with relief. Forget her reasons, what a good sport Paige was to take him in. The polar opposite of Marcy, God bless her, his first wife.

First and only wife: he corrected himself. One Marcy was more than enough. He married her the year before he signed on with Doctors without Borders. After the welcoming get-acquainted tour of the refugee camp in South Sudan, Marcy booked the next flight home to Detroit. The divorce settled; Tony drifted into a lack-luster alliance with a French nurse in Cairo.

The affair over, Tony wondered if any woman was worth the aggravation of conflict and the pain of loss. Aside from spiritual loneliness, celibacy had much to recommend it.

That was life before Paige. Maybe it was time to modify his policy on relationships. Paige was astoundingly super-sensible, not to mention drop-dead good looking. Not gorgeous, mind you. Rather, the strong features of a woman who rolled up her sleeves to clean up the world. The way Tony thought of his own commitment.

A bit troublesome, though, the lilt in her voice when she referred to Zacharias De Leon, one of the Knights, those hot-heads with their brains in the Sixteenth Century. Knights my arse. Was the bloke shagging her? A nutter, if he didn't try.

But before you go off half-cocked, Tony warned himself, wait for a signal from her. A protective maneuver when you're looking down the barrel of fifty with bits 'n bobs of mush around the middle. No cash to speak of, the capital locked in bonds with maturation dates into the next century. And as soon as he was up to it, he'd promised himself he would return to another one of Medecins' shit holes.

Paige's voice carried through the door.

"Sorry?" he called.

The door opened a crack. "Would a Muslim wear a yellow skirt?"

"Under a burka."

"I don't do burkas." The door closed.

A burka an excellent cover if he knew where to buy one.

She emerged wearing black slacks and a baggy black shirt meant for the beach.

"Spot on. Bunch the top, so it looks like you're fat, and put a coat over the whole shebang."

"Are you serious? It's eighty degrees."

"That's the point, love. Keep ladies too miserable to rebel. The Turks wear ankle-length coats. Got one?"

"Let me think. My Burberry's sort of longish."

"Black?"

"Brown."

"Go get it."

Tony held Hamid while in the foyer, Paige faced the mirror and arranged the new silk scarf. Tony went up behind her, and she spoke to his reflection. "I can't fix it like they do."

"Lower the fold at the top almost to your eyebrows, or else we men will go mad at the sight of a naked forehead."

She wound the tails of the scarf around her throat. "Such beautiful silk. You shouldn't have—"

"Done it? But I did. You've been to Corte Ingles? Not Harrods, but close." His eyes caught hers in the mirror. "We best get going." Hamid turned his head from right to left, back again before he howled in protest. "When we hit the street walk a bit behind me," he said, "For authenticity."

"A Muslim woman would carry the baby." She held out her arms.

It was midafternoon by the time they got back from the kennel, lunch in the car at McAuto, and a stop at Carrefour's to stock up on nappies. Paige unwound the scarf and with an exaggerated sigh, slipped off the coat.

"Don't get too comfortable," Tony said. "As soon as the baby gets a square meal, it's off to your Dad's." Tony carried Hamid to the kitchen and with his free hand, drew out the high chair.

"Did you forget to turn off the pole lamp?" Paige called from the living room.

"It wasn't on. We left in broad daylight."

"Strange."

Tony took the milk from the refrigerator while Hamid whimpered. His terry cloth onesie absorbed the thin stream of drool leaking from the side of his mouth. At the counter, Paige said, "I could swear I left Mozart's empty water bowl right here." She looked at the bowl on the floor. "Now it's full."

Tony's eyes met hers. "Someone has been here."

"Who else but Casey would fill the water bowl?"

"Would he steal?"

"Hard to imagine," she replied on her way to the bedroom. Tony heard a drawer slam. "My emergency euros are still in the envelope," she said, returning to the kitchen.

"Over here. He studied a sandy footprint on the white marble floor. "From a trainer."

"A what?"

"I forget you don't speak English. Those soft canvas lace-ups with rubber soles and—"

"Tennis shoes."

"I suppose you could wear them for tennis."

"That's Casey's, all right," she said. "He knows I take Mozart to McAuto's for snacks." She glanced at the Gerber jars, infant vitamin supplements, and the array of miniature plates and spoons on the counter. A copy of *Baby-*

Scene: The First Twelve Months lay beside a pile of clean onesies. "He must have noticed all this and the crib, of course."

Hamid was licking the tray of the highchair. Tony held up his car keys as a distraction. The baby continued working his tongue across the wood. "You said you didn't trust Casey."

At the counter, Paige slid a jar of pureed carrots into the microwave. "Think back when the kidnappers snatched Hamid from the church."

"And?"

"Strike you how Casey stood there, not moving a muscle. Like he expected those guys to show up." Paige lifted a teaspoon. "Maybe because the day before when I asked Casey to come with us to translate—from that moment on he knew where the baby was and had plenty of time to do—I don't know what. Yes, I do. He could have sold the location to the jihadists." She passed the half-filled spoon under Hamid's nose. He waved his fists in the air. "When Casey sees the baby stuff, he'll know he's here."

Hamid slapped at the spoon. "Down the tummy," Paige said. The baby chocked. "Whoops. Wrong pipe." An orange stream hit the bib. "Meaning the jihadists know where I am, too," she said over Hamid's sobs. She tore off a sheet of paper towel. "What if I call Casey and mention, casually, I'm babysitting a friend's kid."

Finished wiping Hamid's chin, she reached for her phone, Tony grabbed her arm. "Wait. In case it wasn't Casey, don't stir up suspicion."

Hamid lifted his head and let out a fierce shriek. Tony backed away and turned to Paige. "Stuff the rest down his trap, and we're out of here."

22

Tony was at the wheel while I sat in the back with Hamid beside me in his car seat. No moon, only the lights from the strip malls. Malls not even on the drawing board when Dad found the summer house. He bought before the European Union when Spain was still on the peseta, and rural real estate went for bargain-basement prices. One look at the lawn of the Alhambra Club next door and the view of Gibraltar, and he said, "wrap it up." To incite the envy of his colleagues, Dad bragged about his villa smack against a golf course on the Spanish Riviera he picked up for peanuts on the dollar.

Tony accelerated to climb the hills of the National Forest. Following my directions, he crossed the bridge and turned onto the road winding past the ruined church. At the entrance to the building, I asked, "Recognize it?"

"Don't go there,"

"Don't be silly. It's too dark and—"

"I meant being so uptight. Think love. How would an Arabic speaker track you down out here?

"Casey?"

"You said he doesn't know your dad's name or where the place is. You think jihadists comb tax records looking for property they don't know you own? You're safe."

The villa couldn't be seen from the road, but the driveway was in full view. Tony pulled up in front of the garage and kept the motor running while I lifted the door—only to lower it after one look at the shingles stacked ceiling to floor. "Tony?"

The driver's side window went down.

"So no one sees your car, park behind those bushes. I'll go in ahead and get the lights."

Carrying Hamid, a minute later, Tony entered the house and swung the door closed with his foot. "Here. Take the little bloke while I unload."

Hamid's face went scarlet, and he howled. "Pampers, quick," I called to Tony. He returned from the car and dropped the king-sized box beside the desk that was now a changing station. No matter how many times I'd done it, the diaper routine it still made me queasy. It did not help to remind myself body fluids were just another disagreeable aspect of the human condition. While Hamid squirmed and shrieked, I stuffed the wet—fortunately only wet—diaper in its packet, flipped Hamid on his stomach and dusted his bottom with a Spanish baby powder that smelled of vanilla. Lifting him from the desk, I sang to him on our way to the sofa, "As I walked out in the streets of Laredo,"

Hamid reached for my lapel and hung on. I sat on the edge of the couch, careful to not slide forward on the slippery leather as I often had as a child. "If you liked that song, wait 'till you hear this one. 'The stars at night/Are big and bright—' My singing voice gave out. "In the heart of Texas," I whispered. In case Hamid sensed oncoming abandonment—he wasn't my kid—I added, "You'll be able to see me from Spain because Texas is as big, bigger than the universe. When I was your age I lived in a house as big as an elephant that looked exactly like—" I glanced at Mom's leather armchairs trimmed with brass studs, the Navajo rug and the Remington bronze reproduction—"exactly like this one."

Tony was back with the crib he had to jockey sideways through the door. "This goes in the bedroom, right?"

"Thanks," I said, and tapped Hamid's nose. "Let's be sure these stars are behaving themselves." I went to the glass wall and lifted Hamid to the view of Gibraltar. Across the Straits yellow lights upon the water reflected the lit shops along the rock's thin strip of coastline. To the west, the sky glowed from the infamous port of Algeciras; the rag-tag hostels, the hole-in-the-wall tapas bars, and the street-front hotels owned by Russian pimps and staffed by Moldavian ladies of the evening. A port where jihadists mingled with Syrians, Somalians, and Moroccans streaming through British immigration. Overwhelmed by the volume of refugee traffic, the harried officers probably admitted dozens of terrorists on their way to join the Emir's Army, soldiers coming for Hamid. The thought contracted every muscle I owned. "Look how the sea's a great big bathtub," I said.

Instead, of looking at the water, Hamid turned his head to the bookcase to watch Tony, who had emerged from the bedroom and was now scanning dad's books.

"An absolutely brilliant collection. He's an archaeologist?"

"As a hobby. I told you he's a surgeon."

Tony read the title "Paleolithic Iberia, Pre-Phoenician Cadiz, The Mysterious Caves of Anacondrai." Tony turned to me. "He had a proper private practice."

"Let's say he got off on breakage."

Hamid, sucking the drawstring on his onesie choked. Saliva oozed down his chin. I wiped it with the edge of his flannel top and once more turned him to the glass door.

A speck on the horizon became the ferry from North Africa. A cold wave tightened my spine as if the ship churned fear in its wake. "Don't be afraid," I told Hamid. "The bad men can't hurt us."

Hamid yawned.

I forced myself to look away from Gibraltar and picture the oilfields and wild meadows of Texas. The grand plains. The long-legged egrets in flight like silver confetti tossed up to the sun. The buffalo grass hell-bent against the wind. Here and there a live oak, its sprawling lower branches and round top making it a giant head of broccoli. No people. Few cars. Only wrought iron arches over dusty roads that led to ranches of a thousand-acres or more.

Dad owned more. Plus, a tiled-roof house, a mini airstrip with two wind-socks, and a day-sailor on his shallow lake. He liked to shoot prairie dogs from the all-terrain-vehicle he tore around in on weekends. From the kitchen window, I'd see him mount his ATV and disappear into the desert. "Target practice is all ground-life is good for," he said. I assumed ground-life included me.

Hamid gurgled in my arms.

Tony came up to the window. "From here you can almost make out Africa."

"Of course you can. There's Lagos, lower east, Johannesburg."

He gave me a strange look. "If you say so. Meanwhile—" He turned to the kitchen, "where should I plug in the bottle-warmer?"

•   •   •   •   •

An hour later, I lay beside Tony in the backyard on the blanket-sized flat stone. The humidity brought out the spicy scent of lantana mixed with the sweet smell of the weed Tony bought at the gas station behind the Supermercado. Carefully he sprinkled shreds onto cigarette paper and rolled it up.

I checked on Hamid next to us, asleep safely tucked into his carry-a-kid. "Just a small hit," I said. Marijuana did nothing except make me dizzy, but so what? I inhaled and hoped for the tangled wires in my brain to uncoil.

Tony tipped his head to the sky. "Listen, love, keeping that baby's not a done deal. Let's say tonight I take him back with me, and tomorrow he goes straight to Zachariah DeLeon. I come back for you, and we're off to Madrid and the Embassy."

"And Hamid goes to the jihadists and becomes one more suicide bomber."

"He's not your kid."

"Neither were the kids you rescued in the Sudan. Why did you do it?"

Tony turned his head and stared at me, then turned away. "The same reason people write music." Another pause and he said, "Some innate longing to improve the world, I suppose. "

"If you believe a better world's possible."

His eyes focused on the single star. "Not a chance."

We have protection. There's a prayer. Listen. "Saint Michael the Archangel, save us from the evil that roams the world seeking the ruin of souls." My memory lost steam. "Something like that."

The weed kicked in. The world slowed. The breeze loitered in the low-growing cactus, and a gecko dozed on a dracaena leaf. Tony's eyes were closed. "You need to be protected?" he asked.

My own voice came from miles away from my own ears. "Absolutely."

"What from?"

"The Emir's soldiers, to name one."

The gecko raised on its spindly bowed legs.

"Name one more."

The sweet smoke answered without my permission. "My father, the doctor. The model doctor, husband, and father? Don't believe it."

Hamid made a sound that could have been a laugh and cradled his penguin. Tony examined what was left of the joint and offered it to me.

"You finish it," I said.

"Are you telling me the old pater got physical? I mean, hit you or—"

"Amputations were his specialty." My thoughts slowly gathered momentum. "I think he was only mildly curious in the difference an arm, leg, whatever, made to someone's life. Like a jihadist wonders how a crook without hands will feed his kids. I mean, the crook after his hands were chopped off."

"How in God's hell—?" Shredding the remains of the reefer into the grass, Tony raised his head. "First you talk Dad. Then jihadist? As if there's a link?"

"It's clear," I said. And incredibly, all at once it was. "Because the link's a feeling, not a thinking thing."

The fear of jihadists, the fear I felt as a child awakening to the thump, thump of heavy footsteps coming from my parents' bedroom. The thump, thumps followed by my mother's whimper. Trembling, cringing, I clutched the top sheet and held my breath, waiting for the footsteps to close in on me. They never did. Which was why I was still waiting.

Tony blew the remainder of the shreds away from our rock. "You're so quiet."

"Sadists," I said finally. "It's as if all the evil in the world has joined forces."

Tony rose and brushed off his jeans. "Too right, love, too right.

Around eleven, I walked Tony to the car and stood in the driveway as the taillights disappeared into the night. Turning toward the house, I caught a flash of headlights and wondered who on earth would be on this dead-end road at this hour. The car slowed as it passed, then picked up speed. Teenagers looking for a place to make out?

I checked on Hamid in the bedroom and went onto the deck to watch the moonlight play with the ruffles of the junipers. The back yard sloped down to a gully of pampas grass. Beyond the gully, railroad tracks divided the field of scrub from the dried-up creek bed. The distant sea shimmered under the stars. I listened to Hamid babbling and smacking the mobile over his crib. Then to the silence of Spain, the eerie quiet of air uncontaminated by the ever-present low-frequency infra-sound of too many wires, factories, satellites, and cell phone towers. I've always thought silence is a form of God's grace. The pause in the mass when the celebrant takes his seat. The catch between notes in a syncopated stanza. For the first time since finding the woman's head on the beach, I felt safe. I took a deep breath. The peace smelled of pine.

I moved from the deck to the bedroom where Hamid, having surrendered to the mobile, slept with his arms around his penguin. I touched his nose. "'Night, mini-munchkin." Somewhere a dog barked and all at once I missed Mozart. His goofy grin and stump of a tail. This afternoon when Tony and I pulled up to the Casa Pero, he refused to get out of the car and Tony had to drag him into the kennel. The minute Mozart saw the play area he charged ahead and began harassing the other dogs.

I slipped off my shoes. In a rare lapse of bad taste, Mom had furnished the bedroom in American traditional. A Sheraton mirror hung over the Queen Anne vanity, and adjacent to the window overlooking the deck, a magnificent Chippendale desk stood on ball and claw feet. What a relief to take off the black shirt and slacks–my Muslim suit. A University of Texas knee-length tee-shirt served as a nightgown. I settled into the four-poster bed—mom's lacy canopy was in storage—and opened the Spanish grammar to the chapter on the subjunctive. Drifting in and out of sleep, I was only vaguely aware the book had slid to the floor.

A dull thump from the deck. I opened my eyes. Either I imagined a shadow or one moved outside the window. A dark blur. A dead branch blown from the eucalyptus tree?

A crash. I sat upright. Cautious footsteps crunched across broken glass: toe, heel, toe. My body shut down, a power failure in a storm. Silent men in black balaclavas moved through the doorway. Weapons hung from straps across their chests. Hard to tell how many. A few prowled around the bed, two circled the crib.

"Get out." My shout muffled by a hand clamped over my mouth. The rough canvas glove reeked of motor oil. Other hands pinned my shoulders to the mattress. When I gagged, the glove drove my head into the pillow. Hamid shrieked, and I fought the arms holding me down.

Hamid's cry became a sustained scream. A burly shadow raised the butt of his weapon above Hamid's head, and the baby's wail broke into hysterical sobs. "Take me instead," I screamed, as the tallest shadow in the group grab the perp's arm. The gun was lowered, and I caught my breath the instant before tape was pressed across my mouth. A ripping sound as the tape was torn from the roll. My wrists were held together while someone clicked on plastic handcuffs. The hand-cuffer leaned and drew down the top sheet. Cool airbrushed my skin, and I heard or thought I heard, a collective intake of breath. Dark eyes slithered up and down my bare thighs. Dizzy, lightheaded, I was hyperventilating.

Would I survive rape? You bet I would. I'd live to kill every single one of these bastards.

The guy fingered my tee-shirt and as if teasing either me or the others, slowly raised the hem. Another gave a shrill falsetto scream. "Haram, haram."

The guy let go of my shirt. My muscles went limp.

Two men tied my ankles with that hairy twine used to bale hay. Hamid howled, and when I struggled to position both feet into a kick, the burly one drew back his arm, slapped me across the face and laughed, his breath hot with garlic. My cheeks burned with humiliation more than pain. I stared up at him, amazed how those gentle brown eyes with their long soft lashes had just estimated the distance between a gun and a baby's skull.

A guy at the foot of the bed held a plastic shopping bag that he turned upside down. A mound of black rags tumbled out. With both hands, he held up a burka, then transferred it to one hand and pointed to me with his other.

Harsh Arabic consonants scratched the air. An argument broke out full force, the tall guy, apparently the leader, pointed to my wrists, then to the rag. Shaking his head, he repeated what I construed as "idiots." Fingers pointed to the garment, then to me, and I gathered the knuckleheads tied me up before realizing I needed to stand to put on the kaftan. "See what happens?" I said. "When you have guns for brains."

Garlic breath motioned to a colleague, who unhooked his weapon and held the muzzle against my temple. The ankle-twine was unwound, the handcuffs, unclipped. Another of their stupid mistakes—I was able to swing my legs over the bed and fling myself against the man with the gun. A knee plowed into my stomach. I doubled over. A kick from the metal toe of a boot landed on the ribs only halfway healed. A flood of liquid pain. They hauled me to my feet, and I was held upright as the tall guy slipped the burka over my head. The cheap jersey fabric covered with lint came with the stomach-churning smell of rancid cooking oil and sweat.

Why the burka? The foggy thought answered itself. Of course. I could be punished their style, stoned or beheaded. As if the method made a difference. The guy fussed with a black drape of some sort, a kind of shawl. Then came a black sheet over my head, nose, and mouth. A screen of stiff mesh fell over my eyes. The ensemble was topped by an elastic headband to hold the grotesque outfit in place. My vision was blocked on both sides. Blinders on a horse on route to the glue factory where it didn't want to go.

I was half-dragged, and half goose-stepped from the bedroom and though the living room. When we passed the hallway, I motioned to Tony's silk scarf, and the dragger took it off the hook, and together we lurched out the front door. One of the guys followed with a screaming Hamid.

The SUV in the driveway was either dark blue or black. The door slid open at the same time my feet left the ground. Thrown headfirst onto the back seat, I landed face down onto cold vinyl upholstery that smelled of burned garlic and charred lamb. Someone climbed in and sat on the small of my back, a sudden terrible weight that forced the air from my lungs. I must have passed out, for when my head cleared the weight was gone and one of the assailants sprawled in the seat beside me.

Grasping the headrest on the back of the front seat, I pulled myself upright. Periodically the SUV stopped, started and crawled forward, leading me to think we must be in Algeciras traffic. Each passing street lamp cast a stripe of yellow light across the man's black jeans. His leather jacket hung open over a dark tee-shirt. Slits, in his balaclava, exposed amber eyes and thin pale lips. I smelled whiskey.

The eye-screen forced me to twist my entire body to see out the back window. Bright headlights tailgated the SUV. Hamid's with the rest of the team, I thought of turning from the blinding glare. When the driver lowered the window to toss out a cigarette, the smell of the sea carried into the back seat. I heard the whine of machinery, the incessant beep of a truck backing up, and the low blast of a horn—a moan that could only come from a ship.

Condensation clouded the window on my side of the back seat. I lifted my handcuffed hands and cleared the glass with my sleeves. We were on the service road along the A7 near La Linea. The sky glowed with an eerie amber light from the refineries. The jihadist sitting next to me partially blocked my view through the window on his side, making me crane my neck to see around him. Whiffs of whiskey rose from his jacket. We turned on to the stretch of highway skirting the harbor. A sign wired to the Cyclone fence read Trans-Mediterranean; the arrow under the words pointed to the ferry embarkation wharf.

A kiosk ahead sat on the median strip. A uniformed watchman sauntered from the doorway, and after a quick exchange with the driver, we re-entered the traffic to poke along behind an eighteen-wheeler lumbering toward the container terminal. The diesel fumes made it hard to think.

Tomorrow morning Tony would find an empty house. He'd call the local police; a sensible reaction, but useless. They wouldn't know where to look. The only hope was Zak and his renegade Knights of San Avila. Would they help? Sure. That's what knights do.

High overhead a forest of loader-cranes was silhouetted against the peculiar blood orange sky, an acrid, industrial color I could almost taste. A minute later, we swung onto an unpaved track ending in a parking lot.

A decrepit palm swayed beside a copse of flags. The engine off, the only sound was of ropes clack-clacking against flagpoles. The Moroccan eagle and the Union Jack flapped in tatters. Not so the Spanish flag that was twice the size of the others and reigned a foot above. An iron fence separated the parking lot from the commercial docks. I made out the hull of the Kara Maru, a Japanese freighter with its name on the bow.

The jihadists' car with the rest of the terrorist team screeched to a halt beside us. All four doors flew open, and the men clambered out. A baby screamed. No other kid in the world had Hamid's vocal range, decibel level, and most of all, his volume sustainability. His recreational scream and I sighed with relief.

The driver of our SUV turned to the jihadist beside me, and before I grasped what was happening, a blindfold was wound around my eyes and tied behind my head. My perfume lingered on the silk scarf Tony gave me, the scarf the kidnapper grabbed on his way out of Dad's house. You'd think terrorists would bring their own supplies. One more indignity, like digging your own grave.

The door on my side opened, and two guys dragged me from my seat onto the ground. The fear in my bloodstream hit a clot, and my knees almost gave out. Hands gripped my elbows and hauled me across the parking lot. The squeak of hinges must have been from the gate on the iron fence.

A fierce gale from the sea plastered the stinking burka to my thighs. I was on a walkway that rattled and swayed with each gust. A gangplank? My handlers steadied me on a landing. My right arm was suddenly free, and I realized I'd lost half my escort team. The remaining jihadist ushered me down a flight of steps. From all directions shouts in Spanish mingled with shouts in Arabic. More turns—funny how quickly you get the hang of intuiting surroundings you can't see. I sensed interior walls on both sides. Each step took me farther from the voices fading in the distance. My escort stopped. A ping of an elevator, the clatter of doors, and I was inside where the feel of the motion told me we were going down.

We landed with a bump. More corridors. My handler left me standing alone while he jingled what sounded like a hundred keys and spit out Arabic expletives until he found what he wanted. A whiff of minty chewing-gum when he bent to unlock the handcuffs. The click of a doorknob and I felt a blast of cool damp air. Behind me, a door closed, and I heard the grate of metal on metal as the bar of a deadbolt slid shut.

The gentle rock and roll of the floor told me the ship was docked and not yet underway. A rustle at my back and when the blindfold came off, I faced a woman in a navy-blue burka.

"*Hola*," she said. "*Me llama Dima*." A veil covered her lower face. Heavy black kohl outlined her huge brown eyes.

I touched my chest. "Paige. *Pero, no Español.* Or should I have said '*nada Español?*

Dima held her thumb and forefinger an inch apart and said, "My English."

The vast room was the size of a warehouse. The air reeked of mold laced with gasoline. Faulty Fluorescent tubes hummed and flicked blueish light over acres of gray cement. A battered Toyota pickup sat along a far wall. From the yellow lines painted on the floor, I gathered this was a decommissioned ferry. In the center of the hold, two women in burkas milled around a plastic table. Muslim women in veils, women I always called burkas for that's the only aspect of their humanity the world saw. Not people, burkas were all they were—what they had become—had allowed themselves to become. An ancient burka dandled an infant on her knee.

Where was Hamid? My palms sweat. He's okay, I reassured myself. Maybe the Muslims were taking him to his imam of a father. That's the case, why bring him to the port in the first place? Don't panic. If you pray, he'll be fine.

In the corner, a tall burka fussed around a hotplate resting on the truck's tailgate. A wire ran from the appliance to the floor where it was met with an extension cord which slithered around a rear tire and up to an outlet on the wall. Beside the pickup sat a toolbox, the kind used as storage for a truck bed. Now it was used as a kitchen countertop. A bag of rice and a few dishes rested on the lid.

The cave, the silent women, the noxious air... Now I know how Jonah felt, only instead of trapped in the belly of a whale, I was in the belly of a boat.

One of the burkas approached Dima and me, stopped, and stared.

"Her name is called Aisha," Dima said in careful English.

Blue-black skin shone between the head wrap and veil. Dark eyes with blood-shot iris's and a subservient slump of the shoulders reminded me of women I'd seen from the sub-Sahara. Mali, Somalia, maybe she was Sudanese. Her burka touched the straps of her sandals worn over white ankle socks which could use a hefty dose of detergent. She made no eye contact but pointed to the mattresses and blankets piled against the green wall. Come to think of it, everything in the cavern was painted a bilious pale green—doors, woodwork, and the exposed pipes that clung to the walls like topiary vines. A staircase spiraled up to a steel door. Dima must have caught my expression for she said, "Not possible."

Nevertheless, first chance I got I'd check if it were locked. Oily stains formed black squiggles on the floor, the residue of the incontinent rust-bucket vehicles the boat ferried back and forth between Europe and Africa. A ship carrying goats, tourist junk, heroin, and good people along with people up to no good. How on earth did terrorists get their hands on a used ferry? And who were the burkas? Bona-fide passengers locked inside to keep out the crew? A typical Middle East solution to relationship problems—women locked in, men locked out. Or were the burkas migrants whose families paid a coyote to smuggle them from the third world to the first. The most sinister scenario, the burkas were slaves trafficked by a middle-man who had them up for re-sale, the ferry used a car-lot for abused women.

Why hadn't the terrorists killed me? Save manpower; kidnapping is labor-intensive. Maybe they wanted to gain popularity by posting my beheading on YouTube. Maybe hold me for ransom. They'd find my mother. And if she paid... I turned back to my surroundings.

No evidence of a washer or dryer, but a hairy thick seamen's rope ran from a support beam to a pipe along a wall. Odd, how the clothesline held no dresses or slacks, only control-top leggings, and knee-high stockings. Under their black tents, the women must be in the only normal-people clothes they owned. I'd heard burkas weren't usually worn in the privacy of home, or when men weren't around. Why did the women keep them on? As I formulated a tactful question for Dima, she came up to me, took my hand and led me to the others as if I were a kindergartner being introduced to the class.

Our first stop was at the hotplate where the burka named Fatima held a wooden spoon over a dented aluminum pot. The sweetness of her smile showed in her eyes. She turned and resumed boiling almonds.

When we came to the old woman and the baby, I learned the child's name was Ooma. I forced a smile. Unbelievable an infant could be so ugly. A narrow head, spikes of orange hair, beady eyes. What was God thinking? In a desperate attempt to fix the kid up, a ridiculous red bow was fastened to an elastic strap around her head. Dima touched the woman's shoulder and said, "Maria," then added, "*abuela,*" one of the few Spanish words I recognized.

And Maria certainly seemed more of a grandmother than a regular mother. Her skin was wrinkled carbon paper above the veil, her eyes clouded as if thickened with brown cornstarch.

Dima showed me the bathroom with its miniature sink and toilet. No tub nor shower.

Spotless, I saw with relief. In a make-shift pantry, a wooden crate held a gallon of cooking oil and a box of mint tea bags. An under-counter sized refrigerator was packed with Spanish stabilized milk—Hamid hates that goo—and Gerber's baby food labeled in Arabic with a blond toddler grinning on the jar.

Now that my hands were free, it struck me I could shed the head-gear. I unwound the screen-thing and veil and wadded them into a ball I tossed on an empty chair. Dima screamed and put her hand where her mouth might be. Maria put her hand over Ooma's eyes while chef Fatima held the spoon in mid-air and shook her head, no. I got the message. The headcover and bottom veil went back on, but not the screen-thing. Enough was enough, I thought, just as the door to the hallway swung open. The instant the four men barged into the room; the women's hands flew to their faces to check their veils were in place.

The men were in leather jackets and balaclavas. Wonderful. The men are masked. The women are veiled. Do these people ever kiss each other? The men were tall, slim, and fit, and glided around the cave with the grace of snakes. I couldn't see the women's faces but sensed their fear. Or maybe my own.

Hamid's okay. He has to be.

One of the men pointed to Fatima's leg, running his finger up and down as if measuring the distance between the hem of her burka and her bare ankle. The other three men gathered around, nodding. The angry one opened his jacket and drew a dagger from his belt. A curved ornamental weapon with artificial emeralds—I assume artificial—set in the mother-of-pearl hilt. He positioned the tip against Fatima's ankle bone. Whatever she shouted, made the guys laugh. Slowly the assailant drew up the blade, lifting the burka along with it. Another guy, the assailant's assistant, held her steady as she struggled to back away. The assailant gave the knife a quick thrust and in one fell swoop sliced her leg from knee to ankle. She screamed and clung to the jihadist holding her upright. The porous cement was unable to absorb the volume quickly enough. The assistant let go and Fatima collapsed on the floor. The men disappeared through the door without a backward glance.

Screaming, Fatima writhed on the bare cement. I knelt beside her. Her burka was soaked with blood. The fabric clung to her flesh. I peeled back the skirt. The wound was a clean slice. I managed to get a grip on her slippery leg and lift it. "Dima, get something to keep this leg up and grab some diapers and a blanket."

As if knowing exactly what was needed, Maria passed Ooma on to Aisha, came over and gently held Fatima's shoulders to keep her still while murmuring to her in Arabic. Dima appeared with a chair that proved to be high enough to support the leg above the heart. She left and returned with a ragged blanket, Pampers, and a threadbare towel. Then she hurried to the hotplate. Why now, of all times, was she scooping the almonds from the boiling water? It took me a minute to get it. Smart girl. Sterile water to clean the wound. I fought to get a handle on my rage. Probing the skin along the cut, I glimpsed white tibia. Fury stopped my breath. Fatima continued sobbing as I fastened the diaper over the cut. The Velcro helped.

"Dima, explain to Fatima why she has to lay still and keep her leg on the chair."

I wound he blanket around the Pampers to form a mock pressure bandage. The seepage of blood slowed somewhat.

By this time, my rage was totally out of bounds. I got to my feet, crossed the room, and banged on the heavy door. "Fucking animals. Get back here with morphine, antibiotics, gauze—" My shouts became a plea. "Please, morphine. Please." I was shouting at rocks. "You fucking shitheads will pay. I will make every single one of you—"

Dina put her arm around my shoulders. I stopped pounding. "Say morphine in Arabic. Say I'm a doctor ordering them to come back with—"

One look told me what she thought; anger was a stupid waste of time. Let it go. Resigned, I dropped my fist and returned to Fatima semi-conscious on the floor.

Bright red arterial seepage continued through the cotton blanket. How to make a tourniquet? Scanning the room, I spotted the tool chest beside the truck. I called to Dima, and after demonstrating how to apply steady pressure, I said, "Take over," and made my way around Aisha who stood and bounced Ooma in her arms.

The bag of rice and dishes atop the tool chest went in the bed of the truck. Trying to tune out Fatima's screams, I opened the chest. Rusted screwdrivers, wrenches, and nails lay among damp shredded newspaper. A partial set of Allen wrenches and a broken tire jack—mirabilu dictu—a jack extender, the smooth iron rod the perfect length. Now for something to use as ties.

The leggings on the clothesline, too Spandexy. The rope itself, too rough for the skin. My glance fell on Aisha's socks. They appeared to be high enough that if tied together. "Take them off," I ordered. A blank stare. I spun around towards Dima and shouted, "Make her take them off." Another blank stare, this one Dima's. I leaned and pinched the white terry cloth between my thumb and index finger. Choosing both words carefully, I said, "I need."

The filthy socks twisted around the rod; the rod positioned on the thigh—I'll never know exactly why the Mickey Mouse set-up worked. The miracle was it worked at all. "There's still the danger of shock," I said.

I bent over Fatima, gathered a handful of the hateful black veil, and drew it off. For a minute, the sobs subsided as if she were distracted by the cool air. A pretty woman, she was about thirty with regular features and jet-black hair. No pallor nor indications of shock. "Get rid of this." I handed it to Dima.

Fatima gave a weak smile as we helped her onto the least moldy mattress we could find. She reached for my hand and held it as she passed out again. God was kind.

"If no infection, she'll make it through," I said. "Through hell."

I brushed a few loose black hairs from Fatima's cheek, knowing that in the hours ahead each cry, each scream, each gasp of her breath would tear my heart to shreds.

Later that afternoon I sat at the table across from Maria who was attempting to shove a mashed grape down Ooma's throat.

It was getting through to me. The hotplate on the tailgate, the ugly baby, green walls, a woman who was peacefully boiling almonds, now half dead. I was an inmate of a medieval madhouse. I corrected myself. This was not a madhouse. The inmates were not crazy. The reality was the inmates, me, perhaps the entire world from Afghanistan to New York were victims of one crazy cult.

Once more, the door to the hall flew open, and one of the jihadists held the screaming Hamid straight out in front the way a person who hates dogs would deliver a puppy to be euthanized. The baby was naked except for the diaper working its way down his thigh. His feet frantically kicked and flailed. A yellow stream ran down his leg.

I reached for Hamid, and miraculously, he calmed down in my arms.

The guy held the crease in his jeans, flipping the fabric back and forth as if trying to dry the wet denim. He looked up and shouted, "*Kess ommak.*"

Dima lost it. When she shouted "*Kess Ommak*" back, he jerked up his head and let go of his pant leg. Calmly, he walked over, drew back his arm, and slapped her with the back of his hand. Her palm flew to her cheek. He slammed the door on his way out.

Dima, her face flaming, eyes red-rimmed, held out her arms for Hamid. I shook my head no, drew him closer, and carried him to a mattress. My soaked burka smelled of a clogged toilet. Dima, God bless her, trailed behind with the Pampers.

Half an hour later Hamid, in a lavender dress donated by Maria, slept in a cardboard box I dredged up from the junk under the staircase. I lay on the mattress beside his box and listened to Fatima gasp as she tossed beneath the blankets. Hungry and exhausted, I found prayer impossible, hopeless until the teeth of anxiety quit gnawing on my gut.

Once again, the door opened.

Now what?

Whatever was flung into the room arced through the air and hit the cement. The door closed. I got to my feet, walked over, and looked down. One of the penguin's webbed feet was missing, the yellow toes of the other foot were black from the oily floor.

23

The ladies crisscrossed the room, back and forth, back and forth, their skirts sweeping the floor with the swish of worn brooms. With nothing to do and nowhere to go, they must be going out of their minds. In the far corner, Fatima lay quietly in a stupor of pain and exhaustion.

A hissing sound from overhead speakers, static, then the call to prayer, "*Allahu Akhbar.* Each burka stopped and bowed her head. The call was harsh, with a hysterical edge. What happened to the magnificent kingdoms of carpets, Rumi, the miniatures of Alyshir Navoi, and Nasser Shamma's that beats the heart from the desert? When had the call to prayer become the sound of a car bomb?

I tucked the penguin beside Hamid, and without opening his eyes, he wrapped his arms around his broken bird. The mattress on the floor beside him was thin as a cookie sheet and just as hard. I hadn't slept since the night before last. I almost dozed off when I smelled sandalwood perfume and heard Dima whisper, "Are you from London?"

I propped myself up on my elbows. "Texas."

I sensed a smile behind the veil. "Cowboy." She sat back on her heels, gave a furtive look at the women pacing the room, and said, "I'm here to warn you."

"About the women?"

"The cameras."

Aha, cameras. Why the burkas wore burkas.

Dima's veil moved in and out with each breath. "We will make talk with my hands as if I don't know English. Be careful. They're going to kill you."

Saliva hardened to crust in my mouth. Dizzy, heart pounding, I finally managed to ask, "How?"

She didn't know.

Hamid squirmed in his sleep. "And the baby?"

"Don't worry."

I had to get off this boat. "Will we ever leave port?"

She pointed to the kitchen and tossed her head as if performing for an audience. "After these women are paid for by the man, we go to Naples to pick up more. Next, Dubai."

"Sex trafficking?"

Dima stiffened and drew back. "My cousin Mohammad is the scientist to fix the engine and tonight he's the watch-duty."

"Watchman," I said.

She rose and brushed at her gown. "We do more talk later."

I rolled onto my stomach and stared over the edge of the mattress. Stared at an oil stain on the floor until it became a black skull.

· · · · ·

No windows and no clock made it impossible to track time. I tried to assemble an escape plan that refused to coalesce. No amount of rational thought could overcome the fact I was going to die. Right here on the good ship hospice. How did other die-ers cope?

Like me, they blocked the picture of how it would happen. Wallowed in life review. Listed every injury received and everyone delivered. I analyzed all the relationships I'd screwed up, patients I'd misunderstood, my husband's suicide I'd failed to prevent. The list went on.

Who would be at my funeral? Wait—no funeral, my leftovers would be fish food. There was my office in Houston. The confidential files. Who would finish my book on medication resistance? Mom was the executor of my outdated will, and I wondered if she could handle selling my house and all the accounting it would involve. Please, God, more time.

I always hoped when my turn came, I would go out on my own terms. But a glance around the room confirmed what I already knew, no weapon, no cliff to drive over, no meds for a liberating overdose.

The door opened, and a masked guy came in carrying an iron cauldron. After setting it on the floor, he strolled the perimeter of the room. The hold was below sea level, nevertheless, he seemed to be checking that no one was digging a tunnel. He looked down at the bloody blanket around Fatima's leg and quickly moved on. Then stopped when he came to Hamid. Dima pointed to me. Without knowing a word of Arabic, I got the message, "infidel."

The guy stroked Hamid's silky hair while chatting up Dima. I recalled Casey telling me jihadists believed establishing a bullet-proof caliphate depended upon next-generation Muslims. Victory by demography. I thought of my own Byzantine Catholics, our elderly parishioners dying in their houses cluttered with icons and rosaries draped over lampshades.

The guy tickled Hamid under the chin and in return got a wide toothless grin. He laughed and held up his index finger in the jihadist salute. The smell of boiled meat drifted from the pot. Goat? I looked down at chickpeas, rice, carrots, and yams swimming in a broth of turmeric. Hamid had settled back in his box and instantly fell asleep. Not knowing the impact harira would have on his stomach, I decided to get my own meal over with, then feed him Gerber's to stay on the safe side.

A burka approached with a measuring cup in one hand and a Carrefour's bag in the other. The Styrofoam bowl and spoon she handed me were stained harira orange. No doubt dinnerware was washed in the bathroom sink—If washed at all. Germs? You bet. Death by sword? Or E-coli? All the ladies except Marie, who was at the table feeding Ooma, sat on the floor around the cauldron. Following Dima's lead, I dipped the cup into the harira and filled my bowl. Not bad. The tremors in my hands eased as the starchy soup went down.

Dima finished before me and motioned to Hamid. When I nodded, she lifted him and picking up a jar of baby food on the way to the table, she joined Marie. A flash of envy when I saw she did a better job than I could sliding the spoon into Hamid's mouth. Each time he turned away his head, she chased it and pounced. Finally, she dropped the empty jar into the filthy oil drum used as a trash can.

That afternoon I created a playpen by shoving the mattress against the wall and blocking the other three sides. Hamid crawled in circles, every now and then getting tangled in the folds of one of Ooma's long black nightgowns—burkas for kids. After an hour of energetic squirming and rolling, he collapsed on his stomach with his arms outspread like the wings of a downed bird. I tried to catch a nap, but Fatima's soft moans kept me staring at the ceiling.

It must have been near ten or eleven that night when the burkas dragged mattresses from the pile. Dima lugged hers to the Toyota where with her head under the tailgate, she was sheltered from the overhead light. Despite promising brief outages, the damned fluorescent bulb never went out.

I was the only one who took off the burka. Under it, I still wore the tee-shirt I was in when the thugs grabbed me. Who cared if the camera caught a foot or a knee? A jihadist's thrill of a lifetime.

When the room settled into a rhythm of Marie's snores and Fatima's soft whimpers, Dima rose from her mattress and came to sit on the edge of mine. "It's okay because my cousin does all-night watch."

I slid upright and rested my back against the wall. "Where'd you learn English? And for heaven's sake take off that veil."

She hesitated, then slowly lowered it where it lay draped around her throat. No lipstick, no makeup except the black kohl. Only white teeth in a brilliant smile. "My father taught languages in the Quaker University in Tangier."

"Why are you on this boat?"

She did her best with the English she had. I organized the bits and pieces of her story into a coherent narrative.

Dima's family were rich. Not just by Moroccan standards, but by international membership in the world of yachts, private schools and what she referred to as their palace. She was twenty-five now. When she was seventeen, her parents married her to Khodaidad, who just graduated medical school in London. The couple had no kids. An admission that came only after she gathered the courage to confess a shameful defeat. "Allah deserted us."

A few years ago, the Emir's Army had overrun Tangier. During their brief reign, Khodaidad was indicted for dispensing Vicodin to a child with cancer. He was convicted of betraying Allah, who relieves all suffering and sentenced to amputation of his right hand. Instead, he bought an Italian passport and made it to Naples, where he waited for Dima. Dima's parents paid Mohammad a hefty bundle of baksheesh—Dima didn't give a figure—to smuggle her aboard this old ferry on its weekly run to Italy.

"My husband's a good man," she said. "Gentle, kind. No craziness. Mohammad and I will help you out of your—"Her search for a word brought, "Condition."

"Situation."

"Situation," she agreed.

Relief came over me as a wave. "You mean get me out of here? Can you do it?"

"Simple. I gave Mohammad a big gift to give to his friends on board, who are sensible. He buys alcohol and sleeper pills. The friend helps Mohammad lower the lifeboat hanging over the back—you saw it on your first way."

"I was blindfolded."

"Oh, I forget. Do you know to work—?" She made rowing motions.

"Oars? Of course."

"In Algeciras, you'll find your own people."

I thought it through step by step. "If the lifeboat's in the water... it's a long way down from the deck."

She gazed over my shoulder at the wall, then faced me. "Somehow they'll drop you."

Somehow.

"Remember, I'll have the baby," I said.

After a pause, she replied, "I'll watch him, and so will Khodaidad, too."

It took a minute for this to sink in. All at once, the offer to help made sense. Hamid in exchange for my escape. In a sense, buying him. I put my assumption to the test.

"How can I ever repay you? Your risk and what you paid the friend?"

She took my hand and folded my fingers onto my palm. "Don't worry. Every day of his life, I'll tell little Hamid about his angel."

"Meaning, no baby, no escape."

She avoided my eyes. "I bring Mohammad." She got up, headed upstairs to the steel door, and knocked.

Cousin Mohammad's English was so-so, but Dima picked up the slack. Introductions: Mohammad bowed, I nodded and after the usual tiresome Middle East overture of 'how are you's? I pinned him down. "What if the captain and the crew wake up while you're arranging the dinghy?"

Spoken slowly enough for him to get the gist.

"Never," Mohammad said. "Inshallah."

Yeah, right. Inshallah.

"He says they won't wake up," Dima said.

"Mohammad, are you sure the oars will be in the dinghy?"

"I, myself, see them when we do the safety in the start."

"He says, yes," Dima said.

"Are there life jackets?"

"What means this?" he asked.

Dima spoke, and Mohammad replied at length.

"He says yes," she said.

"One baby-sized?"

He and Dima exchanged glances. Then came their animated dialogue until she turned to me and took a deep breath. "He wants me to say how it will be in the little boat. Waves." She made waves with her arm. "Bigger boats will crash you." She smacked her fist into the palm of her other hand. "You must keep looking at the red and green going on and off." She flicked her middle finger rapidly against her thumb to imitate flashing lights. "You feel land, you walk to the shore until the water's dry, then push and push the little boat back into the deep." She mimicked difficult pushing. "The boat goes away, and they think the driver's drowned. You'll be okay. Don't worry."

"Providing no-slip, twist the cup and the lip."

"What means this?" Mohammad asked.

"Among other problems," I said. "How do I get from the port to downtown Algeciras with no money, no identification, and wearing only a tee-shirt—" I lifted and dropped a corner of the burka. "Under this."

"Don't worry," she said.

Then she burst out with, "So you see, taking Hamid's not possible. He'll be drowned dead. Say to me, please, where can you leave a baby while you leave the boat? Where's his food? What if it rains? Think of him. We'll keep him safe. Don't worry."

"Will you please stop saying, don't worry?"

She placed her hand on my arm. "Khodiadad's father's a big doctor and owns the building where Khodaidad does his clinic. We give the boy everything he wants. You, like a Christian, can't make him be as good a Muslim as his father can."

That was the whole point. She hit the nail on the head.

"You can't say no to us," she said. "Impossible."

Try me.

"We'll marry him a good girl," Dima said wistfully. "Such a beautiful boy."

But not yours.

Nor mine, either, but I plowed ahead anyway. "You're very kind. Hamid would have a good life, however, no, it can't happen."

"You want him for yourself?"

"It isn't that."

I thought of the mosques popping up everywhere from Denmark to Malta. Headscarves in grade schools and supermarkets. How could I tell a Muslim I would not contribute to the rise of her faith and the decline of mine?

Fatima must have regained consciousness. Her moan followed by racking sobs filled the room. How could I explain I would not risk contributing one more monster to measure the distance between an ankle and the hem of a burka.

"You don't care for him," Dima said, her voice bitter. "You don't care if your idea is all wrong. If you are all wrong."

There weren't enough words between us for me to explain.

"What you do is wrong," she added with a catch in her voice.

I thought of Mother Teresa's advice on the futility of one single person trying to combat evil. She would agree my cause was futile but would say. "Do it anyway."

"You are wrong to keep a baby from his people," Dima said.

"I'll do it anyway," I said as gently as I could.

If Dima grasped a fraction of what I felt but could not express, it didn't show. As if resigned, she quietly watched Hamid chew on the penguin's beak. Slowly she reached into a pocket hidden in her burka and looked at Mohammad who held up his palms as if saying, 'I don't care.' She came over to me and pressed a wad of euros into my hand.

"Please, no." I tried to thrust the money back, but she wouldn't take it.

Instead, she stepped away, and all business now, said, "Be ready tomorrow time at night when the men get the boat for you."

Judging by the decrepitude of ferry, the lifeboat would be a leaking wreck. I had no clothes. Hamid had no onesies or blankets... just then, all the common sense on the planet flooded my brain. Dima was right. It would be impossible to hold Hamid and row at the same time. What about rough seas? Assuming we hit land, how long could he go without food, diapers, and a safe place to sleep?

What did Tony accuse me of? He called it altruism at someone else's expense. Hamid was that someone. Altruism at the expense of a drowned baby?

Hamid's large hazel eyes—which according to pediatricians' maturation benchmarks would later turn brown—followed my hands as I lifted his solid little body while instructing Dima, "Remember, he spits out condensed milk. Hates the stuff."

She looked at me, then at Hamid.

"And if you can get your hands on some crackers, three are okay before bed. Any more he throws up."

It took Dima a minute before she rushed forward with outstretched arms.

"He won't sleep without his penguin," I added knowing full well she wasn't listening as she pressed Hamid close, crooned and swayed back and forth. Mohammad turned from her to me, back to her again and motioned to the stairs. She walked him to the steel door, returned and stood near Hamid's box.

"Of course, you can take it," I said and loaded his cup, blankets, and diapers. Finished, I carried it to her mattress.

Hamid whimpered and rubbed his eyes with his fists.

Was his life beginning? Or was it over?

"Don't worry," I said as if answering the question I hoped he'd never ask.

24

Mohammad came for me in the middle of the night. No blindfold nor guy manhandling me this time. I followed him along the corridor past closed doors, a sort of recreation room where the picture was on, but the sound on the TV off, and past an enormous kitchen where the countertop appliances were covered like birdcages for the night. The smell of dinner was trapped in the air. Halal pork? Farther along, the hallway opened onto the deck, and I walked into foamy white fog. As I got my bearings, there was a sudden break in the cloud cover, and I saw anchor lines dripping seaweed. I had come aboard on a gangplank. Apparently, a tugboat towed us offshore. On the horizon, the cement wharf was bordered with the giant grasshopper legs of overhead cranes—the cranes I'd seen from the SUV on our way here. On the low hill beyond, the port a tiara of city lights crowned the Bay of Algeciras.

The ferry seemed larger than it had when I was in the hold. Another opening in the mist gave me a clear view of the deck. The loading ramp for vehicles was raised full height, forming a metal wall across the stern. Dead center of the parking area an enclosed staircase led to a flying bridge. A lantern slung over an overhead rope swung back and forth; one minute, the rickety planks cast in yellow light; the next minute, in gray. The humid air reeked of Sulphur fumes from the refineries. A figure emerging through the mist became Dima carrying Hamid. A flash of yellow light showed Hamid wrapped in a satin blanket embroidered in gold calligraphy. "We say goodbye," she said. I wondered if she had special privileges, or if this were the first time she'd been allowed above board.

Mohammad's voice came from the darkness. "Everyone is asleep, so we get ready."

Amazing, how quickly my entire body shifted from despair to exhilaration.

True, I wasn't free yet. But I felt filled with strength, hope, and a word I'd coined for my patients—copeability.

Through the swirling fog I made out Mohammad, and another guy huddled around a shadowy mound. I went closer with Dima and Hamid behind me. What looked to be about eight feet of inflatable boat was tightly rolled and fastened with bungee straps. Mohammad hunkered down and read the label aloud—most likely directions—while the other man, his helper, a tall slender guy in a striped djellaba studied the bundle as he would a monster from the deep. In the yellow glow of the lantern, as I watched them move around the deck, I fought an eerie feeling of depersonalization. I was a captive. But was still almost taken in by Mohammad's courtly manners, his soft voice, and soft brown eyes. The eyes of Osama Bin Laden, I reminded myself. If Mohammad and his colleagues were as gentle as they appeared, why was Fatima bleeding to death in the hold? And why were four women locked in the belly of a ship?

Mohammad unsnapped the hooks and an expanse of acrid-smelling vinyl, or rubber, or whatever the material was, sprung loose and uncurled itself. He vanished and returned wheeling a compressor tank. Groping around the vinyl, he unscrewed what looked like a car's gas cap and thrust the wand into the porthole. He flipped the switch, and the ear-splitting roar of the motor shook every plank and winch.

I tugged his sleeve. "Cut it off before the rest of crew's all over us."

"Don't worry," he shouted.

Slowly the vinyl swelled big, bigger until the form took on boat-ness. Finally, Mohammad turned off the compressor, fastened the cap, and ran his hand over it as if checking for leakage. He unscrewed the cap, frowned, and screwed it back on. Meanwhile, his helper came up with a plastic board that turned out to be a bench that he adroitly fastened onto brackets. The board was too long; it stretched the vinyl, creating a bulge on each outer side. The helper ran his fingers through his thinning dark hair, looked over at me and slowly shook his head. In sympathy? Or was I reading feeling into him that wasn't there.

"They make a whole ship," Dima said as if amazed.

Long metal rods were clamped along the gunwales. Oarlocks, I supposed. Sure enough, Mohammad lay a pair across the bench.

Examining their work from all angles, the two men ran their hands over the hull, tested the fittings, and the vinyl's tensile strength. Then they carried it to the edge of the deck, rested, then in one heave rolled it over the rail and into the brink. Quickly the helper tied the line from the bow of the lifeboat to a cleat on the ferry. I looked down at the toy boat bobbing atop churning waves.

The men and Dima stood around me, awkward, as if not knowing what to do next. Dima broke the mood by giving me a quick one-handed hug and telling Hamid, "Wish the lady bye-bye."

I grit my teeth. Please God. Facing the deck with my hands behind me, I drew myself up and perched on the rail, gathering the courage to face the sea. I swing around. My feet dangled over the edge of what seemed like the Golden Gate Bridge. In reality, the drop was about ten feet. Below me, the lifeboat crested a wave, then plunged into a foaming ravine.

I could not do this. I swung back to face the deck. "The lifeboat has to stay put," I told Mohammad. The ferry rocked, and a cleat that should have been mounted on the lifeboat's stern slid across the deck. "You need a line on the back end, too," I said, knowing it was a waste of breath.

Mohammad handed me a clothesline of a rope. "I keep this end. You have the other one for safety."

"I need more than that."

As if inspired Mohammad crossed the deck and opened a storage bin built into the hull and produced a tangle of leather straps and metal buckles, a complicated harness of some sort. After a short consultation, Mohammad approached holding the apparatus the way a rider would hold a bridle as he approached a horse. "You wear this and go down. We hold it on top."

Window washers and linemen wore harnesses like this. I looked it over for rotten leather or splits. "Works for me," I returned it to Mohammad. "I'll need help to fasten the back."

Holding it aloft, he was about to drop it over my head, then stopped and turned to speak to the helper who nodded in agreement and said, "Haram."

"Oh, go ahead and touch me," I said. "Gender isn't contagious."

Mohammad called to Dima who handed Hamid over to Mohammad who took him in his arms with practiced care. The guy's too young to have kids of his own, I thought. Dima took the complex mélange of Velcro, buckles, and loops within loops that went over my head and formed a 'T' in front. A tricky pair of straps meant to go around the thighs would force me to raise the burka hip-high. Forget modesty. This was life or death. I started to lift the skirt—Dima yanked it down. I thought of Fatima bleeding to death in the hold and let the straps dangle loose.

Mohammad showed me the lines that would lower me to the lifeboat. Dima, carrying Hamid, walked me to the rail. Wrapped in his blanket, Hamid squirmed beneath the red satin embellished in gold Arabic words. Something was wrong. On impulse, I reached out.

Dima smiled as I took him from her. "To hug bye-bye," she said.

I loosened the 'T' of the harness.

"What are you doing?" she asked, and when she caught on shouted, "no, no" and lunged. Grabbing the leather band around my waist, she tried to loosen the T-strap while I tightened my grip on Hamid and struggled to get free. "You promised," she shouted. I pried her fingers off the Velcro just in time.

I shouted what she would understand, "It's God's will." Shouted it louder just as one of the crewmen clattered down the spiral metal steps of the bridge. As if still half-asleep, he stumbled to the center of the deck and stopped short to get the picture. Bearded and in a tee-shirt and jeans, he leaned and fumbled under his pant-leg for the pistol strapped to his ankle. Mohammad called out in Arabic. Dima screamed. Hamid shrieked at the top of his lungs. The crewman shoved the helper aside and aimed the gun directly at Dima. Mohammad gripped the guy's arm. The assailant spun and kicked him in the groin. Gasping, Mohammad dropped to the deck and curled into a fetal position.

For some crazy reason, I flipped a corner of the red blanket over Hamid's eyes. The assailant glanced my way, and in that split second, Dima took off for the dark corridor. A shot rang out, and she crumpled on the planks. I started toward her. Another shot grazed my arm. Stunned, I stopped to watch my burka darken with blood. Hardly a tear in the fabric, the bullet just grazed the flesh. Driven half by fear and half by panic, I made my way to the railing. Hamid kicked and struggled against my chest. The assailant blocked my path. I dodged around him as a sudden blow from the helper caught him off guard. The helper then forced the rope in my hand and gave me a boost onto the edge of the hull. I swung my legs overboard.

The helper lowered me to the lifeboat where I threw myself across the bench, pulled myself up, set Hamid free of the harness, and lay him beside me. Over my shoulder, I saw Mohammad grab the assailant, then both men slide below my line of sight. I grabbed the oars and pulled. Nothing, until the helper untied the bowline of the lifeboat from the cleat on the ferry. "Thank you," I called into the wind. One hefty pull and we slid ahead.

Dawn was beginning to rise, but the dark shoreline ahead could have been on Mars. Hamid writhed and thrashed and I fought to keep him in place while I kept on course. At this rate, it would take all night. The bottom of the boat was dry, so I settled him near my leg.

Shouts came from the ferry behind me. *"Tawaqquf. Waqfa."*

Men swarmed the deck. Bullets skimmed the waves, arcs of water kicking up on all sides. I ducked and rowed. The searing pain in my upper arm engulfed my entire body. A bullet whizzed past. A good thing Hamid was safe at my feet. Breathing hard, I rowed with every ounce of strength I had. A sudden gust blew me farther out of range, and the bullets fell short.

Just as Dima described, channel-marker lights blinked red and green. Beyond it, I made out the halogen lights of the concrete wharf. Between each back-breaking pull, I paused and applied direct pressure to the wound until the bleeding let up. Meanwhile the sneakers Marie loaned me began to feel strangely cool—they were sopping wet. I scooped up a damp Hamid and balanced him on my lap. With each stroke, he slid sideways, and I had to wrestle him back. All at once, I noticed the blinking lights seemed to be in a different position. No, it was me. I was lower in the water. Wrinkles puckered the vinyl of the gunwales. I checked the gas-cap and felt a trickle of air. We were sinking.

Something—tape, plastic, cloth to tighten the seal. I lay Hamid on the bench and unwound my headscarf, then rested the oars across my lap, leaned over them and unscrewed the cap using my foot to block the stream of air. A corner of the scarf fit nicely around the thread. I screwed the cap back on. The set up might or might not work. Meanwhile, Hamid had slipped off the bench, and I fished him out of the bilge water. It was impossible to wring his blanket dry.

The wharf slowly emerged from the shoreline. Objects on the horizon morphed from shadows into cranes, loading docks and the Japanese freighter I'd seen on my way here. My arm throbbed. The pain of the wound merged with the pain of my aching muscles. I stopped to catch my breath. The soggy burka clung to my skin. Although his blanket was soaked in saltwater and God-knows-what body fluids, Hamid's screams settled into a whimper. The impact of what I was doing—what I had done—struck. Never mind my arm, Hamid could have been the one hit, and it might as well have me who aimed the gun. Proof of what I already knew; recklessness brings wreckage. The starboard gunwale caught my eye. Once more, the vinyl had puckered and gone soft. We were going down.

A high wall bordered the port's container-vessel zone. Greasy water sloshed against the concrete. Even if I stood in the lifeboat, I would need to climb about nine feet to reach the wharf. I scanned the shore. A quarter of a mile away scrubby pines marked a strip of beach.

The home stretch. I rowed counting each pull. "One." Then, "Two." At twenty, I ran out of steam. As the shore came closer, I saw an Appalachian landscape of empty bottles, tires, and tall weeds sprouting through the coils of a mattress. The foliage on the shrubs shone black from the oily wake of tankers. Behind me, Gibraltar glowed pink in the morning light. Weird, the sight of busses and cars streaming along the coastal road. Drivers off to everyday work on what to them was an ordinary day.

Gliding through shallow water, I bore down on the oars and kept them raised, allowing the trajectory to carry the boat ashore. As soon as the bow scraped sand, I struggled to my feet. Not trusting myself to get Hamid and me off the boat in one piece, after making sure the hull was stable, I lifted him over the gunwale and lay him in a patch of dry scrub. Then I climbed out and gave the rubber craft a farewell shove. Instead of floating out to sea as a healthy boat would do, it exhaled, shriveled, and collapsed slowly into the mud.

25

The Archbishop DeAlba's hacienda—what the locals called it his summer palace, sat midway between Cadiz and Jerez de la Fontera. The estate overlooked pastures where perky goats danced in the grass, their demented yellow eyes following Zak's Porsche as it crept along the fence. A uniformed guard stepped from a kiosk, glanced at Zak's ID and waved him on. The guard paid for by taxpayers? Zak wondered. Or by the diocese? Zak passed a few stone outbuildings, wound through the shadows under a wisteria-draped portal and accelerated onto the driveway. Fields of flowers were separated by low-growing boxwood. In the center of a rose bed, a figure in black raised a hoe high above a floribunda and with one hefty swing brought it down with such force Zak could have sworn the earth cringed. He pulled up on the gravel berm, parked, and picked his way around the rows of thorny hybrid teas. "Sorry I'm late, your Excellency."

DeAlba rested his arms atop the hoe. "Take it up with God." Born in Granada and educated in Salamanca, the Archbishop was well over six foot, and slender to the point of emaciation. Magenta buttons ran from the collar to the waist of his dusty cassock. The wind whipped a few blond hairs from under his zucchetto; tarnish rimmed his pectoral cross.

Zak knelt to kiss the Archbishop's ring, then rose, slapping dust from his slacks.

"These Queen Elizabeth climbers," DeAlba complained. "Prima donnas, typical Brits." With the hoe slung over his shoulder, he waded through a pile of clippings. "The garden gobbles most of my time," he said in a voice as thin as his physique. "But I think outdoor exercise benefits mankind more than my working out in a gym. Agree?" Without waiting for a reply, the

Archbishop turned to the hacienda, started forward and motioned for Zak to follow.

The walled one-story mansion would fit nicely in the suburbs of a Saharan city. Through an arched entry in the limestone wall, the house was built around an inner courtyard, Arabic-style. Zak followed the Archbishop along a tiled walkway and waited while he unlocked, then threw open the massive oak door. The foyer was cool and dark as a wine cellar. The only light came from low-watt sconces. Everyone knew the Archbishop maintained one of the more well-heeled dioceses in Spain: Zak was awed, but not surprised at the opulence. Louis XV armchairs in groups of three, a library table draped in red brocade, matching love seats. Particles of dust rode a beam of golden light shining through the floor-to-ceiling windows. Like walking down a sidewalk on the sun, Zak thought.

The Archbishop rested his hands on the shoulders of a wingback chair. "Sit, please." In the hallway, an elderly woman leaning on a cane—either DeAlba's mother or his housekeeper—loomed in the shadows. "We have a guest," the Archbishop called in his soft voice, then turning back to Zak, offered coffee, tea, or Coke. Brandy was Zak's choice after his Excellency said that's what he, himself, would have, and would pour for both of them. The woman disappeared down a corridor.

"You got my email on Pope Gregory's itinerary, I hope," DeAlba said. "His helicopter will land Sunday on the roof of the hospital, the only helipad around. My staff cobbled together a procession that will accommodate the Pope's entourage. Short and sweet. The only thing His Holiness has to do is cut the statue's paper cover. The dedication prayers, and quick as a button, fly back to Rome."

Zak frowned. "Button?"

"And he can stay in Rome," DeAlba snapped.

So, Zak thought, DeAlba's on the outs with the Holy See. Could have something to do with the fact he'd been passed over as Cardinal. But why be so upfront about it? Looking for support, Zak decided, seeking allies for his next shot at promotion. The Knights were gaining political traction: support from the royal family, albeit covertly, most of Parliament and the conservative CEO's of major players: Zara, Fiat, the Bank of Santander.

The Archbishop drew a bottle of brandy from a Sheraton sideboard, filled two snifters, and came back with the bottle under his arm. He handed one glass to Zak and set the other on an end table. The woman in black limped into the room with a silver tray. Zak helped her lower it to the table. She unrolled plastic wrap from neatly arranged almond pralines.

"Sold by the Sisters of Mercy," the Archbishop said reaching for his snifter. "Cottage industry." He tipped his glass toward Zak, who lifted his own drink. "To the Inquisition." DeAlba sipped, then held the snifter it to the light. "A little woody. From Coruna Vineyards, I won't buy from the British bodegas." Inspecting the glass, he said, "Getting back to this coming Sunday, no slip-ups, agree? No embarrassments, no surprises."

"It's under control," Zak quickly changed the subject. "The Holy Father gives a dedication speech?"

The Archbishop's smile did not reach his eyes. "Wish you hadn't asked. The draft I saw praises the goodwill between the Vatican and the Anti-defamation Islamic Federation and goes on to commend the peaceful relationship between Spain and Morocco, and—

"But it isn't peaceful at all," Zak interrupted.

"Preaching to the choir. The Holy See thinks we can reach the Islamists through love and understanding and wants us to dialogue about the similarities of the faiths." The Archbishop sighed. "Don't look at me like that. It's not my idea. Anyway, the committee on inter-religious relations is responsible for giving His Holiness some very bad advice."

Zak studied DeAlba's flushed face, heard the quiver in the soft voice and decided to make points with DeAlba by throwing the Pope under the bus—verbally, of course. Assure the Archbishop that no way would the Knights support cock-a-mammie dialogues with the jihadists. Publicized discussions guaranteed to show the Christians as slop-headed fools, and the Muslims as models of reason. Zak wondered if the Pope understood, or acknowledged taquiya, the middle-eastern art of the political lie. The irony was, the Muslims were amateurs compared to the spokesmen for the Vatican.

Zak wanted to make it clear that the Knights were solidly in the Archbishop's camp. Show loyalty. His Excellency was writing checks for arms and supplies. "Excuse me, Father, for being so outspoken, but the problem isn't with the advisors to the Holy See. Despite how much his Holiness tries to hide behind his bureaucrats, he, himself, calls the shots."

Zak sat back with satisfaction as he watched DeAlba begin to smile, then catch himself. "The question is," Zak said. "Why is the Pope appeasing the Muslims?" Zak knew he spoke the words the Archbishop dare not say himself. "His silence when a hundred Christians were beheaded in Raqqa."

DeAlba nodded slowly as if grateful to Zak for acknowledging a reality he, himself, could never say aloud.

Zak's pulse quickened. "Look how His Holiness ignores his church in Syria," Zak said, heady with his power to stir shit.

DeAlba's jaw tightened. "The... uhh... parish in Lebanon is being rebuilt by the Shiites. our people getting more help from the enemy—including Hezbollah—than from the Vatican."

"A betrayal of the Papal vows," Zak said.

"Furthermore, while Damascus was being bombed, where was our Holy Father?" DeAlba answered himself. "At the London Hyatt, a workshop on global economic strategies." The Archbishop took a long swallow of brandy.

Too much alcohol all at once, Zak thought.

Silence except for the tick of the grandfather clock. Through the window Zak watched a crow land on the stone wall. A leaf drifted past the glass. "Does the Holy Father know Spain's assertive position on the jihadists?" he asked. "In fact, has he even seen the statue he's about to dedicate?"

"He must have. It was on YouTube with an interview of the artist."

"Then he saw the scabbard on her left side, and Her right hand on the handle about to draw the sword."

"Not handle, hilt."

"His Holiness couldn't have missed the symbol. Our Blessed Mother ready to fight for the faith."

"Ready for this? He says the statue depicts Our Blessed Mother showing us peace by returning the sword to the scabbard. Putting it back in."

Stunned, Zak said, "No, no. She's drawing the sword out."

The Archbishop selected a praline from the tray. "I tried to clarify this with His Holiness. He said the artist was divinely inspired, therefore, there was no argument."

"How does he know what inspired the artist?"

"He's the Pope."

Zak ran his fingers through his hair. "He doesn't understand Spain."

The Archbishop leaned back to brush praline crumbs from his chest. "Oh, yes he does. The mask of naivety. Psychiatrists call it pseudo-stupidity. If you say you don't know what a cobra is, you have no responsibility to kill it."

"Can you communicate with him/" Zak asked.

DeAlba's lips tightened. "I took a vow of obedience..."

Clever, Zak thought. DeAlba's way of saying despite his reservations, he remained a company man.

"But meanwhile, we have to deal with the jihadists and the baby," DeAlba said.

Here it comes.

"A hostage was an incredibly bad move on your part. What were you thinking?" DeAlba asked.

"It's all under control."

"Where is the boy now?"

Zak pretended to examine a burned almond on a praline. How to confess both Paige and the baby had gone missing? Paige not returning his calls. No answer to his pounding on her door. Her father's place was eerily empty. A flash of anger at Paige for putting him in this position. "He's doing fine," Zak said, hoping that would take care of it.

"Father Estaban tells me he's going to place the baby with the Perez family, the Seville Volkswagen-dealer people," the Archbishop said.

Estaban chaired the Board of Catholic Services.

"The child will have a good life," Zak said. More than that, Zak thought with a flash of envy. Private Catholic schools, clothes, cars, university, a profession. A life of living the faith and enjoying the respect of the Christian community.

The Archbishop moved his hand in dismissal. "Money's not the issue."

"I never said it—" Zak began.

"The Perez grandfather contributed ten thousand euros, just like that." DeAlba snapped his fingers. "To carry the mayor's coffin in the funeral procession. The jihadists are lucky their offspring will want for nothing."

"Only I need to warn you," Zak said, "there might be a problem with Tariq, the father, the imam. He'll be very unhappy when I break the news we're not giving the child back. I won't tell him, of course, until the Pope leaves the grounds. We can't put His Holiness in harm's way."

The Archbishop smiled slightly as if considering exactly what the jihadists might do if they acted out what the Archbishop himself would do, given the opportunity. "I assume you've come up with a good reason to tell him why you're not returning the baby as promised.?"

"For the good of the baby's soul," Zak said. "Best I can do," Zak admitted.

"Oh dear, such bullshit."

Zak winced at DeAlba's language. Then felt a twinge of elation as he remembered clergy allowed themselves profanity only in the presence of peers, never around subordinates, so this was a sign the Archbishop considered Zak a colleague. "I'll work on something better," he said.

"The mother will cause a problem, too?" DeAlba asked.

Zak looked toward the window. Decided to lay it all out. "She would have if the Emir's Army hadn't—hate to put it bluntly—chopped off her head." Responding to the Archbishop's sharp intake of breath, Zak went on.

"The Army got the idea she was colluding with the enemy, meaning us, the Knights because one of our own men agreed—the guy's a moron—to take her to the vacant church where we were holding her baby. Naturally, she wanted to be with the kid. Do you know Saint Isadore's cathedral? The bombed-out church Franco—?"

"It's in my Diocese."

"Anyway, on the way there, the Army's goons forced our van off the road. The mother jumped out, and the Muslims caught up with her." Zak ran his finger under his throat. "Trying to find her, our man Bassem lost his wallet. The next morning when he's out poking around, just his luck the American woman walking her dog comes across the mother's head. Our guy spots the American. Maybe she sees him, maybe she doesn't. If she did, she would assume he's the killer."

"Better find out what she saw."

"We tried. The Guardia's men on my payroll tell me she reported the crime. But even though they're computer savvy, they can't access—or find— her statement. We even went to her apartment." Careful, Zak thought. No hint the guys roughed her up. "To ask for her copy of the police report," Zak continued. "She didn't have it."

"Or give it to you," the Archbishop said. "And why should she?"

"Bottom line, we don't know what she knows."

DeAlba's eyes darkened as he studied Zak.

"I see what you're thinking," Zak said. "There could be problems. Maybe not." Keep it vague. "The jihadists aren't all that smart. We'll outfox them."

A dog barked in the distance. The clock on the mantel chimed the first four notes of the Kyrie Elision. The Archbishop peeled off an almond stuck to his cassock and rolled it in a napkin. "I think, son, you're seriously underestimating the ferocity of our Muslim brothers."

"No, I'm not."

"They have guns."

"Ours are better."

The Archbishop shook his head sadly. "On and on. The same war, Christians, Moors, reenactment battles like the foolish Americans do their silly Civil War enactments."

He rose, crossed the room to the window and with his hands behind his back, spoke to the courtyard. "The church hasn't had a good night's sleep since Mohammad came to us in five seventy AD. Now they're swarming the globe. ISIS, Al-Qaida, the Emir's Army, Boko Haram. When Saint Isabella kicked them out, she thought it was done, They're back." With renewed vigor, the Archbishop faced Zak. "Just as we planned, our Knights have to kick them out again. Same old, same old, war without end." He slowly returned to his chair and inched it closer to the pralines.

"Our war won't be like that," Zak said knowing full well that of course, it would be like that. But he didn't want to spook DeAlba. "There's technology. Like the American's Desert Storm. Plus, I've convinced the Prime Minister to double the ranks of the Guardia Civil." Zak's lie almost plausible. "The US Navy in Rota's on alert." He drew back to resist the temptation to lay it on thicker. "If only there were enough Kevlar vests." He stopped. No begging. Just a hint.

The Archbishop raised his head. "How much for each?"

Zak looked beyond the Archbishop's shoulder, pretending to feel awkward. "You've already given so much."

"It's been a good year."

Strike while the iron's hot. "No insurance claims to pay out?" Zak asked.

"Only the usual sand storms in Roccio."

The Diocese was the insurer of its own assets, collecting premiums from each parish, amounts that included processing and administrative surcharges. The Archbishop would then turn and pay a major carrier like, say, Lloyd's of London, for a comprehensive policy. He doled out reimbursement for individual parish's claim as he saw fit. The premiums collected from a hundred and eighteen parishes produced a discretionary slush fund. The best part, the cash flowed with no oversight.

"How much per Kevlar vest?" The Archbishop repeated.

"Kurt has the numbers."

"Your German accountant?"

"Yes, Kurt."

"I'll be waiting for his invoice." DeAlba slapped his knees and stood. "But I'm taking too much of your day."

Zak nodded at the guard in the kiosk and followed the service road to the C 3383. Where was Paige, anyway? Her downstairs neighbor, Casey the Obnoxious, Zak called him, might know. Worth a try.

The Western sun cast the meadow in rosy light. Where's she off to? Along with the neighbor, who else might know? A goat grazed the fence line. "Why in hell would a woman with a baby leave the apartment in the first place?" Zak asked aloud. The goat lifted its head, stopped chewing and smirked as if even if he knew the answer, he wouldn't tell.

26

I watched lifeboat spin slow circles as if being sucked down a bathtub drain. When the surf swallowed the last of the vinyl hull, I pulled myself together and feeling like a mother bird, assembled a grassy nest for Hamid. Physically he was okay except for an abrasion, a dime-sized patch of scraped skin under his eye on his right cheek. Considering what he'd been through the damage could have been worse. Nevertheless, he was screaming his head off.

"I know, I know. Pretty soon we'll go for a wonderful walk to a fabulous restaurant where the chef specializes in carrot mush." Holding my breath against the smell of his sopping pajama's—a potpourri of ammonia, fish and garbagy vegetation—I stripped him down to his diaper which I removed, shook out and disgusting as it was, put back on him as a buffer against the wiry grass. Overhead, gnats swarmed in a beam of sun. Flies buzzed his red blanket and pajamas that I spread over a shrub to dry. After a quick glance to be sure no one was around, I slipped off the burka and draped it beside Hamid's wardrobe. Wearing the same tee-shirt I'd been in since being dragged from Dad's house, I lay down on a wide smooth stone beside Hamid's ragged nest. A minute later, he fell asleep with his thumb in his mouth.

The sun toasted the flat stone under me into a warm—albeit hard—bed that lulled me into a stupor. The breeze died. The world at rest. I slapped a gnat on my arm. The blood on my shoulder was drying into a thick, soft scab. I must have dozed, for when I sat up, the sun had climbed to the summit of the sky. Hamid stirred, yawned, and went back to sleep. Where were we? I looked around. Another huge stone tipped on its side lay a few feet away. Odd, the precise edges, far too precise to have been caused by erosion. I turned slowly to as not to wake Hamid and saw what I missed when we landed, the red and white striped flare stacks of the refineries outside La Linea. We had come aground in the remains of the Roman settlement hidden among the pipes, metal sheds, and storage drums of Cepsa Oil. Tourist brochures advertised the ruins as an attraction. But there were no tourists, for the municipality had fenced off the broken amphitheater and walls. The rock I lay on and those around me were outside the official perimeter of the defunct archeological park. A year ago, I'd bicycled the C34 that bordered the area. Through the spaces in the green wire fence, I had made out acres of rough-hewn stones strewn around as if a giant fist slammed down on the site and sent the blocks flying toward the sea. I pictured a guy in a toga welding a chisel. And here I sat as if sixteen hundred years had not happened between the mason and me.

Suddenly the aftershock of the trauma caught me in its jaws. The fear, the stress, the images of black masks, shining boots, and the white bone of Fatima's leg. I started to shake as if with a fever about to crash. I fought to keep a grip on myself. My breath steadied in time to cope with Hamid's, 'I'm awake' scream. He rolled over and groped the grass beside him. My heart gave a sickening twist. No penguin. Assuming we made it to civilization, I'd buy him a bigger and better one. He lay back and instead of rubbing the bruise, dug his fist into his eye, most likely unable to pinpoint the exact source of what hurt. "We don't want to make that teeny scratch angry, do we?" I drew his hand away. His shrill cries sounded raspy, hoarse as if from a dry throat, and I wondered where I could find water before dehydration became an issue. I got up, lifted the burka from the shrub, and brushed off the sand. A lump within the folds. I sorted through the layers of acrylic— how can fabric be as slimy as egg-white—and pulled out a wad of damp euros. Dima, God bless her. I recalled how she thrust the money into my hand despite my refusal to hand over Hamid. Truth be known, I thought, with a twist of guilt, she would have made a wonderful mother. Giving me money proved her concern for the little boy was greater than her injured pride at being rejected. And maybe she instinctively knew that before Hamid and I reached safety, the money would not only be relevant but downright transformative. I put on the hateful burka, re-wrapped Hamid in his dry red and gold blanket and struck out for the road.

Bleached weeds and emaciated saplings struggled to survive the toxins spewed by the refinery. Not a single sturdy branch where a bird could rest. A gust of wind sent a black plastic bag writhing in the center of the road. I held Hamid in one arm while with the other, I pried his fist from his eye.

"Let's keep Mister Germ out of there," I said, then thought, please, no infection on top of everything else.

A white van came up from behind. The driver gunned it and swerved around me—gypsy, he would think, or some kind of nut. I folded a section of the garish satin blanket over Hamid's head to protect him from the noon sun. He found a corner to chew. I eased it from his mouth. "You don't want that." We passed the Cepsa Oil welcoming sign, the empty kiosk where a guard should have been, and the dusty cars of workmen parked in the shade of a withered eucalyptus tree.

Not a soul in sight. Silence except for the song of Cepsa, its eerie industrial hum carried on a gust that smelled of kerosene. I repositioned Hamid, his weight increasing minute by aching-muscle minute. His large amber eyes roamed the sky, the trees, and the pitted asphalt.

Focus on the task. One foot in front of the other. A mile to the A7. Someone would help—maybe, probably—there must be someone who would not be put off by a ragged Arab woman lugging a baby along the service road of the Autovia. Don't think, I warned myself. But thoughts broke through anyway. Faint and disjointed voices drifting in and out of the earshot of my imagination like voices from a neighbor's radio. The kidnapper's, "Haram, haram." Dima's, "The men will kill you." Mohammad's, "The lifeboat's number one, okay." Overhead the sun burned the world white. I was in an oven baking my brain into a meringue of exhaustion and delirium. I circled a crater of a pothole and returned to the shoulder. Hamid gurgled and in a burst of energetic thrashing tried to wiggle from my arms. "Settle down," I said. "This is no way to thank your rescuer."

Hamid was at his eye again, and I paused to draw away his knuckle. "Infection and sick little boys don't have any fun." He sucked in his breath, exhaled and howled. Bouncing him in my arms soothed him, so I kept it up.

He'd been rescued from the jihadists. Why did God spare me? Maybe this wasn't about me at all, but about Hamid. "Yes, you," I said, looking down at the flushed cheeks. Sweat plastered his thin brown curls to his forehead. His finger moved toward his face, and when I blocked his hand, he batted furiously at my arm. He was certainly no baby Jesus. Yet he seemed a harbinger of hope: his rescue a sign that despite the hate and violence in the world, we would win peace, soul by soul.

The tar burned through my sneakers. Every neurological connection in my brain seemed overloaded—my head a tangle of hot wires. Holding Hamid tightly, I stumbled across a drainage ditch and into a weedy field of industrial waste, where grass grew in the shadow of a pine. I lowered Hamid to the ground, sat, and pulled him onto my lap. With my back against the trunk, I gently rocked him back and forth, slowly allowing my heart to fill with unexpected love for the miniature life in my care. Drool from his lower lip oozed into the neckline of his pajamas. I wiped his chin with the hem of the burka. A wave of shame swept over me when I thought of how I'd resented the diapers, the screaming and the pain-in-the ass-mess that was Hamid when all along I should have been grateful.

A fresh sea breeze momentarily cleared my mind. Mother Teresa you are not, I told myself. With that disappointing reality, I drifted into a shallow sleep interrupted by Hamid's restless sobs. I rose with a renewed sense of purpose, and with the energy, I always seem to cough up when faced with work that had to be done. Babies need food and dry clothes. "Come with me," I said as if the poor kid had a choice.

I trudged along the asphalt until I heard a car behind me and moved to the berm of the road. The car slowed. The woman at the wheel lowered the window of the ancient Ibiza. "*Ayuda?*"

Judging by her pronunciation, she was not a Spaniard. "I'd greatly appreciate a lift," I said.

"Do I hear an American accent?" Hers had an Irish lilt. She leaned to open the passenger side. "I can take you far as the round-a-bout if it's a help."

Balancing Hamid against my hip, I jockeyed us onto the seat and eyed the woman beside me. Her hair was too uniformly red for the age of the smile lines around her eyes. I recognized her sequined tee-shirt from those on the rack at H and M, and she'd bitten for the matching slacks. I looked down and pretended to be busy brushing sand from my sleeve while frantically trying to think of an explanation for why an American was in a burka and carrying a baby. But the woman explained it for me.

"A man, wasn't it, darlin'?"

"A nightmare," I said.

"Aren't they all?" Hamid whimpered, and the woman reached and tickled his chin with her finger. "Cute little nipper. You can call me Polly." She straightened. "As in the name Pauline, me mum took straight from the telly's, "Pauline's Restless Heart." She drew back her hand and shifted into drive. "Got yourself mixed up with one of them A-rabs, did you? Oh, they're cute all right. You was my girl, I'd shoot the bloke."

I tried for a grateful smile.

"I'd drive you all the way to downtown Algeciras, but got to get to the farmacia before they close. Siesta my foot, Spaniards just don't want to work.

Did the boyfriend throw you out? To the dogs, what he did to my Katy, who got mixed up with a sailor. Spaniard, A-rab, they all look alike, skinny as whippets, those sexy eyes and curly black hair and just when they've convinced you they're mister super, it's bam, the old heave-ho and butter wouldn't melt in their mouth."

I thought of the waves in Zak's hair that sprang back into place when I ran my fingers through them.

Polly looked me up and down. "Bet those rags he puts you in are hot as the devil's breath."

"You're right about that," I replied. "Maybe I can buy something in Carrefour's—the one across from the McAuto. Would it be out of your way?"

"No problem darlin'," she said. "Hang on, sharp turn coming up. Here we go." She swerved onto the 112B ramp. A minute later when I stood in the parking lot and was about to close the car door, Polly said, "If it's a few euros you'll be needing, I can—"

"No, but thank you very much." The kindness of strangers, I thought as she pulled away. Or was it the strangeness of kindness.

In Carrefour's I bought a sippy cup, water, and juice to hydrate Hamid. In the bathroom, I outfitted him with Dot-Tot diapers and new pajamas. Taking off the burka, I told Hamid, "We can kiss this goodbye," and changed into a cheap sweater and skirt. Weird to be moving along the aisles pushing a cart with Hamid in the baby seat, as if we were normal shoppers. Possibly no scars showed. The store carried Hamid's carrot mush that I took with me into the restaurant where I ordered eggs, the most food I'd had since the haira on the boat. Finished, I ordered ice-cream. "Just like everybody else," I said wiping sticky stuff from Hamid's hands.

In the store's entrance, a Vodaphone kiosk sold mobiles. With Hamid still strapped in the cart, I took my new Samsung to the parking lot for better reception and waited impatiently while the clinic nurse called Tony to the phone. "I bought the minimum minutes," I said. "Talk fast."

27

Stretched out under a blanket on Tony's sofa, I watched him set a cup of hot water on the coffee table. "Watch don't leave a white ring on the surface," I said.

He moved the cup onto a magazine, and dunked a tea bag up and down in the water. Without looking at me, he asked, "is Zak shagging you?"

The question not entirely unexpected. It had probably been bugging him for some time. Still, I was taken aback and tried for a clever reply. I could act offended, say, 'none of your business.' Act coy: 'who wants to know?' Or seductive—'jealous?' I went for the truth. "Once." I said. "It wasn't pretty."

Tony rested the teabag it in the bowl of a spoon and wrapped the string around it. "I ought to say I'm sorry," he said. "Sorry, it wasn't, as you say, pretty." He squeezed the bag and concentrated, or pretended to concentrate on the color of the tea. "But sorry it didn't work out? No."

Was he critical of my—what? Morals? Judgment? I studied his face to see how much, if anything, he cared. During our harried days of baby-care, I'd begun to think of him as a combination husband and brother. Sometimes when we laughed at Hamid or stumbled over each other during emergency mop-ups, I felt a giddy rush of partnership, togetherness or affection or whatever you call the feeling for a man who was far more than just a friend. Or a brother.

"Why are you staring at me?" he asked.

"Why did you ask about Zak?"

"Curiosity," he said finally. Rude, yes, to speculate on someone's personal life. I'm sorry.

I forced a smile.

He passed me the cup. "And I'm still curious why someone savvy as you—want milk?"

"Straight's fine."

"Why you see anything worthwhile in that daft con-artist who calls himself a knight but is no more than a dangerous piece of living shit."

"And to think you don't even know him," I said.

"The bloke set you up. Conned you into taking the baby he knew bloody well was a hot potato. Figuring if there were a cock-up—and there certainly was—you'd be the fall guy. He—"

Tony stopped mid-sentence. "Forgive my carrying on when you must be absolutely exhausted. You're a bloomin' mess." He leaned and gently smoothed back a few strands of hair from my forehead. "But a super nice one." He glanced at the foot of the sofa. "Agree, Mister Mozart?"

The dog lifted his head.

"He hates when you wake him up," I said.

Tony stood and gathered my empty bowl and crumpled pretzel bag and headed into the galley kitchen. His place was furnished in Ikea minimalism; the Holmsund sofa, Ingatorp table, and Kallax shelves buckling under the stacks of *Lancet* and *British Family Practice* journals. A print of Alexander the Great hung above the fireplace. The carpets were rough North Africans: Marrakesh orange and reds, a black and brown practice rug from a souk somewhere south of Agadir, I guessed. Overall the ambiance of the place reflected someone thoughtful and well-organized, albeit a bit frugal.

The refrigerator door slammed, and Tony returned with a Heinekens and a carafe of orange juice. "Juice for you. Alcohol and pain meds do not mix," he reminded me.

I ran my fingers over the bandage on my arm. "You did a good job. And I appreciate your springing Mo from the kennel."

"If it turned out you didn't come out of this—"

"Alive." I finished the sentence for him.

"I would have adopted him." He leaned and slapped Mo on the back. "Think us bachelors would get along, old boy?"

A sudden memory of the afternoon on the ferry, Dima's expression when I told her I was worried about my dog if I never made it off the boat. Her eyes revealed her thoughts. Only infidels kept a dog in the house. Picturing Dima brought back the hold of the ship, the smell of gasoline and rotten wood, the sound of Fatima's sobs and the footsteps of men in black.

Tony filled his glass and waited for the foam to settle.

"If you only knew how I felt when you pulled up in front of Carrefour's and I knew it was over," My voice trembled. "Don't mind me. I always choke up when I'm being rescued." I motioned to Mozart, the tea and the blister pack of antibiotics on the table. "Thank you."

When Tony pulled up to Carrefour's he'd helped Hamid and me into the car, and as soon as we were in his apartment in Marbella, he'd rustled up blankets, hot soup and something to knock me out while he sutured the bullet wound. Only four stitches. A hot bath for Hamid, carrot mush and now the little guy was ensconced safely among pillows in a big-people bed.

Careful to keep his beer from spilling, Tony returned to his leather lounge chair. "When I saw the broken window at your dad's, I went bollocks. Called the hospitals, hotels, and your embassy." He sat forward. "Oh, before I forget, let me go get it." He went to the bedroom and returned with a brown envelope. "I got Karl to overnight me your passport."

I swallowed hard. There were no words.

Tony resumed his place on the lounge. "The embassy routinely issues replacements. It would take days, weeks, probably never, before the Spaniards to get enough internal clearances to inform the US they've confiscated an American passport. Assuming the police had a legal right to hold it in the first place. Our administrative guy said he wasn't sure about Spanish law."

I ran my fingers over the blue jacket with its gold eagle. On the first page there it was my birth date. My identity reinstated like a migrating robin who finds its way back to the same nest. Was my life still where I'd left it? The god-awful pine paneling in my office in Houston I'd yet to have replaced? My 'don't mess with Texas' coffee mug? Was my house still standing and were the roses holding their own against black spot?

"Blimey, Paige, are you crying?"

I wiped my cheek. "Hot tea makes my eyes run."

"Sure. Right. Hot tea will do that." He came over and put his arms around me.

Every bone in my body softened as I rested my head into the curve of his shoulder, against his firm body and crisp white shirt that smelled of Clorox and that antiseptic Spanish soap.

28

Tony's tiny Panda rattled over the unpaved road to the village of Molino del Santo. He pulled over at the base of a limestone outcrop while I looked up at the fifty-foot statue of Our Lady of Tarifa draped in canvas. She stood facing the harbor, and beyond it, El Ksar on the North African coast. The statue would remain under wraps until this afternoon when the Pope would unveil it.

"You see the preview of the work on YouTube?" Tony asked.

"Interesting," I said. "I've been following the flap on social media about whether her hand is pulling the sword out, or putting it back in."

"Does it matter?" he asked.

"Are you nuts? It's the whole point of placing it on the coast. Is she about to whack off Muslim heads? Or is she showing them we want peace?"

"Whatever," Tony said and put the car in reverse. "Had enough statue?"

I nodded and adjusted the blanket over Hamid. This morning when I'd put him in his car seat, he howled his head off, so I gave in and held him on my lap. I touched his nose, then turned to the passenger side window to watch the wind herd black clouds over the fields. Tony braked at the sign, *centro ciudad.*

Molino del Santo clung to the stony slope of a mountain as if any minute the village might lose its hold on the cliff and tumble into the sea. Capellini-thin alleys wound around a ruined fort until dead-ending at a cobblestone square. A water tower on stilts loomed like an upright spider over the treatment plant. The town crawled with National Police, kids, tourists, clergy, and media-types with name tags on lanyards around their necks. "We're hours early and the place is already jammed," Tony said.

"The new Pope's first time in Spain."

We passed guys in the blue berets of Zak's Constancia Knights. We passed an elderly couple walking a feisty whippet straining at the leash. We passed a man in a black leather jacket leaning against the hood of a Toyota pickup. A cigarette slanted from his lips. His head turned to follow a Guardia Civils' SUV cruising the street.

"He looks like one of the jihadists in the boat," I said. "But men in black leather all look alike. I could be wrong."

"He does appear a bit dodgy," Tony waited for pedestrians to clear the cross-walk and swerved into an alley. "Keep your head down." Then in an exasperated tone, "I told you it was dangerous for you to show up. The bloody sods on the ferry might be the ones the cell sends here to demolish the festivities."

"To tear the place apart," I agreed.

He gave my hand a quick squeeze. "Let's hope the chap's just ducking the missus. You think this dog's breakfast-of-a-town has a place to get tea?"

Tony circled the square where the church of St. Clare of Assisi and the rectory behind it sat in splendid disrepair. Chipped conquistadores marched across the lintel; the angel guarding the portal was one wing short. From the pointed arches and ribbed vaults, I guessed the buildings as late Gothic. The hideous yellow-ochre stone must be from a local quarry and probably cheap, otherwise, why dig it up? A splat of rain zig-zagged down the windshield, leading an advance of bullet-sized drops.

"I see stores," I said, "but no parking. Quick, that Citroen's backing out."

Tony swung into the vacant spot. Opposite the church, a café served croissants and coffee at the plastic tables it shared with the tapas bar next door. A hole-in-the-wall tourist trap displayed dusty mantillas and matador capes on a clothesline strung above the entrance.

Tony unfastened his seat belt. "Stay in the car so the bad guys won't spot you," he ordered. "What can I get you two?"

"Coffee for me and juice for Hamid. No condensed."

Tony plunged into the swirling rain. I looked down at Hamid, who was chewing on his blanket. When he paused for breath, I drew away the cloth and slid a teething ring into his mouth. "Oh boy," I said. "I wish I had one of those." He gazed dreamy-eyed at the dashboard. I too, was lost in thought, running down how we'd hand Hamid over to the church and asking myself what could go wrong? The answer? everything.

Assuming the dedication came off without a hitch, the Knights were to deliver Hamid to the Red Crescent's main office near the hospital. The exchange would be filmed showing the kid alive and well.

The plan was in cement until I threw in the monkey wrench. Me, on my high horse insisting the kid be raised in the church. Me, so devout I rarely got out of bed for Sunday Mass. And here I was grandstanding even though realizing if we did not return Hamid, who knew what the jihadists might do. Why didn't Zak talk me out of my grandiose idea? And why did the others buy in? I must have fed into their secret vanities. If Zak pulled off screwing the jihadist's he'd come out as the new Richard the Lionheart, and the Archbishop could print mass cards for when he made cardinal.

The revised scenario went like this: as soon as the Pope's helicopter lifted off, instead of the Red Crescent, Hamid would be delivered to St. Clare's rectory. Brother Fernando from Catholic Services would take it from there.

A rumble of thunder. I eased the teething ring from Hamid's mouth. His scream could blast the paint off the car. I wiped off the gooey spit and popped the ring back in before he could let loose again. Through the window I watched a mom in a raincoat coax a stroller over the slippery cobblestones. A nun in a full-length habit unfolded an umbrella. A sleek dark-green Mercedes glided past, and I glimpsed Arabic plates. I picked out Tony among the crowd in the coffee-counter line. In his orange *Medicines Sin Frontera* tee-shirt, he was easy to spot

A rap on the glass on the driver's side. What in the world?

Zak, in a denim jacket and blue beret, motioned for me to lower the window. "I'm drowning," he shouted.

He slid inside, drew off the beret and wiped it on his sleeve.

"You're here early," I said.

"So's everyone else. Including your weirdo neighbor. See him under the awning?"

"Casey said he was coming. He wants to join the Facebook conversation of the day. The topic being, is Our Lady drawing Her sword in? Or out?"

Hamid yawned, and the teething ring rode the current of drool draining into his onesie. I slid the ring back in his mouth and bounced him on my knee. "This morning Casey brought my rental car from our apartment building to Tony's place. Remember me telling you we used Tony's car to get to my Dad's the night the jihadists? But you know the rest. I told you on the phone."

"The rest of what?"

"You were so busy complaining about the Archbishop and the Pope you weren't paying attention."

"Yes, I was. Of course. The ferry."

"Anyway, I'll drop off the rental at the airport. Don't forget, I'm leaving the country."

Zak touched my cheek. "Don't remind me." He lowered his hand. "But right now, we have a problem. The Pope's hung up in Cadiz."

"For how long?"

"He might not show at all. The acolyte danced around the issue. The Vatican's usually precise on logistics, which makes me think something's seriously wrong."

"Can the Archbishop pinch-hit?"

"I have a bad feeling," Zak said. "Like when the crazy Catalonians bombed the Marriott."

"Free-floating anxiety."

Zak took a deep breath, held it, and exhaled. "Your clinical observations have a way of trivializing everything." He motioned to the guy in black leather who was now behind Tony in the coffee line. "Every place I look, there's Emir's people. What are they doing here? My tech-guru picked up internet traffic—the word helicopter. And there's too much excitement, downright hysteria among the chat groups. Not good."

"We're okay. The baby's our leverage. That's why we have him, right? The only problem is that the jihadists might not care if Hamid lives or dies. Let me tell you about when I was a consultant for the prison system."

"What happened?"

"This inmate told me a rival drug-lord held his—the inmate's infant son, hostage. "It don't bother me none," he said, 'go ahead and kill the kid. I can make another just like him.'

Like my own father, I thought.

"A real shit." Zak said.

"You got that right."

Zak positioned the beret on his head and ran his finger along the headband.

"It's on straight," I said. "If the Pope doesn't show, what's the worst-case scenario?"

"That he was tipped off that the terrorists will attack."

I thought for a minute. "Wouldn't his handlers warn the public?"

"If that's what his Holiness decides. Here comes your British friend."

Across the street, Tony, holding a plastic bag, stood on the asphalt waiting for the traffic to clear. A teenaged girl on a skateboard whizzed up beside him and dismounted.

Zak gripped my wrist. "Not a word to your friend about the Pope."

"Okay, but why not?"

"Feelings aren't facts."

The girl repositioned her foot on the board and pushed off. When she got to the center of the street, a motorcycle shot from behind a van, missing her by an inch.

She lay on the street with Tony crouched beside her. They rose at the same time. The girl leaned and picked up her skateboard. Gripping her elbow, Tony helped her cross the street.

"An example of why I wouldn't confide in your doctor friend," Zak said. "He should help the cyclist, not the kid who never bothered to look both ways. If we tell him there might be an attack, he'll instigate the mother of all evacuations. If I'm wrong and the Pope does show up..." Zak closed his eyes. "We'll be blamed for a huge fucking mess."

Tony approached the car, stopped midway and stared, probably guessing who Zak was. I pushed the toggle switch to unlock the rear door.

Zak slid from the front, dashed through the rain and settled into the back seat.

Quick introductions and Zak said, "I take it, you're the doctor."

Tony set the bag between his feet and drew out a bottle of orange juice and a paper cup.

"You're just saving refugees," Zak said, "so we can go broke supporting more of them."

Tony calmly lifted a container of coffee from the bag and passed it to me. "Watch, it's hot. I made sure the lid's on tight."

Hamid whimpered and waved his arms. Then came the urgent kicks under the blanket and the predictable red-faced howl. "You have the Dot Tots?" Tony asked.

I reached for the diaper bag at my feet. "Your turn? Or mine?"

"Not enough room upfront. I'll lay him flat in the boot." Tony slung the bag over his shoulder and hoisted Hamid from my lap.

"It's raining," I said.

"I'll keep him under the open lid."

A good as any excuse to get away from Zak, I thought as the door closed.

Zak leaned on the back of my seat. "I need you to help with a favor. A big one." His breath was warm on my neck. "I got Father Arturo—he's the celebrant in the church across the street. He's young but has impressive plans to rehab the rectory and —"

"Zak, get to the point."

"Hamid has to be baptized. Here. Now."

I twisted around to face him "Are you out of your mind?"

"It's best if both a man and a woman stand up for him. Not that we're official godparents, but..."

"No."

"Hamid has to become Christian. Has to, in case the jihadists show up, and he's—we don't want to think about it."

"No."

"Look, if the kid should not, like, survive?"

"He'll survive."

"If he doesn't, what about your conscience? Your responsibility to the faith? You want him to die without the sacraments and—"

"All right, all right." I turned back to the windshield and watched the rain slither down the glass. Bad timing. On the other hand, what's the harm? I thought of Sister Helen, good old Sister Helen with her narrow-lidded eyes and wide grin like a dinosaur's. Sister going into details about the disadvantages of hell.

"Turn around. Face me. You're on board?"

The intensity of his eyes was unnerving. I sighed and asked, "Just so it doesn't take too long. When?"

"Father agreed to do it right before Mass. Short and sweet. Twenty minutes, we're out of there."

Before I could think it through, Zak said, "I'll be back." He slammed the car door and darted toward the café.

In contrast to its outside, the interior of Saint Clare of Assisi was grand as its name. I followed Zak through the massive portal while wondering how many Visigoths, crusaders, king, and queens had darkened these weathered doors. The tabernacle shone gold. Overhead, a Crucifix hung on chains from the vaulted ceiling casting a shadow of the Cross over the tiers of lilies. The leather kneeling pads smelled of well-worn saddles. In a chapel to the right, the baptismal front sat on a stone plinth. It took a team of angels to hold the marble basin aloft.

Turning his beret nervously in both hands, Zak stood beside me while I swayed slightly to entertain Hamid. Father Arturo emerged from a doorway behind the altar. He wore a black cassock, and with the arrogance of a panther, swept down the altar steps carrying a dipper, an amphora, and a book under his arm. He proceeded to set up his equipment on a table near the font and turned to us with the volume in his slender El Greco hands. He spoke in Spanish.

"Father apologizes for his lack of English," Zak whispered. "He wants to know the name of this child."

Name? It hadn't occurred to me. A Catholic kid called Hamid? "Peter?" I suggested. "John's nice."

"Michael," Zak told Father firmly. Then in an aside to me, "Who fought the devil,"

"Okay by me."

I tucked the red satin blanket around Hamid's feet. The calligraphy on it probably read God is great in Arabic. So much for diversity, I thought watching Father make the sign of the Cross. I raised my head when Zak and Father began a dialogue: the obligatory questions asked all godparents; assurances that the new person would be raised in the faith. More prayers and I heard the rhythm of the Apostle's Creed. Then Father leaned to anoint Hamid with Chrism oil. I caught a whiff of sage.

Two acolytes, boys about nine or ten in white cassocks, came from behind the altar and crossed the sanctuary. Each knelt with hurried dips, then quickly rose and began lighting candles. Bells pealed in the tower. A blast of wet air. The doors slammed shut. The first person to show for mass was an old guy who gripped one pew, let go and reached for the pew ahead. Behind him, a teenaged girl pulled off her scarf, shook out the rain and ran her fingers through her hair. The door slammed again and slowly the pews filled.

Father lifted the gold dipper. Supporting Hamid's head gently with one hand, with the other, he tipped the ladle over the baby's head. I tried to keep Hamid from batting the dipper; he scored only one hit before I blocked his arm. But when Father dried the baby's face with a towel, Hamid only lay back and blew a bubble of spit.

My throat tightened. This was wrong, all wrong. Hamid was cheated. No real godparents. No family in the front row. Instead of Zak, the boy's father should be carrying the baptismal candle and white sash. Afterward, there should be cake and balloons, and presents and ice cream.

I pulled myself together and forced a smile while Father made the sign of the Cross.

"Are you staying for mass?" Zak whispered.

"It would be rude not to."

Father gathered the dipper and amphora and disappeared behind the altar.

One trumpet note soared from the choir loft. A harpsichord responded. If not Palestrina, a magnificent knock-off. The congregation rose. An altar boy holding aloft a Crucifix advanced down the aisle. Two others proceeded the deacon, then came Father Arturo; the first shall come last.

Zak and I had taken the second pew from the front. Hamid lay quietly, seeming oblivious to the bustle around him. Maybe baptism damps down the lungs. That or the turbulence of the past few days, was taking its toll. Certainly, I felt it. The congregation sat. Exhausted, I closed my eyes.

The parishioners suffered through the deacon's endless verbiage. Just as we knelt for prayer, a burst of red flared behind the stained glass. A shrill whistle like the call of a tropical bird was followed by a dull, but loud thwump.

"Mortars," Zak shouted. "Get down."

Screams, shouts, the clack of kneelers flipped against their brackets. More flashes: the building shook and seemed to dip, lurch and spin as if it were a plane flying through hell. I gripped the armrest. Another blast and the wood trembled under my hand.

"Get down," Zak shouted again.

I slid from the pew to the floor and threw my body over Hamid's. Silence. A whiff of cool acrid air. I raised my head. A street-level window was a lake of broken glass. Overhead the Crucifix, down to its last chain, swung in a slow circle. Hamid let out an anguished howl, and I realized I had him pinned too tightly against me.

"Haul ass," Zak said, pulling me to my feet.

"Wait for the mob to clear," I said. "Where should we go? Where's safe?"

"The rectory."

"After the church, the first place they'll strike. Will they dare hit the hospital?"

"Technically, no," Zak said. "The Red Cross and Red Crescent share space, and no one's—" His words lost in an earth-shattering boom and roar of tumbling rock. I clung to the back of the pew ahead until the aftershock cleared. A click of falling plaster and I turned to the jagged hole that had become a window onto the cobblestone square and the street and the shops beyond. Orange dust rose in a graceful spiral. The air was thick with grit that smelled of creosote. Fighting for breath, I coughed and choked while draping the blanket loosely over Hamid's nose. Standing amidst the swirling dust, Father appeared as an apparition about to rise through the grainy clouds. His voice transcended the babble of the congregation.

Zak translated. "Father Arturo says we're welcome to leave now or stay through the mass."

The deacon shoved aside an altar boy on route to the door.

"He's going ahead with the service?" I asked.

"His death on the altar would bring life." Zak wiped his streaming eyes on his sleeve. "Life everlasting."

"What incredible faith," I said, awed. Faith that deserved a witness.

Hamid let out a piercing scream. "It would be wrong for us to leave," I shouted above his sobs. "We'll stay." I dried his tears with the fringe on the blanket. His sobs escalated, and I asked myself if I had the right to impose my convictions on this little guy.

"Cut the fucking nonsense." Zak took my elbow.

I yanked my arm away. "How can you turn your back?"

"Watch me," Zak said.

I looked down at Hamid, up at Zak. "Then take him somewhere safe."

Zak's gaze never left mine as he cradled the screaming Hamid against his shoulder and rubbed his back. "Where will you be?"

"After mass, I'll find you." I hadn't the guts to add, 'if I'm still alive.'

Zak stepped into the center aisle and joined the human stream flowing toward the door. He looked over his shoulder. "You'll be okay?" A question spoken as a fact.

The pews were empty. The urns holding the lilies lay on their sides. Silent bursts of fiery light flashed through the hole in the wall. Despite the relentless rat-a-tat of distant gunfire, Father wiped the chalice with steady hands.

I approached the altar.

Father placed the wafer in my cupped hands. It dissolved it in my mouth, as I crossed myself, turned and stumbled toward the door. Broken glass crunched underfoot. Another mortar; a close call somewhere behind me, and coward that I was, I ran down the aisle, panting until I hit the street.

Dazed, I stood in the entrance to the square. A crater gaped in the middle of the pavement. A geyser shot from the town's water tank. No traffic, only a Red Cross van parked on the sidewalk. Screams came from the row of shops. I crossed the cobblestones to where a man in a tracksuit lay face down. The downpour diluted his blood into pink rivulets flowing in the grout between the stones. On the other side of the square, a woman smoked a cigarette in the shelter of the awning. "Poor sod's gone to his maker," she called. "If you want to see a cock-up emergency room, take a look in there." She motioned to the tapas bar and flipped the butt into the gutter where it hissed in the rain.

Inside the bar, one of the concrete walls had been bombed to smoldering rebar. The air stank of sweat, burnt electrical wire, and fear. Too many people—villagers, back-packers, tourists and families—competed for the same oxygen. White plaster footprints covered the wet floor. A fallen bullfight poster lay in soggy sheds.

Wreckage: walls, bodies, and lives. My throat tightened. How long would it take before the bar was rebuilt? Before the wounds on the bodies turned to scars, and before what was left of the broken lives was salvaged. Behind the takeout counter, a man wept with his forehead against a wall. Other victims paced. A few huddled on the floor. An old man sat on a spindly plastic chair. Blood soaked his tee-shirt. He raised his head as if to say something, but instead of words, blood spilled from his mouth. In a bizarre attempt at normalcy, a waiter slowly wiped the bar, the same spot, back, forth and around. I wondered why helplessness is so often expressed in futile action.

A young boy mumbling in Spanish lay twisted on his side. When I tried to determine the source of the bleeding, two aides lowered a stretcher and I moved aside to give them room. A third attendant checked to be sure the boy's arm, severed from his body, was secure in a clear plastic bag at the foot of the gurney.

A Red Cross crew had set up a temporary triage station. A line formed at a folding table. An aide took names and identifying information of those waiting to be seen. I looked around for the crash cart and saw a pathetic collection of torn boxes and red bio-hazard bags filled with used syringes. A trash can overflowed with bloody gauze. When a woman with a caduceus on her jacket hurried past, I said, "Wait. I'm a doctor and can help,"

She stopped and looked me up and down.

"Put me to work." I dug through my bag and held out my ID. One glance at the laminated card, and she shook her head. "*No possible en Espñna. No numero nationale.*"

I hadn't the language to argue.

A familiar voice called my name. I made my way through the labyrinth of overturned tables to where Casey presided over a bottle of Harvey's Bristol Cream. He was in jeans and a red Henley jersey. Running his fingers through his tousled hair, he said, "They're out of Johnny Walker, so I'm rat-assed on sherry. Where's Tony and the kid?"

"Tony said he'd wait in the car while Zak and I were in church. He's not there. Zak took Hamid somewhere safe." I glanced around the room. "Now I don't know where anyone is."

I reached for Casey's Styrofoam cup and downed the rest of his sherry.

"There's a good girl," he said. "Christ on a bike, you see the impressive shit the Sons of the Prophet have? Brand new gear, weapons. His head lolled back and forth as he refilled the cup. And talk about organshun—organization. Gotta' remember the long 'a.' Anyway, their drones came right on schedule."

It took a minute for this to sink in. "Schedule? You knew they were coming?"

He looked at me with red rheumy eyes. "I guessed."

"Guess my ass."

"Okay," he said with a dramatic sigh. "Call it connections." With an exaggerated show of nonchalance, he leaned back and crossed his arms over his chest. "Friends in high places."

"London?" I assumed he had a clandestine career, an undercover life of some sort.

Fortyish was young to retire. Consulting? Training? Or peddling secrets from one enemy to another.

Testing the waters, I asked, "How's your Farsi, Dari, Hebrew?"

Casey held the fingers of his right hand, over his left wrist, his annoying habit of taking his pulse.

"You know the Maghreb dialect?" I asked.

"Oh, bloody hell. You made me lose count." He started over. His lips silently moved... one, two.

Laughter from three Knights next to us. They sat with their heads together, focusing on a phone in front of them on the table. Their blue berets hung on the backs of their chairs. They passed a half-gallon of vodka hand to hand.

Finished counting, Casey said, "I can even speak English and talk to your shirty compatriots on the front line."

"What front line?"

"The world's soldiers of fortune: Americans fight their wars with contractors. No dirty hands. Their blokes who snatched the kid in the church with the ugly old hag and—"

"Kidnapped Hamid? They were mercenaries?"

"Couldn't you tell? Christ, they spoke American."

I reconstructed the events. "They knew where to find us because you told them."

"It wasn't hard."

Whatever that meant. "Casey?"

He lifted his head. "Sorry, I lost your thread."

"Who hired those guys Who's the middleman?"

He put his index finger to his lips and rocked back and forth.

I held my breath until my surge of anger was overtaken by resignation. Plus, an eerie mix of exhaustion and disgust. "You sold me out."

"He is one smart-ass beltway bandit," he said.

I had nothing more to say. Without proof of a conspiracy, there was no crime. Nothing arrest-able. Nothing sue-able.

Outside, the sirens that were in the distance came close, closer.

Casey reached for the bottle. I held his arm. "You've had enough."

He jerked his hand away, and poured.

Through the front window—floor to ceiling glass still in one piece—I watched two Guardia Civil officers pull up on the sidewalk and get out of their Humvee. I could barely make out the head of a passenger in the cage behind the driver's seat. A prisoner, no doubt.

I turned back to Casey, looking for signs of remorse. None. But why was he telling me this now? Drunk, yes. Or maybe he adhered to the notion that confession—even without remorse—eradicates the offense. Confession as a sort of sin-ectomy.

His right hand reached for his left wrist, and once more he began his silent count.

"Knock it off," I said.

Before he could argue, both of us turned to the commotion in the doorway. The Guardia Civil officers were dragging in a teenager with an Emir's Army logo on his sweatshirt. His feet scraped the floor. Blood from a head wound soaked his collar. Medics rushed over and eased him onto a gurney. The officers conferred with the medics and pointed to the clock over the counter.

"*Un hora,*"I heard one say.

"Leaving him here for emergency treatment," I said.

"I hope the doc kills him," Casey replied, then laughed.

As soon as the officers left, the three Knights quickly rose—so quickly one knocked over the chair behind him. Shoving the medics aside, the Knights took over the gurney. A group of high-school-aged backpackers, boys with their dyed hair in fashionable green spikes, gathered around the captive. Wearing tee-shirts emblazoned with the Union Jack, they giggled and punched each other playfully while tagging along behind the Knights who were wheeling the prisoner outside.

It seemed everyone in the room stopped breathing at once. No sound except the rustle of a medic rooting through a box of supplies and the hum of the refrigerated display case.

The door flew open, and one of the boys shot back inside, trembling. "They got the bloke starkers out there," he gasped. Tears ran down his face. "They had a knife what done his eyes. I think I'm going to sick up." A woman in a mini-skirt hustled the kid toward the bathroom. Too late; the sound of gagging echoed from the hall.

"I have to find Hamid," I said, getting to my feet.

Casey motioned to me to stay put. "Hold off, love, until the place calms down soon as the pious jihadists save us from the pious Knights."

29

I had to get Hamid. The rain slacked off, but I was chilled to the bone despite the ninety-degree temperature. I struck off down a cobbled street, not knowing where I was going or where to go.

A woman in a print housedress knelt on a front stoop. Never mind the town was under siege, and that drizzle slicked the pavement. She splashed Don Limpio into a bucket, balanced the scrub brush on the edge, shook off the excess water, and set to work. Helplessness expressed in futile action.

I waited until she raised her head. "Hospital?" I asked.

She wrung out a rag.

"Red Cross? *Gente enferma?* Doctor?" I said, trying for a hit.

She pointed to an alley.

Only the statue of Saint Clare marked the site where the rectory once stood. Red roofing tiles lay over what used to be a yard. Granite blocks, slabs of drywall—the leg of a piano smoldered next to a hot water tank. Where was I going? Trying to recall Zak's exact words brought momentary panic. He did agree the hospital was the safest place, didn't he? Yes, the hospital. Of course, that's what he said.

The inward-facing halves of my eyes—the halves that track imagination and memory, saw Zak with a spoonful of carrot mush. Saw the orange slop sliding down Hamid's bump of a chin along with the carroty slivers that escaped the spoon. The image was reassuring: if normalcy happened once, it could happen again.

The alley widened into a street open to two-way traffic. No signs of jihadis, but flocks of helicopters churned overhead. One khaki low-flyer bore a Spanish flag painted on its flank. Curious pedestrians crept from doorways to check if the bombing was over. A sputtering fire died on a vacant lot.' Morelas ferreteria was now three walls and a charred beam. Two men wheeled a sheet of plywood toward the broken window of the Super-Sol. Against looting, I thought skirting their dolly.

A screech of brakes and an ambulance pulled alongside. Tony leaped to the curb. Wrapping his arms around me, he swung me off my feet and shouted, "Thank God," Stepping back, he asked, "Where's the little bloke?"

"Zak took him somewhere safe."

"He's okay?"

"I don't know."

"We'll find out." Tony hustled me toward the vehicle. A driver in sweats hunched over the wheel. Squawks resembling words crackled through the static on his radio. Tony climbed in next to me on the bench seat. He now wore a waterproof Red Cross jacket.

"You volunteered?" I asked. A pinprick of annoyance when I recalled the bureaucratic doctor who blew me off.

"Wrong not to," he said. In the rear of the van, a medic steadied the IV pole connected to a patient on the fold-out cot. "Cardiac. She's stable," Tony said.

"We've got to get Hamid to the Catholics."

Tony smiled slightly. "Otherwise you'll be stuck with him."

I sat back. "That's so harsh. After all, I am responsible for him."

"He isn't yours."

"You've said that."

The service road to the hospital wound through groves of palms and rose beds. We rounded the curve and came to a brick guardhouse without a guard. An overhead light blinked red. "A camera instead of a person," Tony said. The driver pulled forward on green.

Uniformed security forces milled around the grounds. Guardia Civil, *Policia National*, Spanish Army Reserves and, of course, the Knights of Constancia playing soldier in their blue berets. Parked near the guardhouse, three white SUVs flanked the green Mercedes.

"The one we saw it earlier," I said. "Who's is it?"

"Some Moroccan, judging from the plates."

Our driver slowed at a four-way stop and motioned for a Rolls Royce limousine followed by four black sedans to make a turn.

Tony whistled. "Take a look at that. See the Vatican decal? The black cars must be part of their entourage. Check out the press pennant on the aerial of the lead car."

Our driver swung onto the concrete parking zone at the entrance to the emergency room. He and Tony jumped from the front and went around back.

"Look for Hamid inside the hospital," I called.

Tony disappeared into the building and came back with a gurney. He and the medic wheeled the patient and her IV pole through the swinging doors. I slid from the high seat onto the ground. The driver got out, circled the hood, and lit a cigarette on his way to the smokers' shack.

In the waiting room, patients lay cheek by jowl on stretchers, on chairs shoved together as make-shift beds, and on the floor, while nuns in old-fashioned white habits bustled back and forth. Sharp-eyed *Policia National* scrutinized the crowd. The overheated air reeked of urine and burnt coffee. A corridor beyond the waiting room led to exam cubicles. "Let's go check," I said.

"You would need Spanish ID," Tony said.

A desk in a far corner was mobbed by a hysterical crowd harassing the clerk with shouts, threats, and desperate pleas. Tony plowed through the milieu and signed a clipboard. When he made his way back, I said, "How on earth will we find Hamid in this mess?"

Across the room, a boy about five or six on tip-toe tried to reach a drinking fountain. Tony went over and lifted him up.

"Tony, for God's sake," I shouted. "Get Hamid."

The kid raised his head. Water from his mouth dripped onto Tony's shirt. "What did you say?" Tony called.

He should be checking the roster, checking the exam cubicles. "Goddamnit." I lit into him, not caring who heard me. "All you think about is your self-importance." Knowing I was being irrational spurred me on. "He could be dead while you're so busy saving mankind—" My attention swung to the other side of the room where an attendant pushed a gurney along the wall toward an exit. A body bag rested atop. Ordinarily, a hospital's service door was blocked from the public, but today the partitions lay stacked against a wall.

Tony's eyes followed the gurney. "It's not a baby-sized body. It's an adult," he said stiffly. "Meanwhile, staff might have Hamid in the nursery on the third floor. Physical therapy would have mats for kids. Getting you an ID in this madhouse would be dodgy. Wait here."

I nodded.

On his way to the elevator, Tony turned. "And bugger all, Paige, the next time you want to improve my character, fuck off." He entered the lift without a backward glance,

I sat on the edge of a table that held magazines. I opened one with a glossy cover, flipped through the pages and closed it. A typical waiting room rag advertising expensive meds—drugs the National Health Insurance would never approve.

Where was Hamid? My stomach churned. Dead? He and Zak could have run into jihadists, been hit by a grenade. My placating inner voice warned my imagination was running amok. Hamid was fine. The Knights were armed. Zak wouldn't allow anything to happen.

Panting, Tony pushed through the crowd. "I took the stairs down. He's not here. The place is on lockdown, and every guard has his knickers in a twist." He put his hand on my shoulder. "Steady on, Paige. It's simple. Zak saw the cock-up in here and took the baby into town, that's all."

I choked down a wave of panic. "I've got to—"

"He's not your kid," Tony snapped.

"Will you stop saying that?"

In a softer voice, Tony said, "Look, we'll get my car and drive to the square where we saw Zak earlier."

If Tony's matter-of-fact tone was intended to trump my anxiety, it didn't work. "If we can't find him straight off," he said, "we'll leave a note on his windshield and say where we'll be waiting. What's he drive?"

"Porsche."

"Let's get cracking."

The downpour had settled into a pesky drizzle. Tony stopped, took off his waterproof Red Cross jacket, and draped it over my shoulders. "Oh, please," I said feeling like a shit after the way I'd lit into him. "You need it."

"A thank you, will do nicely."

"Thank you."

Halfway down the road, a deafening overhead clackety-clack was followed by a cyclone of wind tossing the tops of the pines. Gulls veered off course. Tony and I stopped in our tracks. The helicopter came in low: the gold on the Vatican's coat of arms on the aircraft shone through the rain The wind from the whirling blades stirred the trees. A paper cup tumbled from an overflowing trash can and rolled across the cement. The big bird roosted on the hospital's landing pad.

A roar of diesel engines and I watched a convoy of Ford 250s swarm the parking lot. Brandishing rifles, Jihadis jumped from the beds and ran in all directions. Some wore turbans; others, khaki berets. The rag-tag army was in sweats, track suits, and jeans. The cry, *"Allahu Akhbar,"* rang through the trees.

Tony spun around. "Quick, back to the ambulance."

"The hospitals safer," I shouted, trying to keep up with him.

"They'll go for the Pope on the roof." He paused, panting. "A vehicle might get us out of here."

The ambulance was where we left it. Tony swung open the rear doors and boosted me inside a minute before the first grenade hit the building. The ambulance rocked, then regained balance, as if righting itself after a blow.

I crawled inside the ambulance's hold. A metal shelf was bolted to one panel. "Get underneath," Tony ordered. His head low, he made his way through the narrow opening between the rear and the driver's seat and slid behind the wheel. He slapped the dashboard. "Fuck it all. No keys. Soon as this shit lets up, we'll make a run for my car."

I lay on my side, facing the swing-away cot. The shelf six inches over my head sagged from the weight of the bins of supplies. The sharp whine of a rocket, the rumble of man-made thunder and the crash of stone on stone. My brain went numb. No thought, no reason, just a darkness too thick to think through.

"They sound like M-67s," Tony said.

My teeth chattered, and I took deep breaths until my head spun from hyperventilating. Each blast set our vehicle wobbling on its tires. Flashing red balls bounced off the oxygen tanks, during a lull, I raised my head to see through the windshield, my vision partially blocked by the back of the front seats. The sky was on fire. A flurry of spinning sticks sailed over the pines as the tail of the helicopter vanished into the fog.

"So much for the papal visit," Tony said. "The bird never landed."

"Can you make out where the jihadists are?" I asked.

"Damn window won't come down without keys," Tony opened the door and stood on the running board. "They're holding our police at gunpoint. The rest of the bastards are getting in the trucks."

"Where're the Knights?"

"Who cares?"

"Zak might be with them."

"Get ready to make a dash." After a minute he said, "All clear. Give it a few seconds to be sure. Funny, the Vatican motor entourage pulled under the palms. Look near the fence."

"I can't see anything."

"Oh, right. Ready?"

I jumped from the back and stared at the hospital through the phlegmy mist. The exterior walls on three sides of a wing were gone revealing a stage-set of a nurses' station. The counter, torn from its anchor, upside-down gurneys, chairs, and carts every-which-way. Staff must have rescued the patients before the bombs hit.

"Are you coming?" Tony called.

The road we were on intersected with the main drag that led to the entrance of the grounds. The intersection was blocked. The entire area around the brick guardhouse was cordoned off with yellow tape stretched between stanchions. A virtual barrier, not a real one; the tape only about four feet from the ground But I knew the well-disciplined Spaniards would never challenge a boundary. *Policia National* paced the inside perimeter, their long black rain-capes shone like patent leather through the fog. An officer trotted up to us, shouting. Perez, the name on his shield.

"We're going for our car," Tony said.

Perez eyed Tony's *Medicine Sin Frontera* tee-shirt. "*No Francoise.*" he said.

"English?" I asked.

Perez unclipped a phone from his belt and spoke in heated, fierce Spanish with frequent gestures to the Vatican's entourage. He closed the phone and pointed to the sedans flanking the Vatican's limo.

We hiked the two hundred yards or so to the lead car. The back door opened, and a man in a gray suit clambered out. Tall and burly, the elegant-looking guy had brown eyes and a black beard. The mist brightened his hair and darkened his jacket of raw silk. The ID on the lanyard around his neck identified him as 'Simon Cerrone,' followed by an impressive line of credentials in Italian. "I'm with the Papal Delegation," he said. "Public relations, the backup crew."

"The Pope's gone," I said. "Who's in the limousine?"

"Archbishop DeAlba, along with the rest of the support team," he said. "Now, it's the drive back to Cadiz. Hope the rain slacks off for good."

"You sound American," Tony said.

"The seminary sent me to Catholic University. Georgetown, Blues Alley..."

"Seminary?" I said. "We should call you Father Cerrone?"

"Nope. A Marist Brother." He nodded to the cop watching us. "The *Policia* said you needed an English-speaker."

"It's our car, we'll be needing," Tony said. "We're doctors and—

Two shots came from the guardhouse.

"Dear God," Cerrone said and took off toward the barrier with Tony and me at his heels.

Cerrone and Perez yelled to each other over the yellow tape. Cerrone translated. "A sniper, a fanatic cop who wasn't supposed to shoot fired into the guard-house."

"Can't they stop him?" I asked.

Cerrone shrugged. "Maybe they don't want to. One way to solve the problem."

Tony tipped his head and said, "Sorry?"

"You don't know what's going on?" Cerrone asked.

"We just came from the hospital," I said.

"A Spaniard whacko barricaded himself in the guard-house. He has a baby, can you believe? Won't come out until we—we meaning the church— agrees to take in the kid. Says he won't come out until then."

I swallowed hard. "Have a name?"

"Something like De Leon."

An aneurysm of panic flooded my brain. My head throbbed. Everything around me lost definition, Tony, trees, the stanchions, a blur.

I hardly heard Tony shout, "Look."

In a daze, I watched the green Mercedes followed by its cadre of white SUVs pull up a short distance from the Vatican's limo. I looked back toward the guardhouse, but a group of *Polica* blocked my view.

Cerrone patted his inside jacket pocket. "Forgot my phone. I gotta' get back. "When he turned to leave, Perez immediately raised the tape and stepped under it to our side and blocked Cerrone's path. "Guess I'll wait here," Cerrone said. "Spanish Gestapo," he muttered under his breath.

"Who's that getting out of the car?" Tony asked.

A Moroccan in a white robe emerged from the Mercedes at the same time a priest emerged from the limo. They shook hands. "The one in the collar's Father Roberto," Cerrone said. "Our hostage negotiator. The Arab, I'm not sure. Probably someone to collect their kid."

"Please, Mister Cerrone," I said. "Tell your folks to take in the baby and let DeLeon go."

"Obviously you don't know the whole story," Cerrone said.

I wanted to hear his version. "So, tell me."

"The Knights kidnapped the kid," Cerrone said, "promising to give him back. They reneged.

How does he know these things? I wondered. Then recalled the relationship between the Archbishop and Zak.

"The jihadists got wind of the betrayal," Cerrone continued. "Even before the betrayal had time to happen." Cerrone glanced at the demolished hospital. "They took it to heart. The Pope ordered the Archbishop to intervene. To apologize, say the church had no intention of not keeping its word. Of course, they'd return the child, and the jihadists could come get him."

Everything Cerrone said boiled down to one fact. The church. My church, I thought with a sickening feeling. The church Zak was willing to risk his life for, threw him under the bus.

I glimpsed Father Roberto advancing toward the guardhouse. He lifted a megaphone to his lips. "Senor DeLeon," Father shouted.

I zipped up my jacket and tried to put the situation into some sort of order.

Zak betrayed the Muslims. The church betrayed Zak. Which was worse? Which side was I on? Zak broke a promise, sure. But to whom? To animals. Look at the hospital.

I drew the hood of the jacket over my head and tightened the drawstring.

On the other hand, the church broke its promise to Zak. Worse, its moral obligation to Hamid—now Michael—a new life baptized in the faith. The Archbishop's betrayal was a failure of loyalty to his own. The underrated virtue of loyalty, I thought. The unsung virtue that brought order and peace. I pictured my father's disloyalty to his own child, and at that moment I knew why the world was in chaos.

Father Roberto's pleas carried through the palms. I still couldn't discern the words. What were the textbook techniques of hostage negotiation? I recalled Zak's pig-headedness, his one-track mind, and his conviction he had all the answers. Maybe he did. At any rate, he had the courage to hold out. Alone.

Before I realized what I was doing, I lifted the barrier and called to Tony, "Zak's by himself. I'm going out there to be with them."

Tony grabbed my elbow. "Are you out of your fucking mind?"

I yanked my arm away.

"*Cuidado, Señora.*" Perez raised his rifle.

I backed off.

Cerrone paced, now and then stopping to watch the *policia* watch the guardhouse. I walked over and looked up into his eyes. "You tell DeAlba to stop screwing around."

"No one tells the Archbishop anything."

"He's a coward." Anger bordering on fury drove my words. "The Pope's 'yes' man."

"Now, really, Doctor—"

"Cool it, Paige," Tony said.

"Mister Cerrone—" I checked his name-tag. "Simon. You're not stupid. This baby's a line in the sand." Words that made no sense, but I went on. "The Muslims are bombing our cathedrals, our art, our lives, Bach, Rembrandt, Louis Pasteur..." Stumped for more examples, I added, "Next it will be Disney."

Cerrone smiled slightly. "Don't think I don't disagree." Spoken like the Vatican bureaucrat he was.

Shots came from the guardhouse. "Can you see who fired?" Tony asked Cerrone.

He craned his neck, "The sniper's on the roof. In a Guardia Civil uniform."

Standing on tip-toe, I saw a soldier atop the guardhouse.

Three quick shots. "Are they coming from Zak?" I asked. A wisp of gauzy smoke curled into the fog. "Can you see?" I asked Tony.

"Better not look, love."

The universe fell eerie, quiet.

After a few minutes, Tony said, "They seem to be packing it up."

I heard the click of weapons being fastened back onto slings. The guards spoke softly as one by one, they drifted from the restricted area and joined their captain. I now had a clear view.

Zak lay on the grass. The turf gradually darkened as it absorbed blood from his chest. The Guardia soldier who had been on the roof emerged from the guardhouse holding something against his shoulder. An unmistakable howl—

"Hamid." I shouted lunging toward the tape.

"Stay back," Tony ordered.

The soldier carrying Hamid kicked Zak's ankle as he passed.

"Look. Something's happening over there." Tony pointed to the far side of the roped-off area, where a Guardia Civil officer was dragging away a stanchion. The green Mercedes turned onto the wet lawn, churned through the opening in the tape, and skidded to a stop near the kiosk. Three men jumped from the rear seat. The tallest wore a white robe and white skullcap. The other two, bodyguards I assumed, were in black leather jackets.

The Guardia Civil officer walked over to his colleague carrying Hamid, and both of them headed toward the Mercedes. The soldier carrying Hamid approached the guy in the white robe, and ceremoniously handed the baby over. Hamid screamed, his hands flailed. The white-robed jihadist tightened the blanket, binding Hamid's arms. The howls escalated. The guy gripped the back of Hamid's neck and shook him.

"Stop it," I shouted.

Tony put his arm around me. "Steady on."

The guy in white nodded at one of the bodyguards who took Hamid and carried him into the car.

"He's mine," I shouted. I yanked the tape, tore it loose and dashed into the clearing, Tony behind me.

"Mine," I repeated. Tony grabbed my shoulders and held me tightly against him as the Mercedes bounced across the rough terrain.

Hamid was lost.

Gone to where he would learn rage, anger, and violence. Learn enough hate to blow up a city, to desecrate tombs and to decapitate a mother for committing an act of love.

I pressed my forehead against Tony's chest.

"You did your best," he said.

I raised my head. "And lost him anyway."

"He was never yours to lose," Tony said.

I drew back and looked out at the road where Guardia Civil soldiers were clearing rubble from the road.

"We're getting wet," Tony said.

Yet my heart was arid, parched. How it was possible that the absence of pain could hurt so much?

I felt abandoned, lost. And I wondered if somewhere out there in this vast and lonely world—that wherever he was—Hamid felt it too.

Fine mist bled from the gray sky. Drops slid along the branches of the oaks and dripped into cups formed by the leaves. Tony lifted a strand of wet hair from my temple, tucked it behind my ear, and reached for my hand.

Note from the Author

Word-of-mouth is crucial for any author to succeed. If you enjoyed the book, please leave a review online—anywhere you are able. Even if it's just a sentence or two. It would make all the difference and would be very much appreciated.

Thanks!
Carolyn

About the Author

Carolyn Thorman is the author of the novel *Holy Orders.* Her work has appeared in numerous literary magazines, and she was prior nominated for a Pushcart Prize. She's also received three Works-in-Progress grants from the Maryland State Arts Council and the State's Literary Fellowship. She holds degrees in Law and Anthropology, and divides her time between Houston, Texas and Malaga, Spain.

Thank you so much for reading one of our **Political-Thriller** novels.

If you enjoyed our book, please check out our recommended
for your next great read!

Jihadi Bride by Alistair Luft

"A timely edge-of-your-seat terrorism thriller that plays on every parent's worst fears. This cinematic thriller is destined for TV."
—*Best Thrillers*